MURDER AT WESTMINSTER

THE KITTY WORTHINGTON MYSTERIES, BOOK 2

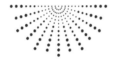

MAGDA ALEXANDER

HEARTS AFIRE PUBLISHING

To my darling granddaughter, Alicia,
The epitome of sweetness and kindness

CHAPTER ONE

LONDON 1923

WORTHINGTON HOUSE, MAYFAIR

*L*ONDON'S SOCIAL SEASON WAS NOT FOR THE FAINT OF HEART.

Debutantes required the stamina of a Boadicea to endure the endless rounds of balls, afternoon teas, picnics alfresco, scavenger hunts, and whatever other festivities a clever hostess devised. Paraded as they were like prize mares at county shows for eligible bachelors to consider their worth as a wife, it was a wonder they weren't weighed, measured, and asked to show their teeth. And all done for the sake of securing a husband. As if that was a goal devoutly to be achieved.

Such a frantic pace was bound to take its toll. Barely a month into it, we'd already experienced several casualties. Lady Gertrude Stanley, who suffered from a nervous

1

complaint, collapsed weeping in the middle of a quadrille. Apparently, the intricate dance steps had proven too much for her. She'd subsequently withdrawn to her Yorkshire country estate where her only companions were sheep. And they, of course, did not dance.

Lady Lydia Campbell, on the other hand, had proven a luminary on the ballroom floor. She'd mastered not only the old-fashioned dances the grand dames so dearly loved, but the more modern ones they eschewed. Unfortunately, she hadn't reckoned with that clodhopper of an earl, Lord Gardiner and Tyne. During a Viennese waltz, he'd trodden on every one of her toes breaking her left foot. Not one to go down in defeat, for she was made of sterner stuff, she'd insisted on keeping to the demanding schedule. Until, that is, her physician warned her she risked losing the ability to walk altogether if she carried on this way. And so, she'd returned to her remote castle in the Scottish Highlands where she would live to dance another day.

Miss Sara Cogsburn, our third casualty, was the only child of an investor who'd made pots of money on railroads and tin mines. She'd suffered no injuries, at least none that were visible to the naked eye. But without so much as a soupçon of a warning, she'd suddenly fled town. Rumors, of course, ran rampant about the cause, which only grew to a frenzy when her engagement to Baron Donne's third son was announced. But soon that particular mystery was solved. While the gentleman in question had neither fine prospects nor an admirable physique to boast of, he possessed something which some ladies prized. He was an expert in the amorous arts. A fact which, gossip had it, Lady Lydia had learned first-hand. One could only hope her connubial bliss made up for his deficiencies in other areas.

While as for me, I kept to the furious gallop, for Mother would not have it any other way. As a result, my season had become a resounding success. Much to my consternation, hardly a week went by that Father didn't entertain numerous requests for my hand in marriage. While some were issued by respectable lords and gentlemen who were serious in their pursuit, others were offered by rogues, rakes, and ne'er do wells who were more interested in my substantial dowry than my humble self. Regardless of the intent, every proposal was respectfully turned down after Father consulted me. But the thing of it was every refusal somehow spurred others to do the same, as if they'd determined it a contest to see who would win the prize mare, er, me.

Of course, Mother was in her glory, for she devoutly wished to see me walking down the aisle, preferably to someone with a title attached to his name. It didn't matter which. Any title would do. Alas, I was bound to disappoint her for I had no wish to marry. At least not at this time. But hope sprung ever eternal in Mother's breast.

As I approached the dining room for the chief reason which had driven me to rise this morning—breakfast—its door opened, and my sister Margaret emerged, followed as ever by her faithful squire, Sebastian Dalrymple. The militant expression on her face told me I was truly in the soup.

"Have you just risen?" she asked, all pinched mouth and scrunched brow. "It's after nine."

"I didn't make my bed until three. You know how late balls go." Having experienced her own season two years ago, she was familiar with its hectic nature.

"We have much to do for the women's march, Kitty." That august event, part and parcel of the social agenda Margaret embraced while at Oxford, sought to gain suffrage for women over the age of twenty-one. As the law currently stood, only women who had attained the age of thirty and owned property were entitled to vote. That left out many a shop girl, factory worker, and domestic servant, never mind myriads of others

3

who toiled for a living. "You knew I needed you bright and early, fresh and ready to go. You should have come home sooner."

If she was trying to make me feel guilty, she was doing a brilliant job. "I'll be there. Just let me enjoy breakfast first."

The edges of her mouth turned down with disapproval. "Very well. Join us as soon as you can." And then she veered toward the ballroom where the march preparations were being made. An amused Sebastian winked at me before trailing in her wake.

He was a dear, truly. One would think he would resent Margaret ordering him about. But he never did. His easygoing style was the opposite of Margaret's martinet ways. But then she was carrying a lot on her shoulders since the women's march was to take place in little more than a week. While the leaders handled the publicity, garnering the public's support through the press, Margaret had volunteered herself and our home to organize the effort. During the last two weeks, she'd trained volunteers and managed supplies, while ensuring the work proceeded smoothly. She was to be lauded for her efforts, and I admired her for them. I just wished she was less forceful about it.

A footman carrying a tray of food drifted by capturing my attention.

"Is that bacon?" I asked. The enticing aroma wafting from the platter made my mouth salivate.

"Yes, Miss."

"Ummm." I followed him into the dining room where I found my parents engaged in a spirited discussion.

"That young man seems to have become a fixture around the house," Father said. "Can't move two feet without stumbling into him."

Mother cast a worried glance toward the door. "Edward, please keep your voice down. Sebastian may hear you."

4

"He can't, Mildred. He's already left the room."

Two weeks earlier, Sebastian had escorted Margaret to my birthday celebration and for all intents and purposes had practically moved in. Oh, he slept in his own bed for he had lodgings nearby. But he never missed a meal at our house, appearing daily before breakfast and remaining until after supper when he would bid adieu and go merrily on his way. Margaret referred to him as her 'friend.' Heaven forfend if my tongue slipped and call him her beau. Even though it certainly seemed that way.

Mother, whose fondest desire was that at least one of her children married into the aristocracy, was overjoyed Sebastian continued to grace us with his presence. After all, he was the heir to a dukedom. Even though nary a hint had been dropped, she'd begun to hear wedding bells being pealed for Margaret and her beau. Pardon me, friend.

Father, on the other hand, seemed to have developed an objection to Sebastian's presence. Odd, if you asked me, since they only came face to face at breakfast and supper times. Father was too busy with his financial business, Worthington & Son, which he managed along with my brother Ned, while Sebastian's satellite revolved around Margaret's sun. Still, Father did have a point.

As I approached the groaning sideboard, my heart leapt with joy. Laden as it was with shirred eggs, bacon, sausage, potatoes, mushrooms, and tomatoes, it was a wondrous sight to behold.

"Why is he here anyway?" Father asked. "A young man with all his prospects should be out and about enjoying pursuits in London."

"He's working with Margaret on her project, dear," Mother said. "You know how important that is to her."

"Women's suffrage. Yes, I know." He put down his fork. "I

don't see what all the fuss is about. They already have the vote."

"Not all of them. Your own two daughters don't."

He pinned his gaze on me. "What could Margaret and Kitty possibly be concerned about that requires them to vote?" He was a dear, really, but he had no understanding of women's plight.

"Employment equality, health issues, self-determination, just to name a few." I took a seat at the table along with my plate of chosen fare. "Why, a woman cannot even open a bank account in her own name. She needs a man to do it for her. That's a recipe for disaster."

"But—"

"Try the coffee, Edward," Mother suggested. "Cook managed to obtain a special blend—Colombian, I believe."

"Oh, jolly good." As soon as he took a sip, contentment rolled over his face.

I smiled into my own cup at Mother's clever ways. She'd mastered the art of dealing with Father a long time ago. Coffee, food, and a change of subject usually did the trick.

Unfortunately, Father was not quite ready to let the Sebastian issue go. A few bites later, he returned to this morning's topic du jour. "Where does he lay down his head at night?"

"Porchester Place," I volunteered.

"Excellent," he said slicing into a sausage. "Shouldn't take him but a tick to drive there."

I took a bite of the bacon and sighed with bliss. "He doesn't drive, Father. He walks."

Father paused with the sausage halfway to his mouth. "He walks?"

Mother, who preferred Father remain ignorant of Sebastian's circumstances, tsked her disapproval at me.

"Why ever for?" As far as he was concerned, a gentleman

did not stroll anywhere. That's what modern transportation was for.

"He doesn't own a motorcar," I said, reaching for a blueberry muffin from the basket on the table.

Mother twitched a warning, a clear signal not to pursue the subject.

"Couldn't he hail a taxicab?" His disconcerted gaze told me everything was not right with his view of the world.

"He would but—"

Mother's twitching grew to a frantic pace.

"But?" Father prompted.

"He's on a rather tight leash," I said, tasting the muffin. Delicious. Cook had really outdone herself.

"But he's the heir to a dukedom. He should have plenty of funds to support a comfortable lifestyle."

"I'm not familiar with the particulars of his situation, Father. But apparently his quarterly allowance does not extend to such luxuries." Or as least, Sebastian had hinted that much without coming right out and saying so.

His mustache quivered with indignation. "That's outrageous." Deep in thought, he tore off a piece of sausage and fed it to Sir Winston, our Bassett Hound, under the table.

Mother put down her fork. "Edward, I wish you would stop feeding that dog. You know what sausages do to him."

As did everyone in the household. Sir Winston suffered from digestive issues. When given food that did not agree with him, he emitted malodorous airs noxious enough to clear a room. But Father being Father tended to ignore such home truths.

He tossed another piece of sausage to Sir Winston. "No hound should live off a bland diet. He needs spice in his life. Don't you, boy?"

The hound in question barked while adoringly gazing at him.

Mother's downturned brow evidenced her disapproval, but she said no more on the subject.

"I'll have Ned look into it," Father said.

"The veterinarian has already done that, dear," Mother said.

A frown line surfaced between his eyes. "What does the veterinarian have to do with Sebastian?"

"What are you talking about, Edward?" Mother asked.

I bit down on my lip to keep from smiling. Not the first time they'd talked at cross purposes, nor would it be the last.

"Sebastian's situation," Father said. "It makes no sense that young man has to traipse about London on foot and eat his meals at someone else's house. Not when his grandfather's the Duke of Wynchcombe."

Dismay reigned in Mother's visage. "I wish you wouldn't meddle in his affairs, Edward. Surely, it's not our concern."

"Isn't it, Mildred?" he gazed fondly at her. "We must understand his situation before things progress between Margaret and him. No sense letting her get her hopes up if his finances are not what they ought to be."

Not hard to see where he was coming from. Upon Margaret's twenty-first birthday, he'd settled a quite generous amount on her, same as he'd done with me. Even if Sebastian proved poor as a church mouse, which I extremely doubted, she would be able to afford a comfortable lifestyle. Still, he did not wish anyone to marry my sister for her dowry.

Mother let out a long-suffering sigh. "Yes, dear."

Father laid down his serviette. "By the way, Kitty, two more of your admirers approached me seeking permission to call on you. One, I turned down, clearly a loose screw. There's bad blood in that family. But the other might be worth considering."

"Which gentleman?"

"Lord Fairbottom. A Marquis."

I shuddered. Lord Fairbottom suffered from a squint, and he sniffed all the time. "Please offer my regrets."

Mother grumbled under her breath.

"Are you certain?" Father asked. "Townhouse in London off Eaton Square. Family seat in Kent. Adequate fortune. No skeletons in the closet, as far as I can tell."

"His mother is a harridan, Father. A widow who's set her mind on being part of her son's household. Aside from that, I couldn't stand to be addressed as Lady Fairbottom the rest of my life."

"Ummm, a fair point. Very well. I'll offer your regrets." Done with his meal, he rose. "Well, I better go. Ned must be wondering where I am. Excellent breakfast, my dear. My compliments to Cook." After dropping a kiss on Mother's cheek, he strolled out whistling 'Yes, We Have no Bananas,' his faithful hound by his side.

For a few minutes, silence filled the space while Mother and I addressed our meal. But the quiet did not last long. "Don't forget, dear. We have an at-home today."

How could I ever forget? We held them every Tuesday. "Yes, Mother."

"Lord Pippin appears to be quite smitten with you." She was hedging her bets in case Margaret and Sebastian's 'friendship' came to naught. But that was Mother all over. Why settle for one bird in the bush when there could be two in the hand?

"Umm," I murmured. Lord Pippin was a dear, but he did not excite my intellect, or any other part of me for that matter. Although I'd remained civil, for that was the proper thing to do, at no time had I encouraged his attentions. Unfortunately, he'd misconstrued my politeness for interest and pressed his suit at every social event I attended, including every one of my at-homes. That, of course, had given Mother room to hope.

Last thing I wished was to be tied to a dreary marriage where I was expected to pop out an heir and a spare—in double quick time if you please. I wanted to visit jazz clubs, drink fizzy cocktails, dance the Charleston. Last month, I'd put aside those ambitions to investigate a murder that threatened to put a noose around my brother Ned's neck. But since that had been satisfactorily solved by yours truly, I was now free to have a jolly good time. Well, as much of a jolly good time as I could manage while attending all the events of the season which, heaven help me, included every one of my at-homes. Four down, eight to go.

"Wear your deep rose chiffon, Kitty. It looks splendid on you. Oh, and your pearls." On my birthday, Lord Rutledge, one of Father's dearest friends, had presented me with quite a stunning necklace of perfectly matched pearls. It'd been handed down through generations of his family. But since he was unmarried and had no relatives to inherit it, he'd gifted it to me.

"Don't you think it'd be a tad ostentatious to wear them during the day?"

"Nonsense, dear. Pearls are meant to be displayed, not tucked away in some dusty drawer."

I sighed. "Yes, Mother."

CHAPTER TWO

AT HOME

*P*ROMPTLY AT TWO, a horde of callers streamed into our home, each carrying a bouquet of flowers or a small token of appreciation. One even brought a gardenia plant. In no time at all, our drawing room resembled a florist shop, redolent with the scent of lilies, roses, and other blooms. Not unpleasant by any means, but a bit overwhelming. As the at-home progressed, every gentleman enjoyed a few minutes with me before giving way to the next. I was told I resembled Venus, Aurora, Helen of Troy. One compared me to his horse.

"Your horse, sir?" I inquired, totally baffled by this.

"She's the most beautiful creature I've ever beheld," he said, a dreamy look on his face.

Lord Pellegrine was definitely . . . odd.

"I . . . see. Well, thank you for that, milord."

Another gentleman, a viscount I believed, knelt at my

feet. Hand to heart, he begged. "Miss Worthington, may I recite an ode to your beauty?"

"Another one?" I offered a tight smile. He wrote the most execrable poetry. At another at-home he'd penned one to my orbs. The similes and metaphors had been so convoluted, I never determined what he'd been talking about.

"Yes, my goddess. I titled it, "To the Star that Lights the Firmament."

"Oh, please." I'd meant it as 'no, not again.' Unfortunately, he took it as approval.

Clearing his throat, he began, "To the star that lights the firmament."

So far, so good.

"To the one who shines in the sky."

Wasn't that the same thing?

"To the beauty who sparkles with dew."

Was he saying I perspired?

"I bestow my heart to thee." He held out his hand to reveal a paper cutout of a red heart.

"That was splendid, Lord—" *Heavens!* I'd forgotten his name.

In a panic, I gazed at Mother. Wise woman that she was, she tapped the wall.

"Lord Wallingford. Thank you."

"My angel." He captured my hand in his. As he reverently kissed it, a blond curl fell across his brow. Very romantic. Unfortunately, he had bats in his belfry.

Mother must have realized I'd had enough for she politely informed the gentlemen we had a supper party to attend that evening and I needed my rest. Within a few minutes, the room cleared out.

"Thank you, Mother. I really could not stand to hear another sonnet to my beauty or my orbs. I never know

whether he's referring to my eyes or" —I glanced down—
"some other part of my anatomy."

"Kitty!" She tried to sound stern, but her laughter rippled
out. "He is the most nonsensical man. He's also a marquess."

I firmed my lips. I had to cut this off at the bud. "No,
Mother."

"I know, dear. Now you really do have to rest. Go have a
lie down so tonight you star may shine in the firmament."

The look I bestowed upon her could not in any way been
deemed loving.

Concerned about the gardenia plant, which I knew
required special care, I headed toward the ballroom where
Sebastian was sure to be found. A junior research fellow in
agriculture at Oxford, he was spectacular at nurturing
anything green.

I found him explaining the tasks that needed to be done
for the women's march to a group of new volunteers. Most
recruits attended because they believed in the women
suffrage cause. But others had started to join when word
spread that Sebastian was part of the effort. I didn't blame
them for wanting to catch a glimpse of him. Blond, blue-eyed
with an athletic physique, heaven knew he was a lot to take
in. Add to that the fact he was an heir to a dukedom, and that
drew women like a moth to a flame.

I waited until his speech was done and tasks had been
assigned before addressing him. "I've been gifted this lovely
gardenia plant. Knowing how finicky they can be, I thought I
would bring it to you."

His eyes lit up. "I say. What a lovely specimen. But you're
right. It requires delicate handling. Heat and humidity and
plenty of light. Should I make room for it in the
conservatory?"

"Absolutely." Although we had a gardening staff, they had
enough to deal with the grounds and had no time to dedicate

to that space. As a result, the conservatory had been sadly neglected. Sebastian had brought it back to life, adding not only flowers, but fruits. Orange and lemon trees now flourished in the conservatory, as well as a whole host of other blooms. The room had gone from benign neglect to a place where the family gathered for afternoon tea to enjoy the fragrant scents and, when the weather allowed, the warm sun.

"Let's away, you beauty," he said lovingly to the plant. Every woman within hearing distance sighed, probably wishing he would address her in the same manner.

"Done with your at-home?" Margaret asked, approaching me.

"Yes, finally. Lord Wallingford delivered another ode to my beauty— 'To the Star that Lights the Firmament' or some such drivel."

Margaret laughed. "He wrote one to me as well. He compared me to Athena, as I recall."

"He didn't propose?"

She hiked a brow. "I told him I could never look favorably on a poet. That put paid to that notion."

"Clever you." Margaret's season had been notable for her lack of proposals. But then she hadn't wanted any since she'd wished to attend Oxford and obtain a degree, a feat that had only been made possible for women by that world renown seat of learning since 1920. Marriage would have prevented her from attaining that noble goal as she couldn't expect to be a wife and attend university simultaneously. Or so I'd been told.

"Thank you for offering Sebastian the gardenia to nurture. He's been a tad despondent."

"Really?" I glanced toward the exit he'd taken. "He seemed his usual happy self to me."

"Oh, he hides it well, but he's been rather unsuccessful at

healing the rift between him and his grandfather. Yesterday, he visited Wynchcombe House and was denied entrance. Again."

I was aware of Sebastian's attempts to reconnect with his grandfather, the Duke of Wynchcombe, but not the reason behind the breach. Sebastian didn't speak about his family, and Margaret had forbidden us from asking. "I don't understand why the duke shuns Sebastian when he's the heir. You'd think he'd welcome him."

"The duke is a difficult man," she said, evading my gaze.

"To say the least." Clearly, she knew more than she was letting on, but she wasn't telling. Understandable, as Sebastian wouldn't want any confidences he'd shared to be spread about. Exhaustion suddenly made itself known, making me yawn. "Well, I'm off to my lie down. Toodle-oo." I turned to leave.

"We could use your assistance," she said, stopping my progress.

I faced her once more. "I helped this morning after breakfast. Besides, you don't need me." I waved my arm at the room which was a beehive of activity. "You have enough volunteers."

"It's not with the march, itself, I'd like your help. At least not at the moment. I want you to demonstrate your special skills."

I had no idea what she was talking about. "What special skills?"

"The ones you learned at finishing school."

"How to tell a fish fork from a meat one? I don't think most of the volunteers need worry about that." Sadly, most of them lived with limited means which meant they were lucky to eat one decent meal a day. More than likely that would not include two courses.

She smiled in response to my humor before turning serious. "That's not what I want you to teach them."

"What then?"

"I'd like you to show them how to defend themselves." She glanced around the ballroom. "This space is ideal for that. We could announce the class and invite all our volunteers to attend. After the march, of course."

During my year at finishing school, I'd taken a self-defense class and become quite proficient at it. Teaching such a workshop would not be a problem but getting permission for holding it here would be. "Do you think Mother would approve such a thing?"

"I've already obtained her blessing." She made a face. "In exchange for my attending even more social events this season."

Mother had allowed Margaret to use the ballroom for the march preparations, but only if she joined us at some of the afternoon teas and balls. Now it seemed our clever Mother had upped the stakes. If Margaret wanted further use of the space for instruction, she would need to socialize more with members of the upper class. After all, if circumstances played out the way Mother wished, Margaret would find herself married to a duke. And duchesses were expected to entertain.

"It would only be a demonstration or two," she explained.

"More like three or four. Self-defense is not learned in a day, Margaret. And I've never taught before."

"You wouldn't need to demonstrate anything elaborate, only enough for them to get out of a perilous situation." When I hesitated, she went on. "It's important to me, Kitty. Say you'll do it."

How could I say no? She was so passionate about it. "Of course, I will."

"Brilliant." Her smile transmitted pure bliss. "We'll plan for it after the march, then."

I glanced around the room where society ladies were happily chatting with shop girls and factory workers, every one of them dedicated to the cause. Margaret had done this. She'd created a hospitable environment for the fellowship of women. Unless I missed my guess, it was her calling. "You're going to make this your life's work, aren't you? Helping women?"

She nodded. "As much as I can, Kitty. So many of them need so much and have so little. If I can make their lives a little easier, I'll do it."

A thought occurred to me. Self-defense training was one thing, but there was another area of particular interest to her. The subject of the brochure she'd sent me at finishing school.

"You're not planning to teach them about" —I lowered my voice— "birth control?"

She firmed up her chin and looked me straight in the eye. "Yes, I am."

"Mother won't approve." Of that, I was certain.

"She won't have to. The organizers are planning to open a women's health clinic in London where free information, as well as counseling, may be obtained."

"Like the 'Yoke of Womanhood' brochure?"

"Among other things."

"Such as?"

"Supplies."

"Condoms?" *Heavens*! If Mother got wind of that endeavor, she'd have a thing or two to say about it.

She nodded. "I wouldn't be running the clinic, though. All I can do is help establish it before I return to Oxford in the fall. Someone else will manage it."

"My dear sister."

She glanced half defiant at me.

I smiled. "I'm so proud of you."

"Oh, Kitty." She hugged me. "Thank you for saying that. It means the world to me."

Another yawn got the better of me. "I better go. We have another supper to attend tonight. If I don't get some sleep, I may drop off in the soup." I sighed. "I would give anything for a quiet evening at home."

"Dearest, you really need to let Mother know not to demand so much of you."

"I can't. She gets so much pleasure out of showing me off."

She sighed. "If only Emily were here." Our beloved sister who'd died of the Spanish Flu five years ago.

"She would outshine the both of us," I said, pressing her hand.

"Yes, she would."

"Well," I said, pushing away the sad thought, "at least Lord Marlowe will be there. He's always entertaining."

Tilting her head, she studied me. "But you're not looking favorably upon him."

I gave her my usual response. "We are friends. Nothing more."

"And someone else has caught your interest. A certain inspector from Scotland Yard?"

She'd always been too perceptive for my comfort. "I know not of what you speak."

Her only response was a knowing smile. I wasn't giving up my secrets. But then, neither was she.

CHAPTER THREE

TEA AND SYMPATHY

*T*HE FOLLOWING DAY found the Worthington distaff contingent at Lady Clinton's afternoon tea. Held every Wednesday, it provided the upper class with the opportunity to meet friends, catch up on gossip, chat about the latest fashions and scandals, and most of all, be in the right place among the right people. Or so it was perceived.

While the tradition had died down during the years of the Great War and the Spanish Influenza, Lady Clinton, being a prodigious gossip, had revived it with great success. It had truly become the place for women of the nobility and those with means to see and be seen. And most importantly, if you had a daughter of marriageable age, you attended Lady Clinton's afternoon teas.

Mother with not one, but two, unmarried daughters did not dare miss the event, no matter how busy we were. Like clockwork she attended every Wednesday, dragging me along. Margaret would much rather have remained at home to work on the women's march, but she'd promised Mother her attendance. And she would never go back on her word. That did not mean, however, she would exercise more than the merest effort. Once she greeted Lady Clinton at the entrance to the drawing room, she quickly moved on.

I, on the other hand, was not getting away so easily.

"Miss Worthington, how very nice of you to join us," Lady Clinton exclaimed, all her teeth on display. Clearly, she wanted something from me.

Plastering on a smile, I curtsied. "Thank you for the invitation, milady." I sought to make as quick a getaway as Margaret, but Lady Clinton soon disavowed me of that notion.

Laying her hand on my elbow, she took me aside and whispered, "I've been meaning to ask, how did you know who'd murdered that woman on the train?"

Word had spread amongst the nobility that I had featured prominently in solving Rose Trevvyan's murder. I had, of course, but that was not something I was willing to admit, especially to Lady Clinton, inveterate tattler that she was.

"Why, Inspector Crawford apprehended the culprit, don't you know?" I explained, wide-eyed and smiling. "It was in all the newspapers." I had it from a good authority she subscribed to every gossip rag in the business. She would have had to be blind to have missed it, which she certainly was not. Every front page had featured the photograph of Inspector Crawford leading the handcuffed murderer to jail. Nor did it end there. Knowing a good thing when they saw one, the newspapers continued to pursue the story, the latest being an article with a snap of the accused on the dock. The upcoming trial was bound to be a spectacle of unusual proportions.

Not satisfied with my answer, Lady Clinton's mouth

twisted with disapproval. "Yes, I know, but rumor has it you were the one who figured it out."

I laughed. "*Heavens!* How would I have done that? No, milady. I'm afraid the rumors are wrong." I glanced around the room for a way to escape the inquisition and found it. "Oh, there's Lady Emma. I haven't seen her in an age. If you will excuse me." I curtsied once more and headed toward my friend on the far side of the room.

"Lady Emma, how pleasant to see you again," I said, once I'd reached her. I'd met her at one of the earlier balls where she'd been rooted and potted along the wallflower wall. Eager as I'd been to give my weary feet a respite after dancing every set, I'd struck up a conversation with her. Her intelligence and amiability had made it easy to become friends.

Her face lit up in greeting. "The pleasure is all mine, dear Kitty." She shifted on the cream-colored settee to make space for me. As she did, a servant materialized with the tea service which he placed on the small table in front of us. It contained thinly sliced cucumber sandwiches, scones with clotted cream, preserves, cakes and other pastries, as well as a silver teapot and delicate bone china cups and plates. Say what you will about Lady Clinton, she knew how to serve a grand spread.

We helped ourselves to the fragrant Oolong and tempting fare before settling into a discussion. "How did Maurice work out for you?" I'd recommended one of the best hair stylists in London to her.

"Splendid. As you can see." She tossed her head from side to side, sending her mahogany curls bouncing. Her heavy tresses had been trimmed away, leaving her with a much shorter coiffure. The result was absolutely charming.

"Gorgeous. I was so sorry I was not able to accompany you, but—"

"You were occupied with the preparations for your ball. Totally understandable."

My birthday celebration, held two weeks before, had been a resounding success. I was glad more for Mother's sake than my own as she'd worked so very hard on it. "It was such a crush. Hope you enjoyed yourself."

"Absolutely! I danced every set." Her brilliant smile told me she was a wallflower no more.

"Splendid." A wonder what a mere hair trim could do.

"I've also taken your advice and visited Angelique's."

"How wonderful." Angelique, one of the best couturiers in London, had styled my wardrobe for the season. She possessed a singular ability to fashion frocks that perfectly suited each individual client, so no two dresses looked the same.

"She's making my gown for the Torrance Ball."

I squeezed her hand. "I'm sure you'll look marvelous in it."

"I have high hopes. No more old-fashioned gowns for me." Lady Emma's wardrobe had been chosen by someone with an older sensibility. Unfortunately, those gowns made Lady Emma seem a Victorian frump. So, I was very glad she'd assumed command over her fashion choices.

After taking a sip of tea, she nodded toward Margaret, who'd perched herself in a barely visible alcove. "It must be nice to have your sister home." She paused while she studied Margaret. "You resemble each other."

"We do, don't we?" Growing up, the tomboy in me had aspired to Margaret's beauty, so Lady Emma's remark pleased me no end. "She's a trifle shorter, and her hair a shade lighter, but other than that—"

"You're two peas in a pod."

I nodded. "We do possess quite different personalities, though. She's the bookish type. While I'm—"

She laughed. "Not the bookish type."

"No, I'm not." Where Margaret tended to overthink matters, I often leaped without considering the consequences. That character flaw had gotten me into trouble more than once.

"Quiet she might be," Lady Emma continued, "but she managed to capture the attention of the Marquis Thropplethorpe."

I almost blurted out 'Who?' before I realized she was referring to Sebastian. As the heir to the Duke of Wynchcombe, he held that courtesy title. Not a surprise Emma knew. After all, Sebastian had made an appearance at my birthday celebration. Anyone with a working eyesight would have seen he was fascinated with Margaret. "I often forget Sebastian is referred as such."

"Sebastian?" Lady Emma's brow arched in surprise. "Is that what you call him?" she asked, not unkindly.

"He insists." I helped myself to another scone. Breakfast had been hours ago. And since we'd skipped our midday meal to work on Margaret's project, I was starving. "Feel free to refer to him as such. Thropplethorpe is such a mouthful."

As she settled her gaze on my sister, her mood turned somber. "Such a sad story that." She turned back to me. "Sebastian's, I mean."

Well, that perked up my interest. "You know his history?"

"Oh, yes. My brother Nicky was in Oxford at the same time as him."

There was so very little we knew about Sebastian. And Mother and I had been prevented from discovering more after Margaret cautioned us against inquiring about his life. We'd honored her request, but that didn't mean I wasn't eager to learn as much as I could. For my sister's sake, of course. "Oh?" I asked, hoping to encourage more confidences.

She lowered her voice. "Sebastian's father married the gardener's daughter."

"Did he really?" I asked in a hushed tone.

Lady Emma nodded. "The Duke of Wynchcombe did not approve. You see, the title goes back to the fifteenth century. Henry V, or was it Henry IV? Anyhow one of the Henrys awarded him the title for bravery in battle. He takes great stock in that. So, for his son to marry a commoner with no blue blood in her? Well, it was not to be borne."

I hung on to her every word while sipping the tea.

"He insists on everyone showing him deference, loves to lord it over every other duke, never mind someone lower in rank. Why" —she huffed— "if he had his way, he'd probably ask people to kowtow to him."

"How do you know all this?"

"Father. Since he's a mere earl, the duke ignores him every time they meet. As far as the Duke of Wynchcombe is concerned, anyone below a ducal rank is not worth acknowledging."

"He'd be lonely then. It's not like dukes are that thick on the ground. At last count, maybe twenty-four?"

Lady Emma darted a questioning glance toward me.

"Mother," I explained. "She made me memorize *Debrett's*."

A honking laugh escaped Lady Emma. "How very droll."

"I love her dearly, but she's a tad obsessed with the nobility." An understatement to say the least.

"She must be thrilled about your sister's . . . acquaintance with Sebastian then."

"She's hopeful." And that was all I would say on the matter. "What happened after the duke's son married the gardener's daughter?"

"The duke told them never to darken his doorstep again, or some such drivel. Apparently, they'd already planned to set up residence in Edinburgh where the son's wife was born.

Her father, the gardener, joined them after leaving the duke's employ. The family, apparently, led a happy life. But then disaster struck."

"What happened?"

"Sebastian's parents died. They got lost in a blinding snowstorm and fell off a cliff."

My breath hitched. "How tragic."

"By all accounts it was, but it didn't end there."

"How so?" I asked, after helping myself to a slice of cake.

"The duke would have ignored Sebastian's existence if it had been left up to him. But the gardener grandfather traveled to the duke's estate with Sebastian in tow and threatened to proclaim the duke's shoddy behavior to everyone far and wide if he didn't acknowledge his grandson as his heir."

"Good for him."

"Well, the duke being the proud sort of man he was did not wish for that to happen, so he agreed to do so. But that was as far as he was willing to go."

"What do you mean?"

"He would only recognize Sebastian as long as he kept his distance."

No wonder Sebastian couldn't gain admittance to Wynchcombe House.

"I would have thrown the offer back to his face, but Sebastian complied. You see, he has a younger sister, Lily. She was three at the time."

"He does?" Why hadn't Sebastian told us? But then again, maybe Margaret knew and hadn't shared it with Mother and me.

"Yes. His gardener grandfather was ill and unable to care for someone so young. So, Sebastian made the duke promise he would provide for her necessities, including her education. If the duke didn't treat her like a princess, Sebastian swore he would cause a scandal the likes of which the duke had never seen. He was only eight at the time."

"Dear heaven." My opinion of Sebastian increased several fold. To face down a duke at that age was downright heroic. "How did this information get about? I can't imagine Sebastian would have spoken about it." He certainly hadn't breathed a word to us.

"Servants." She sipped her tea and placed a scone on a plate. "They know everything."

That was certainly true in our household. Our butler, Carlton, and our housekeeper, Mrs. Simpson, were certainly aware of everything that happened at Worthington House. Well, most of it. There were some things I'd managed to keep from them.

"There was no love lost between the duke's staff and the duke," Lady Emma continued once she finished her scone. "Word got about pretty quickly about what had happened."

"And Sebastian kept his promise all this time in exchange for his sister's wellbeing?"

"Apparently."

"Where is she?"

"She lived most of her life at Wynchcombe Castle in Hampshire, the duke's family seat. But about two years ago, the duke's son, Lord Percy, convinced his father to bring her to London to gain some town bronze. There's only been the occasional sighting of her, though. The lending library, the park. Absolutely no social events."

"She's not out?" Since Sebastian was five and twenty, she had to be twenty. Old enough to have made her debut.

"No. Rumor has it the Duchess of Torrance, whose husband is a crony of the Duke of Wynchcombe, offered to sponsor the sister, but the duke turned down her offer. Apparently, he didn't want to spend any more money on the chit. His words."

"How very sad." If Lily was as beautiful as Sebastian was handsome, she would be a popular debutante. But, of course, the duke had only agreed to provide her with the bare necessities. She'd been fed, housed, and educated. As far as he was concerned, that was probably more than enough. "I gather the duke kept his promise to Sebastian and paid for his education as well?"

"Yes. He attended Eton and Oxford. Once he was old enough to travel on his own, he spent his holidays in Edinburgh, in the very home he'd lived with his parents. All alone, by all accounts. His other grandfather had passed on by then."

"How very lonely he must have been." No wonder he'd taken to our family like a duck to water. We were the antithesis of the duke. We might be loud and opinionated, but we truly cared for each other. "And you learned all this information from your brother?"

She nodded. "It's common knowledge at Oxford, apparently. After Sebastian matriculated at the university, the whole sorry tale unfolded. That institution has a very long memory."

"I can imagine."

Her gaze drifted back to Margaret. "I see Lady Kingsley has joined your sister."

Lady Emma was right. The older maven was seated next to Margaret. "She sponsored her, and me, at our court presentations."

She turned back to me. "Your sister will want to encourage that connection."

"She's a friend of our family, most especially Mother," I explained.

"I understand. But Margaret will need her support. I don't know if you've noticed, but ever since she arrived, the tabbies have been busy."

I glanced around the room. My eyebrows rose as I noticed the surreptitious glances darted toward Margaret, followed by mad whisperings behind teacups.

"It surprises you?" Emma asked.

"It does. Margaret was roundly ignored by most everyone during her debut."

"Ahhh, but she's now captured the interest of the Duke of Wynchcombe's heir. Circumstances have changed. Everywhere she goes she will be watched assiduously. Every one of those matrons, and their unmarried daughters, will wait for Margaret to make the smallest faux pas. Once she does, they'll pounce on her."

"*Heavens!*" More than likely Margaret wouldn't give a fig. Still, I would need to warn her.

"Indeed," she took another sip of the tea which had been refreshed by a footman. "Now tell me about this march of hers. Any chance I can assist?"

"Absolutely." We spent the rest of the afternoon discussing the women's suffrage project. By the time we parted, she'd agreed not only to help with the preparations but participate in the march.

Knowing Margaret would frown on a discussion about Sebastian, I waited until we arrived home before secreting with Mother in her personal parlor to share what I'd learned.

She was as upset as I was. "That's outrageous. That young man is the duke's heir. Is he supposed to live at Oxford until his grandfather passes away?"

"Apparently."

"And his sister Lily?" She shook her head. "Is she to remain in that house with no female to support her?"

"No idea, Mother."

"There must be something we can do."

So much for not prying into Sebastian's affairs. But deep

in my heart I knew we needed to act. "Should we discuss our options with Margaret?" I asked.

Mother took a moment to ponder the question. "We will, but not now. Best wait until the women's march is done."

As it turned out, events soon overtook us; and by then, the damage was done.

CHAPTER FOUR

HOORAY FOR WOMEN

*W*ITH THE MARCH ONLY TWO DAYS AWAY, our ballroom had become a very busy place. We were expecting hundreds to march, all of whom would carry 'Votes for all Women' signs, as well as wear sashes and rosettes with similar messages. While some volunteers were putting finishing touches on the items to be worn, others were hammering the signs to posts. The din was so loud you could hardly hear yourself think.

By now, Mother probably regretted giving her permission. But since she'd exchanged Margaret's participation in social events for the rally organizers to use our home as their headquarters, she couldn't renege on her word. At least, we didn't lack funds. Many benefactors were contributing to the cause.

As everything was proceeding on schedule, we had high hopes for the march. The leaders responsible for getting the word out were emphasizing this would be a peaceful rally, nothing like the militant efforts of previous years. The marchers would simply parade in front of the Palace of Westminster, proceed to Victoria Tower Gardens, where a few speeches would be given, before marching to Buckingham Palace where the rally would end.

Their purpose in insisting this was to be a strife-free rally was not difficult to ascertain. Some of the previous marches had ended with suffragettes imprisoned and force-fed after they'd staged hunger strikes. The current leaders wanted to avoid violence of any kind. But, as they say, plans can often go awry.

Too excited to stand still, I picked up one of the 'Votes for all Women' sign I'd designed, slung on one of the sashes, and pinned a rosette to my shoulder. Turning toward Margaret, I paraded in front of her. "What do you think? Do I look like a proper suffragette?"

She frowned. "This is not a fashion show, Kitty. It's serious business."

"Don't you think I know that? Spoilsport," I whispered underneath my breath.

"I heard that."

I should have remembered she had the ears of a bat. But soon, a sense of shame filled me. As hard as she'd been working, she did not deserve my rude remark. Reaching around her, I embraced her and kissed her cheek. "I apologize. I shouldn't have snapped at you."

Her shoulders drooped. "If anyone's been acting rudely, it's me. Sorry, Kitty." Turning, she hugged me back.

That's when I noticed how tense she was. "Let's go have a cuppa, shall we?" The kitchen staff had set up a food table where tea, sandwiches, and all kind of sweets were continuously being served. Every volunteer had been more than welcome to help themselves.

"But—"

"Margaret, you need a respite from all this. Five minutes to get your bearings is not going to hurt anything." I grabbed her hand and pulled her from the chair. "Come."

Giving in, she smiled. "All right. If you insist."

"I do."

After we helped ourselves not only to the tea, but slices of cake, I asked, "Where's Sebastian?" He'd been missing for the last hour.

"He had to attend to a personal matter."

I could very well guess what it was. "He's gone to Wynch-combe House?" Again.

Margaret nodded and then she gazed at me. "He has a sister. Lily."

"I know. Lady Emma told me."

"Did she?"

"Yes."

"I suppose you know the whole story then."

"She told me what she knew. Got the whole sorry tale from her brother. Apparently, it's common knowledge at Oxford."

She sighed. "Yes, it is. I'm sorry I couldn't share it with you."

"You wanted to keep his confidences to yourself." I pressed her hand. "I understand. Truly."

She gazed off into the distance. "All he wants is to see his sister, talk to her. But he keeps getting barred entrance. He travels over there every day, sometimes twice a day, only to be turned away."

I never hated a human being in my life, but I'd developed a strong dislike of the Duke of Wynchcombe. The man was an utter beast to keep brother and sister apart.

"What does his grandfather hope to gain from stopping Sebastian from seeing his sister?"

"Control. Power. Who knows?" She gazed into her cup as

if the answer was to be found there. "I fear what may happen if the duke doesn't relent."

"What do you mean?"

"I can't see Sebastian allowing this situation to continue. He came to London expressly to see his sister."

That was not the only reason why he'd come to London. He also wanted to be close to Margaret. In my opinion, they were more than friends, not matter what Margaret said. Occasionally, she'd gaze at him, and the full strength of her feelings was there, right in her eyes. As sure as I was sitting here next to her drinking tea, she was in love with him. And so was he with her. Unlike her, he never hid his emotions when it came to Margaret. The love on his face was apparent whenever he looked at her.

"Well, that's that. Back to work," she said, coming to her feet. "Where did you find the sashes?"

"In the corner." I pointed to the boxes which had been delivered in the last hour.

"Can someone take a flat iron to them?" Margaret asked in a loud voice. "We want them nice and crisp."

"I'll do it, Miss Worthington," my maid, Betsy, said. She'd just delivered a plate of sandwiches to the refreshments table. Eager to participate in her first march, she'd proved invaluable as an intermediary between the staff and the march volunteers.

To affect the family as little as possible, the volunteers had been asked to present themselves at the tradesman's entrance in the back of the house. Because they came and went as their time allowed, there was constant traffic through the kitchen and the servant hallways to the ball-room. The constant disruption to the household routine had caused many a ruffled feather among the staff. But Betsy had proven herself a champ at smoothing them out.

As Betsy headed toward the sashes to take on the ironing

task, Mother arrived in a frazzle, her favorite gossip rag, *The Tell-All,* in her hand.

"What's wrong?" Margaret asked.

Rather than answer, Mother responded with a question of her own. "Where is Sebastian?"

"He's gone on an errand. What's the matter?"

"Not here. My parlor." Filled with volunteers as the ballroom was, it was not a place to share what precipitated her upset.

When we arrived at her private space, she showed us the cause of her agitation—an engagement notice between the Honorable Lily Dalrymple and Viscount Tottingham."

"Viscount Tottingham?" I shuddered. "That old man we met at the theatre? The one with the loose, false teeth?"

"Yes," Mother said, wringing her hands.

I stared at her in horror. "He has to be in his sixties."

"And she's not yet twenty-one according to the newspaper."

Margaret's lip curled. "That's disgusting."

"I'm afraid of what—"

But before Mother could finish her thought, Sebastian strolled into the room, cutting off what she was about to say. "Were you looking for me, Mrs. W?" He'd taken to calling Mother by her first initial. Mother had decided to be charmed by it.

"Yes, Sebastian, dear. There's a . . . notice in the paper that pertains to your sister." Unable to continue, she held out the newspaper to him.

"How did you find out about Lily?" he asked Mother, an intense look on his face.

"Society gossip." Mother pointed to the paper. "Read, dear."

His eyes widened as he took in the words. Before too long, he exploded. "That miserable bastard."

"Sebastian, language," Mother gently chided.

"I beg your pardon, ma'am. But he can't do this. He can't force her to marry this, this . . . It's obscene."

"I agree," I said.

"Kitty." Mother shook her head. No sense adding more tinder to the fire, her gesture seemed to say.

"Lily will not be forced to marry a man three times her age," Sebastian exclaimed. "I won't allow it."

"You know she's being coerced?" Mother asked.

His great strides ate up the small parlor space. "I know my sister. I may not have seen her for several years, but we correspond. She's young, innocent. She wishes to enjoy life, not marry this, this." He punched the newspaper again, ripping it in two this time, causing the remnants to flutter to the floor.

I bent to pick up the pieces as we would need to carefully read it for clues.

"You have to gain an audience with your grandfather and persuade him to change his mind," Margaret said.

He ran a restless hand through his blond curls, tossing them into disarray. "How am I to do that when the servants won't allow me entry into Wynchcombe House?"

"There may be another way, Sebastian, dear," Mother said in a soft voice.

Sebastian stopped his mad pacing and turned to her. "Which way is that?"

"Come with us to the Duchess of Torrance's ball tonight. Her husband is an old crony of your grandfather's. More than likely the Duke of Wynchcombe will be there. If he attends, you can approach your grandfather and ask him for a private audience to discuss the issue with him."

She didn't have to say it, but she probably hoped the public setting would lend its weight to a civil discourse. Seeing how shabbily he'd treated Sebastian, I thought there was as much hope of that happening as the sun setting in the east. But maybe the duke would surprise us all.

While he pondered Mother's suggestion, Sebastian resumed pacing the floor. After a few moments, he stopped in front of her. "I don't have any formal wear," he confessed, rather red-faced.

Made sense with his tight allowance.

"That doesn't present a problem," Mother responded with a smile. "You and Ned are of a similar build. He can lend you some clothes. Now shoes." She stared at his feet. "Your feet are larger. Must come from all that walking, Sebastian, dear. Let's see what we can find, shall we?"

A force of nature, Mother was in her element. There wasn't a problem she encountered she couldn't solve. She tugged the bell pull, and our butler Carlton appeared post haste. More than likely he'd determined the way the wind was blowing and anticipated the summons.

"Carlton, please contact John Lobb, the shoemaker. Tell him" —she paused— "tell him the Marquis Thropplethorpe is in dire need of footwear for a ball this evening."

"Please, don't." Sebastian choked out. He was referring to the title, of course. He hated to be called that.

Mother fixed him with a hard stare. "The title will magically open doors for you, Sebastian. Use it."

"But I—I can't." His face retained the color of a muted shade of pink. "My funds. They're not what they ought to be."

"Nothing to worry about for we have an account there. That's where Mr. Worthington buys all his footwear. Now go. Neville, our chauffeur, can drive you. No more walking today, mind you. You simply don't have the time."

Tension eased from him as his jaw unclenched, and his mouth relaxed. "Yes, Mrs. W." Holding her hand in his, he kissed it. "You're an angel on earth."

She blushed. "Go on, lad."

"Yes, ma'am." He bowed and, with a newly found confidence, walked out of the room.

She turned to me. "Kitty?"

"I'll call Ned and alert him to Sebastian's need for formal wear. Heaven knows he doesn't need it since he never goes anywhere. It's probably collecting moths in his clothes press."

Mother stiffened. "I most certainly hope not."

"Not to worry, Mother." I grinned. "He has an excellent valet who'd rather endure the fires of hell than allow Ned's clothes to suffer such a calamity."

She grinned. "Go on with you, then."

"What do you want me to do, Mother?" Margaret asked, her restless hands and shortened breaths clear signs of her turmoil. She might downplay her fondness for Sebastian all she wished, but her body gave her away.

"You will have the most important job of all. This evening, you are to stick to Sebastian like glue. Don't let him out of your sight. Keep up his spirits. We can't allow him to burst into the kind of anger he just displayed when he faces his grandfather. If he does, it will prove fatal to his cause."

"Yes, Mother." She kissed Mother's cheek. "Sebastian was right. You are an angel."

"Stop pouring the butter boat over me."

Margaret simply grinned.

"I'll ask Mrs. Simpson to prepare a room where he can change after he returns. Oh, and Margaret, go and find your father's valet. He'll need to assist Sebastian with clothes and such."

Expecting further instruction, neither Margaret and I moved, but apparently she was done. "Well, go on, both of you. There's no time to waste. Not if we want to succeed."

Jumping to her command, Margaret and I dashed out of the room.

37

CHAPTER FIVE

BALL REVELATIONS

*T*HAT EVENING, we stood with bated breath at the bottom of the staircase waiting for Sebastian to appear. We'd done everything that could be done. Black tie wear and formal shoes had been acquired. Father's valet had been dispatched to assist him in dressing for the ball. Now all we had to was wait for him to materialize.

Sebastian did not disappoint.

We watched in wonder as he descended the steps, so handsome he almost took my breath away. He'd certainly stolen Margaret's. Our happy-go-lucky Sebastian Dalrymple had vanished. In his place, from his shorn curls to his footwear, he was every inch a lord. What a duke he would make!

"Mrs. Worthington." He bowed to Mother, this time using the formal mode of address.

Mother held her hand to her throat. "Oh, my." Even she was taken aback.

After giving everyone a few minutes to take in Sebastian, Father cleared his throat. "Shall we go then? The carriage is waiting to take Cinderella to the ball."

I choked back a laugh.

"Edward," Mother gently chided before turning to Sebastian. "Ignore Mr. Worthington's ill-placed humor, Sebastian, dear. I always do."

"If you say so, ma'am." He offered Mother his arm, and she took it with her head held high. To be escorted by a future duke, well, it didn't get much better than that.

While Sebastian and Mother led the way, Father, Margaret, and I brought up the rear.

"The puppy cleans up rather nicely, what?" Father whispered sotto voce.

I bit my lip to keep laughter from spilling out.

Margaret had quite a different reaction. "He's not a dog, Father."

"No, dear, he very much is not. As I've learned. We need to talk."

She swiveled toward him. "What do you mean?"

"I looked into Sebastian's background."

"You didn't!" Outrage poured out of her.

Which Father took in stride. "As your father, it is my responsibility, Margaret."

"I wish you hadn't," she said in a hushed voice.

"Well, it's done. Discovered some rather interesting information. Tomorrow will be soon enough to have a chin wag about it."

He already knew what we'd learned at Lady Clinton's afternoon tea since Mother had shared the information with him. It had to be something new. I was curious to learn what he'd discovered, but chances were, I wouldn't. The 'chin wag' was bound to include only Margaret, and my sister would never spill the beans.

As Torrance House was in the same area of Mayfair, the drive did not take long. Even though Sebastian wasn't invited, Mother believed he would not be denied entrance. No hostess in her right mind would turn away the future Duke of Wynchcombe.

Once we arrived, Mother insisted he enter by himself. A wise decision on her part. That way, all the attention would focus on him. As soon as the Marquis Thropplethorpe was announced, a sudden hush fell over the room. Everyone, and I mean everyone, ceased what they were doing to stare at him. To his credit, Sebastian took it all in stride, greeting his host and hostess, the Duke and Duchess of Torrance, with the manners of a fine lord, well-versed in etiquette.

The hosts were overjoyed by his presence, especially the duchess, for she spent several minutes talking with him. But she finally allowed him to move on to make room for her next guests—us. While she was politeness itself, her greeting lacked the effusiveness and warmth she'd shown Sebastian. But we hadn't expected it. After all, we were not members of the nobility, merely rich.

As we advanced into the ballroom, some guests dismissed us with a glance. Not a surprise as some thought of us as nouveau riche. But many more smiled and nodded in acknowledgement. Even if I were not as popular as I was, they wouldn't want to insult Father, the person who managed many of their fortunes.

The ballroom itself was the stuff of fairy tales as huge chandeliers sparkled above, their crystals shedding light on the guests gathered below. Flowers cascaded from tall, stylish vases around the perimeter of the room, while musicians played a classical tune—Mendelssohn I believed—on the far side of the space. When a footman suddenly appeared by our side with a tray of gilt-edged wine goblets and champagne flutes, Father and Sebastian helped themselves to the spirits. The Worthington women, however, opted out. The evening was bound to be long, and we would need our wits about us.

Gentlemen soon crowded around us, jostling each other for prominence. When Margaret was asked to dance, she politely declined. I, however, could not let the side down, and my dance card was soon filled.

While I took turns around the dance floor, Sebastian remained with my family, clear proof of his high regard for us. If anyone wished to talk to him, then by God, they would have to do it in the company of the Worthingtons. Plenty took the opportunity to approach him. Some, I could imagine, were old school chums. After all, between his years of study and research fellowship, he'd been at Oxford for seven years. But others were clearly matchmaking mothers eager to introduce the coveted prize to their daughters.

Lord Marlowe, my current dancing partner, commented on the sight. "Poor sod. He's in for it now."

Even though I knew what he meant, I asked, "Is he?"

He nodded toward the grouping. "Those matchmaking mothers swarming about him would love to land a future duke as a son-in-law."

I could tell them it wouldn't do any good since his interest was all for Margaret, but for once I kept my counsel to myself. After all, nothing was settled between them. It could all very well come to naught.

"What about you, milord? Any news about a future Lady Marlowe?"

He fake-shuddered and returned his gaze to me. "You know my attention is all for you, Miss Worthington."

It was so smoothly done, anyone would have believed him. I, however, knew better. "We've had this discussion before, milord. You're using me as a shill to ward off those matchmaking mothers." A turn closer to other dancers kept

41

me silent for a second, but then he spun us away once more. "You'll have to marry at some point, you know."

"That point has not been reached. I haven't finished sowing my wild oats." He meant it as a joke, but I took the point seriously.

"Be careful, Lord Marlowe, lest sowing your wild oats result in damage to the stalk." I paused as I pondered the anatomy of the plant. "Or is it the stem?"

He barked out a laugh. "And what would you know about such a subject?"

"Plenty. Margaret is a fountain of information. But I'm not sure which part of the wild oats would best match your physique. I should ask Sebastian. He's a botany expert, you know." I started to break away.

But he pulled me back before I could take a step. "Don't you dare. My reputation would be damaged beyond repair." He barked out a laugh. "Damaged stalk indeed."

"Lord Marlowe." I pinned him with a hard stare. I was not about to be dissuaded from the subject.

"Miss Worthington, I can assure you every precaution has been taken to protect the, er, stalk from damage."

A grin bubbled out of me. "That's very good to hear. I'm glad that little Lords Marlowe will be assured." In total charity with each other, we continued dancing.

But then I caught a glimpse of Lord Newcastle, not too sure on his feet, wandering the fringes of the room. Usually spotlessly attired, he now appeared disheveled. Not only that, but he'd lost weight, resulting in his suit fitting him ill. As I watched in dismay, he stumbled and leaned against the wall for support.

I nodded toward him to alert my dance partner. "Newcastle. Over there."

Following the direction of my nod, Lord Marlowe frowned.

"He doesn't appear well," I said. "Could he be—?"

"Drunk as a lord."

Why would Newcastle attend a ball in such a state? Could he be looking for another confrontation with Lord Wakefield? Last month, Newcastle had punched Lord Wakefield after Lady Wakefield appeared bruised at a ball, the outcome of her husband's punishment for not providing him with an heir. Subsequently, a *détente* of sorts had been reached when Lady Wakefield retired to the country while her husband remained in town. But bad blood still existed between the two aristocrats. It wasn't beyond the realm of possibility that Newcastle was itching for a second round. After all, he was still in love with Lady Wakefield.

"Is Lord Wakefield present?" I asked in a rush.

"No idea. He very well could be. He's a friend of Torrance." For a few seconds, he watched Newcastle bumble his way across the room. "I think I better—"

"Yes. Please do."

After he escorted me back to Mother, he rushed to catch up with Newcastle. Hopefully, Marlowe would keep the earl from causing harm, whether to himself or others.

It wasn't until an hour later, however, that the real excitement began. The Duke of Wynchcombe arrived, accompanied by someone who had to be Lord Percy, his son. I gasped when I saw them. Why had no one remarked upon the strong resemblance between the duke, his son, and grandson? They were the very spitting images of each other—one old, one middle-aged, one young. Everyone in the room held their breath when Sebastian approached his grandfather. Apparently, word had spread about their strained relations.

"Your Grace." Sebastian bowed to his grandfather, whose arrogant gaze raked over him.

"What the blazes are you doing here?" the duke spit out.

Ignoring his grandfather's rudeness, Sebastian politely

said, "There's a particular subject I wish to discuss with you, sir. If we could retire somewhere—"

"There is no subject I wish to discuss with you, whelp," the duke blared loud enough for the entire ballroom to hear. "Now leave."

"Father," Lord Percy interjected. "Maybe you should hear him out in private."

"No one sought your opinion, Percy. And you—?" His fulminating gaze settled once more on Sebastian.

The tension in the room was sky-high. Everyone waited with bated breath for the duke's next words.

"—Get. Out. Of my sight."

"Not before I've had my say, sir."

"How dare you? No one gainsays me."

"It's about Lily."

"What about her?"

"I want to ascertain if this marriage is something she desires."

"And what if it isn't? I've made the arrangements. And it's final. She will marry Tottingham. As soon as it can be arranged."

Sebastian had stood half hunched over while paying obeisance to his grandfather. But he now rose to his full height to tower over the duke. "No, Sir. She will not."

"And who's going to stop me? You?" The duke threw his head back and wheezed out a nasty laugh. "You're nothing. Less than nothing. I am her guardian. I get to do with her as I will."

Sebastian's control slipped, and anger spilled out. "It's one thing to belittle me, harm me, thrust me away, but I'll be damned if I allow you to marry Lily to that old lecher."

"And what are you going to do about it?"

"Whatever I have to. Sir." And with that he whirled

around and left his grandfather fuming, spittle dripping from the corner of his mouth.

As Sebastian rejoined us, clearly shaken, our family surrounded him in a protective circle. Margaret, in front of him, reached out to take his hand. I stood to his left, Mother to his right. Father at his back glared at the duke with a look of disgust I'd never seen on him before.

"Who are those people?" The duke's voice thundered across the room.

"The Worthingtons, Father," Lord Percy answered.

"Worthington?" He hitched up his chin. "I don't recognize the name."

"The patriarch, Edward Worthington, is the financier."

"Common as dirt, I suppose." The duke sneered.

"Father!" Lord Percy exclaimed. "Mister Worthington is a well-respected member of the finance community with an excellent reputation for managing funds."

"Doesn't matter. He still doesn't have a drop of blue blood in him."

The Duke of Torrance wisely chose that moment to step into the heated atmosphere. "We've a spot of gambling set up in the card room, Wynchcombe. Why don't you join us?"

"Yes, the air here has suddenly become quite noxious." After one last sneer, he turned and made his way through the throng that had collected around him while his son and the Duke of Torrance followed behind.

Sebastian was still shaking with rage while Margaret stood quietly by his side. A misguided lord suddenly appeared and asked her to dance. She shook her head. "My apologies, but I'm not dancing tonight."

She'd cut a lord. But then her priority was all about Sebastian. If there was any question in anybody's mind that these two were destined for each other, her action should put paid to all doubts.

"We should go," Mother said with quiet dignity.

"Please don't leave on my account," Sebastian said in a strained voice.

"I've suddenly developed a headache, Mother," Margaret said.

She and Sebastian gazed at each other. It could burn bridges, that look.

"Me as well," I announced.

"I'll go arrange for the Rolls then," Father tossed out, in effect ending that discussion.

"Thank you, Edward," Mother said.

Father led the way while Sebastian, with Mother on his arm, followed. Margaret and I quietly trailed in their wake, leaving a roomful of shocked guests behind.

CHAPTER SIX

VOTE FOR WOMEN RALLY

*W*ITH THE VOTE FOR WOMEN RALLY scheduled for the next day, Margaret and I couldn't dedicate so much as a thought to the plight of Sebastian's sister. But thankfully, Father had. Taking Sebastian in hand, he'd introduced him to a solicitor to obtain his advice. Unfortunately, the advice was not what we hoped it would be.

Since Sebastian's grandfather held the purse strings, Sebastian didn't have a penny to his name. Under these circumstances, no court would award him guardianship over Lily. But the solicitor did offer a glimmer of hope in the way of a legacy created by Lily's grandmother, the former Duchess of Wynchcombe.

Believing her husband would support the male offspring of their union, she'd created a trust to benefit the female issue of her sons. Since Lily was the only descendant which fit that description, she would inherit quite a sum, but not until her twenty-first birthday. At that point, Lily could do whatever she wished. But her birthday was not until September which explained why the duke was in such a hurry to marry her off. On that day, her new husband, not Lily, would control those funds. And there poor Lily would be, stuck in a marriage to a man three times her age, poor as a church mouse, except for what her husband chose to share with her. The thought was not to be borne.

The problem then became how to stop the wedding from taking place next week. We had no idea how that could be achieved, but we vowed to do everything possible. Privately, I thought a good old-fashioned rescue would do the trick. It wasn't like I hadn't done a bit of breaking and entering in the past. But knowing what my family's reaction would be, I kept that novel idea to myself. For the moment.

On the day of the rally, we were up earlier than the birds as there were plenty of last-minute things to do. But with all hands on deck, as it were, everything was soon resolved to Margaret's satisfaction. We'd set the staging area at the statue of Boadicea and her daughters. Located on the north side of the western end of Westminster Bridge, it was the perfect location to gather and begin our march to the Palace of Westminster where Parliament met. We would then stroll to the entrance of Victoria Tower Gardens situated at Westminster's southwest corner where some of the rally leaders were scheduled to speak. Afterward, we would proceed up Birdcage Walk to Buckingham Palace where more speeches would be given.

At the appointed time, we sorted the signs, sashes, and rosettes into several motorcars. And then we headed out with Margaret, Betsy and I piling into my Rolls Royce Silver Ghost, as well as dear Sebastian, of course. He'd volunteered to be our beast of burden and help carry and pass out the signs.

We arrived at the statue to find not only an excited crowd of rally participants, but newspaper reporters as well. After we distributed the march paraphernalia, the leaders reminded everyone of the planned route and order of events. And then, with heads held high, we proceeded to Westminster Palace, singing 'The March of the Women,' a song composed by Ethel Smyth in 1911 to promote the suffragette cause.

Since we'd given notice to both the newspapers and the police, a sizable crowd met us at Westminster. Photographers had set up their cameras in front of the building, no doubt to get the best snaps. Some in the crowd cheered, others booed. Ignoring the naysayers, we continued on our way smiles plastered on our faces, holding our signs high. Since we'd decided only women should participate in the march, Sebastian was not part of the parade. But he walked alongside cheering, far enough away it was clear he was not one of the marchers.

Unfortunately, his grandfather did not see it that way.

He, along with others, whom I could only assume were members of the House of Lords, stood in front of Westminster, frowns on their faces, watching us pass. When he caught sight of Sebastian, his frown turned into speech. I was too far away—and the chanting and singing were too loud—to hear their altercation, but it was clear from their gestures that Sebastian and his grandfather were exchanging heated words. The argument seemed to reach a crescendo when his grandfather raised his hand as if to strike Sebastian, but he took a step back before the older man could land the blow. After a last sour look, Sebastian veered away from him and caught up to us.

Unfortunately, the photographers had captured the disagreement. And one of the reporters had been close enough to more than likely hear their argument. There was no hope for it. Their altercation would make front page news.

The drama did not end there. We arrived at the entrance to Victoria Tower Gardens to be greeted by a number of rabble rousers, every last one of them a man. Not content to boo, they hurled slurs at us. We tried to ignore them, but soon they shoved their way into our group to tear down our signs. When one big bully went after Margaret, Sebastian knocked him out. In no time at all, the peaceful march turned into an all-out melee with the march women giving as good as they got. Since someone had destroyed my sign, I only had my stick for defense. When a dastard came after me, I hit him as hard as I could, unfortunately breaking the stick into tinder. Unable to use it any more, I resorted to kicks to a certain part of the male anatomy to defend myself.

Soon, police whistles were screeching as London's finest surrounded us. Within minutes we were rounded up and carted off in police vans. With my hair tossed every which way and my lip bleeding, I was probably a sight to behold. Lady Emma had not fared much better. But she had a militant light in her eyes I hadn't seen before. Unfortunately, Margaret had not fared as well for she was gingerly holding her arm against her chest. It did not appear to be broken, though, so maybe she was only suffering from a bad sprain. Sebastian had been taken up with the men, so I didn't see what happened to him. But regardless, it appeared I was headed for the clink. Again.

CHAPTER SEVEN

A STINT IN THE CLINK

*I*T TOOK NO TIME AT ALL to arrive at the Thames constabulary, situated as it was in the same area as Westminster Palace. We descended from the van, a little worse for the wear, but with our heads held high. Familiar with the drill from my previous arrest, I asked a rosy-cheeked officer, "The detention room, I suppose?"

"Yes, Miss. This way, please," he responded, surprise apparent on his face.

"Of course, Officer. Come on, ladies. Follow me."

Someone started belting 'The March of the Women,' and soon all of us were singing along. I was so proud of them, proud of us. We may have been temporarily down, but we were not out. But when we were shown into the station and the seriousness of the situation struck them, everyone quieted down.

Constable Peters, who'd processed me during my previous misunderstanding with the law, explained the procedure. Our fingerprints would be taken, photographs would be snapped. We would then be led to holding cells where we would remain until someone bailed us out. The leaders, anticipating such a contingency, had set aside funds for bail money. No marcher would be left in jail. A person assigned to that task would make sure every one was released.

But I was pleased to see the police was not eager to keep us in prison, at least not permanently. No wonder. Having gotten so much backlash the last time women marched for the vote, all they wanted was to release us as quickly as possible.

"Any questions, ladies?" Constable Peters asked, polite to a fault. Someone must have ordered him to treat us with kid gloves. When no one spoke up, he said, "Now, who would like to be first?"

Two of the leaders stepped forward. Since they'd been through this process during the right to vote protests of several years ago, they probably wanted to show the marchers there was nothing to fear. I wasn't so sure. Everyone arrested would have a police record which could be used against her when seeking employment or a place to live. But they'd been made aware of the possible conse-quences, which made them brave indeed.

The leaders, along with Constable Peters, disappeared into the processing room where they would be fingerprinted, their photographs taken, and an arrest card completed.

I would have volunteered to go next, but Margaret's arm needed attention. If her drawn expression was anything to go by, she was hurting. But as was her wont, she did not complain. So, I would do it for her.

"Officer?" I asked the fresh-faced policeman we'd met upon our arrival.

"Yes, Miss."

"Can you fetch Constable Peters? I wish to speak with him."

"Of course, Miss."

Constable Peters soon emerged from the processing room. When he saw me, his eyes grew wide. "Miss Worthington."

"You remember me." Not only did he recognize me from our previous encounter, but more importantly, he was aware of my connection to Scotland Yard Detective Inspector Robert Crawford.

"Yes, Miss."

Good. "My sister is hurt. She needs a doctor."

"Aww, Miss. We don't—"

"Never mind, Constable. I'll handle this," a deep voice answered from behind me.

I knew that voice. It made regular appearances in my dreams. Turning toward its owner, I said, "Inspector Crawford." Tall, dark-haired, dark-eyed. As handsome as ever. Should have known I would run into him.

"Your sister is hurt?" he enquired, his gaze showing concern.

"Yes. Her arm."

His gaze took in the pain on Margaret's face, apparent to anyone with two working eyes. And his never missed a thing. He nodded. "I'll get someone down here. In the meantime, let's get her more comfortable."

"Thank you."

Without acknowledging my gratitude, he thrust open a door clearly emblazoned with the superintendent's name and escorted us into the room. "You can wait here while I fetch a physician."

Emma, Betsy, and I accommodated Margaret in the only comfortable chair, the one behind the desk. As she took the seat, her face turned an even whiter shade of pale.

Alarmed by the change in her, I turned to Inspector Crawford. "Is there some water she can have?"

"I'll ask one of the officers to bring it. I'm afraid Superintendent Jackson only favors whiskey." And then he was gone.

The water appeared in a glass that didn't appear too clean. One look, and Margaret refused it. I didn't blame her; I would have done the same.

It took maybe fifteen minutes for a doctor to appear alongside Inspector Crawford. The police must have had someone waiting nearby in case the march turned violent. Hopefully, he wasn't one of the sawbones who performed autopsies. That would have been a bit macabre.

His examination of Margaret's arm confirmed my earlier deduction. "Wrenched, but not broken." He put her arm in a sling and retrieved a small medicine bottle from his doctor's valise. "Laudanum for the pain. Put five drops in a glass of water. Drink the mixture every four hours for the pain."

"I don't—" Margaret started.

"Thank you, doctor." I fixed my gaze on Margaret. "She'll take it because she wouldn't want to upset Mother."

I washed the glass previously offered with soap and distilled water retrieved from the doctor's valise. Under his watchful eye, I mixed the water and the medicine before administering it to Margaret. He then excused himself as there were others who needed his services.

The laudanum would not only take away Margaret's pain but make her drowsy which meant she needed to be home. With that thought in mind, I turned to Inspector Crawford. "Can we please leave?"

His gaze filled with regret. "You know the drill, Miss Worthington. Not before you're processed."

"We did nothing wrong. It was a peaceful demonstration until those ruffians started tearing down our signs."

"I know." A look of understanding rolled across his face.

"They've been rounded up and will be charged with disturbing the peace and other crimes."

"So, why are we suffering through this indignity?" I fumed.

"Orders from high up." Apology shown in his eyes. "I'm sorry. Truly."

Someone powerful had put his thumb on the scales of justice. Someone who resented women getting the vote. Sebastian's grandfather and his cronies had stood in front of Westminster with sour expressions on their faces. Were they responsible for those rabble rousers? And the arrests of the marchers? Or was it someone else? There was nothing I could do about it right now, but I vowed to find out who was responsible.

"In that case, take Margaret first. And then Betsy, Emma, and me. We can share a cell."

"You know the rules."

"Only one person to a cell." Something I'd discovered during my previous stint in the clink. "But surely an exception could be made in this case? Margaret can't manage on her own. What if she tried to rise and fell? She would suffer further injury."

A muscle ticked in his jaw. "I'll see what I can do."

While we were processed, he made sure we suffered as few humiliations as possible. I was most grateful for the care he took with Margaret, for she was barely aware of her surroundings. The laudanum had done its job. When it came time to put us in the cells, he ordered Constable Peters to put Margaret and me together, as my sister was too ill to fend for herself. After ensuring she was comfortable, he bid us goodbye, explaining he had other matters to attend.

While we waited for someone to spring us from prison, I considered Inspector Crawford's actions. He'd been kind to us. No. More than that. He'd been caring when he didn't have to be. Maybe he'd done it out of a sense of compassion or because of our connection to his mentor, Lord Rutledge. But I sensed it was something else. A harmony existed between us. One which had sprung to life during the Rose Trevvyan murder investigation and carried through to my birthday celebration. As Margaret had deduced, I was attracted to him, and I believed he was attracted to me.

But he was, as Lord Rutledge once told me, a servant to the law who brooked no interference with that role. Still, he'd bent the rules in my favor. Once when he'd returned my arrest papers from my previous stint in the clink. And another time when he'd met with me to discuss the Rose Trevvyan case. I doubted those discussions would have been approved by his superiors at Scotland Yard. And then there was tonight when he'd ordered Constable Peters to put both Margaret and me in the same cell. He might be a servant to the law, but apparently the law could be regulated.

A couple of hours later, we were finally released after Ned paid our bail. Between him and me, we assisted a sleepy Margaret to her feet and escorted her out the door, with Betsy bringing up the rear. Unfortunately, the press was waiting outside. They managed to snap quite a number of photographs before we climbed into the family's Rolls. More than likely, those photographs would feature front and center in tomorrow's morning editions.

"Did Emma get bailed out?" I asked once we were on our way.

"I don't know. My concern was with the three of you. I assume her family was notified as well."

I couldn't fault him for that comment. Still, I wished I knew how she was faring. Although Mother had come to accept she had two firebrand daughters, Emma was not so lucky. She'd been born into a conservative family who would be horrified about today's events. She'd known the possibility of a possible disruption, and yet, participated in the march anyway. It proved not only the strength of her convictions but provided ample demonstration of her courage. As soon as it was possible, I would discover if she'd suffered any repercussions. In the meantime, I needed to find out how Ned found out we'd been arrested. "Who notified you?"

"Inspector Crawford, same as before. I informed Mother as soon as he did."

Of course. She would have been anxious about us. "How did she take it?"

He looked pensively at me. "To tell you the truth, she was not as upset as I thought she would be."

I let out a soft chuckle. "She probably half expected us to be arrested."

"She wasn't as calm, though, when I told her Margaret had been hurt. Inspector Crawford shared it was only a sprain, so it mollified her somewhat." He cleared his throat. "Doctor Crawley is waiting at home to examine Margaret. You as well, and Betsy."

"I'm right as rain, sir," Betsy piped up from the front seat into which she'd slid so she could be next to Neville, her beau. "No need to worry about me."

"I'm afraid there's no help for it, Betsy. Mother insists."

"Yes, sir. Thank you, sir."

"Do you know which constabulary Sebastian was sent to?" I asked.

He shrugged. "No idea."

"We need to find him, Ned," Margaret mumbled from her half-asleep state. The laudanum had truly done its job.

"Once I get you home, I'll make a few calls."

But it wasn't until the next day we found out where Sebastian had gone.

CHAPTER EIGHT

THE RALLY AFTERMATH

*T*HE FUROR THAT ERUPTED from the march was extreme to say the least. The newspapers, knowing a juicy story when they saw one, blasted the front pages with photographs of the melee as well as the marchers being hauled off to jail. And even worse, the organizers were blamed for the riot, though we'd had nothing to do with it.

Nor did they stop there. Our names had been plastered front and center in the early morning edition, branding Margaret and me as the Worthington Rowdies. Someone had even managed to capture one of my roundhouse kicks with the words 'Scandalous,' 'Indecent,' and 'Shameless' printed below the photograph.

"Worthington Rowdies," I scoffed. "What a pitiful use of the English language. At the very least, they should have called us the Worthington Warriors or Worthington Wenches. Those have a nice ring, don't you think, Mother?"

All I got for my quip was a death stare. Clearly, she was not amused.

Unfortunately, that was not the end of it. Threatening letters, unsigned of course, were left at the tradesman's entrance in the back of the house. 'We should be horse-whipped' was one of the kinder epithets hurled at us. Lady Emma sent around a note thanking us for our efforts and apologizing she could not come in person, but her father had forbidden her from leaving the house. A temporary measure, she assured me, which would blow over in a few days' time. But for now, she couldn't visit. After we received similar notes from other young ladies of noble birth, Mother announced it was all a storm in a teacup. Things were bound to turn around. I wasn't so sure.

Someone had determined to scuttle our efforts. After a night spent cogitating that issue, I'd surmised it'd been members of the House of Lords afraid of what it would mean to them when all women over the age of twenty-one earned the right to vote. They were right to fear us for we would elect liberal members to parliament who would enact measures to benefit all, not just the ruling class.

Rather than join the family, Father had taken his break-fast in the study. He acknowledged we hadn't been at fault. That it had been the rabble rousers who instigated the melee. Still, the current situation, including our stint in the clink, was bound to affect his business. So, he was more than likely making telephone calls to assess the damage from the nega-tive press.

Of course, my debut was once again in peril. For myself, I did not care. But Mother would suffer if our invitations dried up. She was a social creature, not only for the family's sake but that of the Ladies Benevolent Society which depended entirely on donations. Being banished to the fringes of society, or denied access altogether, would hurt more than one person or cause.

And the thing was that it was all so unfair. During our planning sessions, we'd taken great care to emphasize the importance of marching peacefully. But now, after those ruffians had caused the commotion, we were being blamed. Of course, it hadn't helped that a photograph of me beating a brute over the head with my sign had made the front-page news. But what was I supposed to do? Let the barbarian beat me to a pulp? Not while life breathed in me, I wasn't.

Regardless of the whys and hows and who was to blame, we were all stepping lightly around the house. Not only that, but Mother had cleared out all evidence of the march. Signs, sashes, pamphlets—all gone. Not one item proclaiming a woman's right to vote could be found in the house.

In one way or another, we were also the walking wounded. True, I'd suffered nothing more than a small cut on my lip and a skinned knee, but Margaret's wrenched shoulder pained her. Betsy, feisty thing that she was, had come away relatively unharmed with only some bruised knuckles. Thanks to four older brothers who'd taught her how to fight, she'd been well prepared to fend off the brutes. I shuddered to think how much worse everyone would have fared if the Metropolitan Police hadn't stepped in. Although I was not happy to suffer through another arrest, at least we'd been safe in jail.

Sebastian finally reappeared mid-morning, bearing scandalous news. Joining us in the drawing room, he explained that he, as well as the men who'd caused the ruckus, had been taken to a different constabulary. His release had not come until dawn when somebody clued in the superintendent-in-charge as to who he was. But his time in jail had not been wasted. While in custody, he'd discovered the men had been paid to disrupt the rally. Just as I'd surmised. Although he'd probed them as to the identity of the one who handed over the blunt, no one knew who'd paid.

"Have you eaten, dear?" My ever-practical mother asked him.

"No. I . . . stopped at my lodgings to clean up and—"

"Well, let's get you something. Can't have you fading away."

Not a chance of that happening in this household. Mother made sure of that.

"Thank you, Mrs. W," Sebastian said.

She tugged on the bell pull. When Carlton appeared, she requested sandwiches and tea.

While we waited, Sebastian related the rest of his tale. "My guess, it was one of those who stood in front of Westminster watching the march. It wouldn't surprise me if it was grandfather himself. He objected strongly to women getting the vote in the first place."

"Really?" I asked.

"Yes. He's never approved of women enjoying any freedom, much less becoming enfranchised. As I understand it, my grandmother, the duchess, lived her entire married life under his thumb. She wasn't even allowed to travel anywhere on her own."

Glad he was finally sharing something about his life, I encouraged him on. "How did you learn this?" I asked.

"From my father. When I was little, I asked him why we never saw the duke, since Seanair, my Scottish grandfather, was ever present. That's when he explained the circumstances of his life."

"The duke never visited you in Scotland?" Margaret asked.

"No. The first time I saw him was when Seanair brought me to the duke."

"That's so sad," Margaret said.

"It wasn't, I assure you. I enjoyed quite a delightful life. We lived in a small cottage, surrounded by flowers and trees. My parents, Lily, and I were a happy family until . . . they passed away."

A footman arrived with a tray laden with enough food to feed an army battalion. By necessity, we paused while Sebastian satisfied his hunger.

But once he was done, I asked, "Can you tell us how that happened, Sebastian? If it's not too painful, that is." I'd learned the general details from Lady Emma, but not the particulars.

The corners of his mouth turned down. "It will always be painful, Kitty. But the ache does lessen with time." He took a deep breath and proceeded. "Mother was a midwife. A wonderful one I might add. Very much in demand in our community. Well, one day she was called out on a particular difficult delivery. Father accompanied her because of a pending snowstorm. She made it in time to deliver a healthy baby and keep the mother from slipping away. They thought they could make home ahead of the storm, but it was not to be. Somehow, they lost their way. Days later, they were found at the bottom of a cliff. At least" —he swallowed hard — "at least they died together. I think they would have hated going on living without the other."

"I'm so sorry, Sebastian," I said while Margaret pressed his hand.

"It was hard. One day they were there. The next day they were gone. Lily especially did not understand."

Caught up in the tragedy, none of us said a word.

After a minute or two, he went on. "Seanair notified the duke about their deaths. But when he didn't hear back, he brought me to Wynchcombe Castle in Hampshire. A great mausoleum of a place. The duke was not happy about it.

Barred us entry, he did, but grandfather would have barged into the devil's den itself to get what was due me."

"Did your sister accompany you?"

"No. The journey would have been too long and arduous for her. Besides, Senair did not know how we would be received."

"How old was she?"

"Three." A small smile bloomed across his face. "She was a sweet child. Blond, unruly curls, big blue eyes. Ever smiling." He sighed heavily. "I had to give her into the duke's care."

"How old were you?"

"Eight. It was hard on me, but at least I understood what was happening. Lily did not. All she knew was that everyone she loved had been taken away from her. It was a devil's bargain. But then the duke was a devil."

"What was the bargain?"

"He would recognize me as his heir and pay for my education and see that Lily was fed, dressed, and educated. As long as I never darkened his doorstep again. If I did, Lily would suffer the consequences."

"And you agreed?"

"What choice did I have? Seanair was in ill health. He couldn't care for Lily. But the duke could. So, the bargain was struck." His demeanor changed, turning hard as stone. "But forcing Lily into an undesirable marriage was never part of the bargain. As far as I'm concerned, the arrangement is off. I'm old enough now to care for her. I'm not too proud to work for a living. I'll enter service if I must. It might not be what Lily is used to in the way of luxuries, but she will have a roof over her head and a full belly. That much I can promise her."

Father who'd arrived in the drawing room toward the end of Sebastian's speech had stood by the door in silence while Sebastian had his say. But now he stepped forward. "You can come work for me, lad."

"Sir!" Sebastian glanced toward him in surprise. "But I know nothing about the business world."

"You can learn. I won't allow that man to get the upper hand, even if he is a duke. You have friends, Sebastian, not only here in our home, but among the elite. I spent the morning making some calls. Plenty who witnessed your grandfather's outrageous behavior at the Torrance ball want to help. We'll sort you out."

Father offered his hand. In friendship and support. Seemingly overwhelmed by the offer, Sebastian nevertheless accepted it with good grace. "I don't know how to thank you, sir."

"We'll say no more about it. First thing you must do is get your sister away from your grandfather. Now that you have an offer of employment, the solicitor can help set that up. It would help if Lily no longer desires to live within the Duke of Wynchcombe's household."

"She doesn't. Her situation has become untenable. The last two years have been especially miserable. But this forced marriage with—"

"Viscount Tottingham?"

"Yes. She's terrified."

"He's been married twice before, and neither marriage was fruitful," Mother piped in. "His eagerness to wed a young woman for the sole purpose of begetting an heir is heinous. The circumstances are too horrible to contemplate."

"I agree, Mildred," Father said. "A marriage should not be based on a woman's ability to procreate but love and respect." He sent her a loving look. "As ours is."

Mother colored with pleasure. Their marriage may have been borne out of love and respect, but it had also been fruitful for Mother had borne five children. But even if she'd been unable to have any, Father would have loved and cherished her. Of that, I had not doubt.

"I've made an appointment with the solicitor for this afternoon, Sebastian. No promises, but he does think it will help that your sister is willing to walk away from her grandfather's protection. He can't keep her a prisoner at his home, no matter who he is."

Carlton walked in with today's afternoon edition of *The Tell-All*, a lugubrious expression on his face, and presented it to Mother. After a quick perusal, she exclaimed "Oh!"

"What's wrong, dear?" Father asked.

"An announcement. The wedding between Lady Lily Dalrymple, granddaughter of the Duke of Wynchcombe, and Viscount Tottingham is set to take place in three days' time."

Sebastian gnashed his teeth. "Should have known my grandfather would act in such a way."

"We should go to the solicitor's office," Father said. "Clearly, there is no time to waste." With determined looks on their faces, he and Sebastian marched out of the room.

I prayed they'd get the answer we hoped for.

While we waited for them to return, Margaret retired to her room to rest, for her arm was still bothering her. Restless as I was, I couldn't do the same. So, I fetched Sir Winston and, with Betsy for company, took him for a walk at the park.

Several hours later, Father returned. Alone.

"How did it go, dear?" Mother asked.

"Not well. The solicitor can't work as fast as we need to stop this wedding. It will take at least ten days to obtain a hearing before the court."

"But she's getting married in three days."

"I know, dearest. We traveled to Wynchcombe House, but they refused Sebastian admittance. He did manage to get a note off to Lily."

"Where is Sebastian?"

"He headed for Westminster to try to gain an audience with his grandfather. That's where the butler said he was. Sebastian will let us know if he was successful."

But word didn't come, and Sebastian never returned.

CHAPTER NINE

MURDER MOST FOUL

*T*HE NEXT MORNING, the family, sans Sebastian, had barely sat down to breakfast when a footman entered carrying a salver on which a newspaper rested. He walked up to Carlton and bowed.

How very odd. Breakfast was sacrosanct in our family. Nothing and no one were allowed to interfere. So, if something in the newspaper had been deemed important enough to interrupt, it had to be catastrophic news.

Our butler took one look at the paper, and his usual bland expression turned to shock.

What on earth had happened? I didn't have long to find out as Carlton soon presented the salver to Father. "My most sincere apologies, sir."

Father took stock of the headline and blanched.

"What is it, dear?" Mother asked, a tinge of alarm in her voice.

He glanced up, a horrified look on his face. "The Duke of Wynchcombe is dead."

A chorus of "What?", "How?" and "Oh, my," rang out.

"He was found last night in Black Rod's Garden at Westminster, a dagger through his heart."

My stomach roiled as that image materialized in my head. Fighting off the nausea, I joined the rest of my family as we gathered around Father to read the newspaper over his shoulders.

For once the gossip rag reported only the facts, leaving out the more lurid details. The duke had been discovered at midnight by an employee of Parliament who'd been charged with locking the garden gate. As he was performing his usual inspection to ensure no one remained inside, he came across the body, a knife stuck in his chest. After ascertaining the duke had expired, he alerted the police. An inspector from Scotland Yard had taken charge of the investigation. The inquest would be held in three days' time at the Westminster Coroner's Court.

Father glanced up. "Where is Sebastian? Shouldn't he be here by now?"

"He hasn't arrived," Margaret said in a trembling voice. Her edges were fraying right before our eyes.

"Carlton. Send a footman to his lodgings. Immediately. Have Neville drive him. Sebastian must be located as soon as possible."

Carlton bowed. "Of course, sir."

A footman was dispatched, but barely a half hour later he returned without Sebastian. No one had come to the door when he'd knocked.

"Blast it," Father exclaimed. Rather than leave for the office, he telephoned Ned to apprise him of the situation and asked him to manage things. "Where's the lad? Of all days to be missing." He asked after joining us in the drawing room.

No one had finished breakfast as we'd all been too upset to eat.

No answer came forth as none of us had the foggiest idea of Sebastian's location.

It wasn't until an hour later that he finally arrived wearing the same clothes of the day before. He looked ghastly and smelled none too fresh.

"Where have you been?" Father demanded.

Rather than respond, Sebastian asked a question of his own. "Is something amiss?" His gaze raced from one of us to the other. No one answered as Father was managing this inquiry.

"Just tell us where you've been since last time I saw you," Father said, in a calmer tone.

Sebastian raked a hand through his blond curls. I doubted they'd seen a comb today. "Well, Sir, I couldn't locate the duke at Westminster, though I searched high and low for an hour. During my quest, I encountered a friend from Oxford who works for one of the committees. Foreign Affairs, I think. He asked me to join him for supper. Since I had no luck finding the duke, I accepted."

"You should have returned here to let us know, dear," Mother said. "We were worried about you."

Sebastian bowed his head. "You're right. It was unforgivable of me. It's just" —his gaze, filled with contrition, found Mother— "I've presumed upon your friendship for so long, laid my troubles on your door so often, I thought a night away would be best."

"Of all the muddleheaded thinking," Margaret exclaimed. "As if you'd ever—As if we could—ugh." She turned away clearly upset with him.

"You're not imposing, dear," Mother explained. "We care about you. We want to help you and your sister."

Margaret swiveled back to confront him, so upset she was shaking. "Don't you ever do that again."

Father cut in on the theatrics. "Where did you go to supper?"

"A private gentleman's club. Cherubs, off Piccadilly."

"Never heard of it."

"It was not what I expected, I must say." He appeared . . . abashed.

"What do you mean?" Father asked.

"It seemed more of a tavern than anything else. There were low" —he cleared his throat— "women, sir, and goings-on."

Margaret would not approve of that.

"Carousing?" Father inquired.

"Yes, sir."

A disgusted snort emitted from Margaret. So much for her and Sebastian being just friends. She wouldn't give a hoot he'd been entertaining women if she didn't care for him.

"And you stayed?"

"I felt compelled to do so. Supper had been served by that point."

Father urged him on. "What happened then."

"I woke up this morning. At Hyde Park. Beneath a tree. Can't remember anything else."

Father's expression turned to stone. "That's a hard thing to believe, young man."

Sebastian stood up to his full height which easily matched Father's. "It's the truth, sir." He brushed a hand across his brow as if he was trying to decipher what had occurred. "I don't know what happened. One moment I was right as rain eating supper with a friend. Next I woke in the open air with leaves and dirt stuck to me. Went home for a wash and clean clothes, but police were stationed at my door. So, I decided to come here. Now, I've answered enough of your questions, sir, could you please tell me what's going on?"

"I'm sorry to tell you this, but your grandfather, the Duke of Wynchcombe, was murdered last night."

The shock on Sebastian's face was clear for us to see. "Murdered? How? Where?"

"He was stabbed. Through the heart, apparently. He was found at Black Rod's Garden. It's next to Westminster Palace."

"I know the place."

Father's gaze narrowed. "Do you?"

"Yes. I haven't been inside, though. It's reserved exclusively for members of Parliament."

After a quick knock on the door, Carlton walked in and bowed. "Begging your pardon, Mr. Worthington. Chief Detective Inspector Bolton, is asking for an audience."

"It's Sebastian he wants to see," I said. "I knew it wouldn't take long for someone to show up at our door. Everyone knows about Sebastian's connection to us." One of the gossip rags had printed a photograph of Sebastian striking one of the rabble rousers in defense of Margaret who lay injured by their feet. The accompanying article would have left no one who read it in doubt of his closeness to my sister.

"Where did you put him?" Mother asked Carlton.

"In the receiving room, ma'am."

"Bring him coffee and food and make sure he doesn't take a notion to explore the house," she ordered. "Lock the receiving room door if you have to."

"It shall be as you wish, ma'am." Without turning a hair at the request which called for him to imprison a Scotland Yard inspector, if need be, Carlton left.

Having taken care of the Inspector, she addressed Father, "If I may make a suggestion, dear."

"Of course." Father nodded.

"Sebastian should go upstairs and make himself presentable. We still have the clothes he was wearing prior to the Torrance Ball. Cleaned and pressed, of course. Could you ask your valet to assist him? Sebastian will need to present himself as a proper gentleman to Inspector Bolton."

She was right. Sebastian had the look of a lord who'd been out carousing until all hours of the night. It would do nothing to endear him to the good inspector. If anything, it would make him appear suspect.

"Always thinking, my dear," Father said with a soft smile before turning to Sebastian. "Go. I'll ring for my valet."

"Yes, Sir."

"Send up some food as well, Mother," Margaret spoke thru gritted teeth. "After last night's *carousing*, I'm sure Sebastian needs sustenance to get him through the day."

"Megs, I didn't—I would never—" Sebastian pled. He was in trouble with her, and he knew it.

"Now is not the time for recriminations, dearest," Mother addressed a sullen Margaret who, in a fit of pique, turned her back on Sebastian and walked away from him.

"Sebastian, go up to the room you used before. Mr. Worthington's valet will join you there with your clothes."

"Yes, ma'am." After one last tortured look at Margaret, he departed, wearing a miserable look on his face.

And that was the last we saw of Sebastian for some time. Once he was properly groomed, Chief Detective Inspector Bolton bore him away to Scotland Yard.

CHAPTER TEN

INQUEST

*O*N MONDAY, the public gallery at the Westminster Coroner's Court was packed. Needless to say, every newspaper worth their salt had sent reporters. But since photographers were not allowed inside the courtroom, artists had been dispatched to sketch the witnesses and coroner. Thanks to Inspector Crawford, who'd volunteered his assistance, Margaret, Mother, and I had front row seats in the gallery. Sebastian, however, was to be found at the front of the courtroom, along with several police officers and Chief Detective Inspector Bolton.

Two days ago, after being interrogated by the inspector, Sebastian had been released. Needing his rest, he'd headed to Portchester Place where he discovered his lodgings were no longer available to him. The police had declared it a place of interest that needed to be searched. At that point, he thought to move to Wynchcombe House. After all, he was now the duke. But the criminal solicitor Father had engaged while

Sebastian was being interrogated cautioned Sebastian against moving into that residence. It would infer he'd been eager to lay claim to it, when just the opposite was true. Sebastian's interest lay in reaching his sister, not laying possession to the house or, for that matter, the other Wynchcombe properties.

The solicitor also warned him about contacting his sister, as he wouldn't want her suspected of any wrongdoing. So, in the end he'd come to us for advice on how to proceed. Since, first and foremost, Sebastian needed a place to stay while the investigation played out, Ned had generously offered to share his lodgings with him. After all, he had plenty of space in his townhouse. While that solved one problem, others remained—mainly what do about Lily.

Sebastian had written her a letter explaining the circumstances, that he wouldn't be able to speak with her until the matter of their grandfather's murder was resolved. He was devastated he could not talk to his sister for that is truly what he wished to do. But as matters stood, it was not something he could do. We tried to cheer him up. But the happy-go-lucky Sebastian was no more. His situation was downright dire, and it was about to get worse.

The first witness called was the Wynchcombe House butler, a Mister Temple. When asked to describe his whereabouts on the night in question, the butler said he'd enjoyed his supper with the rest of the staff at six, their normal time. Since the duke opted for a tray, his usual preference, and Lady Lily, his granddaughter, had done the same, there was no supper served in the dining room that night. After eating his meal, he'd retired to his office to work on the household books as they were to be turned into Mister Nevins, his grace's personal secretary, in the morning.

"Did anything unusual happen that night?"

"It did. One of the footmen knocked on my door. He'd

found a note addressed to the Duke of Wynchcombe in the front hall. It was marked urgent."

"What time was that?"

"Shortly after 9:30."

"How was the note delivered?"

"Well, sir, that's a puzzle. Whoever brought the envelope did not ring the front bell. We would have heard it in the servants' hall. Which we did not. I can only guess it must have been dropped through the letter box." He hitched up his chin and stiffened, as if he was affronted by that. "Highly irregular, if I may so, Your Honor."

The coroner made a notation of this. "What did you do?"

"Well, sir, normally I would have waited until the duke returned, but since the note seemed important, I thought it best to deliver it to His Grace. He was playing cards at Viscount Tottingham's."

"Is that what you did?"

"Yes, sir. I would have sent one of the footmen; but, since the envelope was marked urgent, I took on the task myself."

"Very well. Go on."

"I hailed a taxi and arrived at Viscount Tottingham's house shortly after ten. Upon my arrival, I handed the envelope to the butler, a Mister Harrison which he took to His Grace. I remained in the entrance hall in case His Grace needed me to perform some other service."

"How did the Duke of Wynchcombe react?"

"He was furious. Down the stairs he came, face like thunder. Whatever was in that envelope did not suit him at all. He questioned me, effusively I might say, about who'd delivered the note but I could not provide any more information than I have given now. His Grace was not pleased."

The coroner made another notation before asking, "Did he say anything about the contents or name the person who'd sent it?"

"No, sir, he did not. He yelled, 'Damn impudence,' and then asked me to hail him a taxi."

"A taxi? Didn't he have his own transportation?"

"He most certainly did, Your Honor—a motorcar and a chauffeur which were stationed outside. But when I reminded him of it, he dismissed my suggestion. 'Just fetch me a taxi, damn you.' Forgive the language, Your Honor, but that's what he said."

"We want the facts in this courtroom, Mister Temple, even if they offend the rules of propriety. Any idea why he didn't wish to use his own motorcar?"

"The only thing that came to mind was that he didn't want the chauffeur to know where he was going. It was the first time he'd had me arrange for a taxi, if I may add."

"And were you able to obtain one?"

"Yes, and I put His Grace into the taxicab myself."

"At what time?"

"About twenty past ten, Sir."

"Very well. Tell me, Mr. Temple, this note that he received, did it have a return address or any identifying marks?"

For a moment, he hesitated. Was he trying to remember? Or to find a way to evade the question? A few seconds later, he answered, "No, Sir. It was made from quality linen, though. That much I noticed."

I suspected he'd noticed more than that.

"What happened to the note?"

"He took it with him. The envelope as well."

"Was that the last time you saw him?"

"Yes, sir. It was."

"Very well. Thank you, Mr. Temple. That will be all."

The coroner then called to the stand the Westminster employee responsible for securing Black Rod Garden.

He testified he'd been asked by the Black Rod himself to

open the garden gate at ten and return to secure it at midnight. A very unusual request since the gate was normally locked up nice and tight at eight. When he returned at midnight, he'd walked through the garden to ensure the place was empty. The usual procedure to ensure no one got locked in for the night. That's when he found the Duke of Wynchcombe.

"You knew who he was?"

"Oh, yes, sir. He's a well-known figure at Westminster."

"Where did you find him?"

"On the bridge, sir."

"And what was his condition?"

The employee gave him an odd look. "Why, he was dead, sir."

Laughter rumbled through the crowd.

The coroner hammered down his gavel. "Silence."

The room went quiet right quick.

"How did you know he was dead?" the coroner asked.

"He was not moving, and there was a knife sticking out of his chest."

More snickering erupted.

Frowning, the coroner addressed the gallery. "If respect is not shown in these proceedings, I will clear the room." When those present quieted down, he turned back to the employee. "Go on."

"Well, sir, as I was saying, it was quite evident he was no longer among the living."

"Did you check to see if he was breathing?"

"Oh, yes, sir. He was not."

"So what did you do next?"

"I ran to get a police officer. Several are posted around Westminster. Day and night. To guard the palace, sir. After the police officer saw the state of the body, he left to alert Scotland Yard. I remained in the garden to watch over the duke. Wanted to make sure no one would muck it about. Sometimes, people do strange things. Why, I remember one time—"

The coroner cut him off. "We don't need any extraneous information. Keep to the facts."

The employee's face turned a mottled shade of pink. "Sorry, Your Honor. Won't happen again. As I was saying" — he paused, probably to remember where he'd stopped— "Sometime later, Inspector Bolton showed up. After I gave my account, he said I could leave."

"Very well. Thank you. Inspector Bolton, please step forward."

After the inspector stated his name and position with Scotland Yard, the coroner asked, "What happened the night of May 31st?"

"A little past midnight, I was notified that the Duke of Wynchcombe's body had been found at Black Rod Garden, and the death appeared suspicious. My lodgings are not far from Westminster, so I arrived" —he consulted his notes on a pad he pulled from his suit's inside pocket— "at thirty-seven minutes past midnight. After I ascertained there was no life left in the body, I ordered the officers who accompanied me to secure the scene."

"Did you know who it was?"

"Oh, yes, sir. I'd dealt with the Duke of Wynchcombe before, so I recognized him immediately. The police officers knew him as well. We were all paying the proper respects. Other than to determine he was no longer alive, we couldn't examine the body until the medical examiner arrived. But it was clear what had killed him. He had a dagger protruding from his chest."

"When did the medical examiner arrived?"

He consulted his notes again. "Twenty after one. After he

was done with his examination, the duke was placed in a stretcher to be taken to the mortuary."

"Thank you, Inspector. You are dismissed but please remain in the courtroom. I may have further questions."

"Yes, Sir."

"Will the medical examiner come forward?

Once he had done so, the coroner said, "Please provide your name and position."

"Dr. Michael Tompkins. I'm London's Chief Medical examiner."

No run of the mill medical examiner, but the chief one. Made sense seeing the importance of the victim.

"Have you performed a post mortem examination of the Duke of Wynchcombe?"

"I have."

"In your opinion, what was the cause of death?"

"He was stabbed with a dagger through the heart. The weapon was thrust between the fourth and fifth ribs with such strength it pierced right through the chest wall into the left ventricle. A saw-and-sweep motion was then employed to destroy a massive amount of tissue. His heart would have stopped beating within a short period of time."

"How long?"

"He would have become unconscious within fifteen minutes, and death would have occurred shortly thereafter."

"No one mentioned any blood on the scene. Wouldn't such a stabbing cause blood loss?"

"Well, yes and no, Your Honor. Because the blade remained inside the body, the blood loss was internal. It'd been raining as well. If any had escaped, it would have been washed away. But, in any case, I saw none."

"Why would anybody leave a dagger behind, do you think? After all, it could identify the murderer."

"I can't know the mind of the killer, but given how deeply

it was imbedded, he may have had a problem retrieving it. The cross guard was caught between the ribs, you see."

The coroner made a notation as to that.

"In your opinion, could this have been self-inflicted?"

"Oh, no, sir. It was done by someone else. And that someone was left-handed as the thrust came from the left."

"Could a woman have done it?"

"Not unless she was especially tall and powerful. The assailant was at least six two and fit."

"Going back to the dagger, did it have any distinguishing characteristics?"

"Yes indeed. It is quite unique. About seven inches long, with a beautiful crest on the hilt."

"A crest?"

"Yes, sir. Inspector Bolton can shed more light on the subject. But I understand he's identified the crest as belonging to the Wynchcombe family."

A ripple of excitement surged through the crowd. Curiously, the coroner did not hush them this time.

"Do you mean to tell me the Duke of Wynchcombe was stabbed with his own dagger?"

"I don't know about that, sir. But it bore his ducal crest."

"Was the dagger tested for fingermarks?"

"It was. There were none."

"The killer must have worn gloves."

"That would be my guess, sir."

"Were you able to ascertain the time of death?"

"Sometime between ten and midnight. Death, as I said, occurred a very short period after he was stabbed."

"Very well. Thank you, Dr. Tompkins. If Inspector Bolton could retake the stand."

Once the Inspector resumed the seat, the coroner wasted no time. "Well, sir, have you had a chance to ascertain the provenance of the dagger?"

"Yes, sir, I have. Once the body had been removed from Black Rod Garden by the medical examiner, I visited Lord Percy Dalrymple, the Duke of Wynchcombe's son, to notify him of his father's death. As you can imagine, he was suitably distraught."

"Only proper. Did you inquire as to Lord Percy's whereabouts that night?"

"I did, sir. He told me he'd enjoyed supper with Lord Mountford. Subsequently, I was able to verify that fact."

The coroner made a notation. "Go on."

"When I described the dagger to him, he thought it was one of two his father had commissioned years earlier. He'd given one to each of his sons. I asked him to produce his dagger and discovered it was very similar to the one that had been used to kill the duke."

"Similar, but not the same?"

"I could not confirm that at the time, sir. So, I asked Lord Percy to accompany me to the mortuary. Not only did we need to officially identify the body but to learn if the dagger was one of the two his father had commissioned."

"And did he do so?"

"He affirmed it was. It was identical in every way to the one in his possession."

"Who had the second dagger?"

"It'd been originally given to his oldest son, Thomas Dalrymple, who has since passed away. I was given to understand by Lord Percy that the dagger had been inherited by Thomas Dalrymple's son, Sebastian Dalrymple."

As a ripple of excitement surged through the gallery, Margaret's hands clenched on the banister in front of us. Her complexion grew deathly pale.

"Did you question Sebastian Dalrymple about the dagger?"

"Yes, sir, I did. He verified he'd inherited it after his father's death."

"Did he produce it?"

"No, sir. He did not. He claimed it'd been stolen."

This time the gallery roared.

"Thank you, Inspector Bolton. I call to the stand Sebastian Dalrymple."

After slowly coming to his feet, Sebastian walked to the chair the inspector had just vacated.

"Please state your name and your relation to the Duke of Wynchcombe."

"Sebastian Dalrymple. The Duke of Wynchcombe was my grandfather."

"Did you have in your possession a dagger handed down to you by your father?"

"At one time I did, but I no longer have it."

"Why not?"

"I believe it was stolen from my room at Oxford University. I'm a Junior Research Fellow in Agriculture there. Someone broke into my chamber earlier in the spring."

"When did you find out the dagger had been stolen?"

"Last month. I planned to come to London and went looking for it. When I travel, I like to carry it for protection. That's when I noticed it was missing."

"Did you report it to the police?"

"No, I did not."

"Why not?"

"I did not hold any particular affection for it. I carried it more for safety reasons than anything else. I decided I would obtain a similar one after I arrived in London. I never got around to it, though."

"You would replace a valuable dagger, a family heirloom, with something you could purchase at any shop?"

"As long as it could provide protection. That's all I cared about."

"And you came to London why?"

"My sister is here. I was hoping to see her."

"Was that the only reason?"

"No. I was escorting someone."

"Who?"

"Margaret Worthington. She was coming home at the end of term. We'd become . . . friends."

Reporters scribbled like mad. That pause of his couldn't be missed. It suggested he and Margaret were more than friends.

"Very well. Where are you residing while in London?"

"Portchester Place."

"Not in the Duke of Wynchcombe's home?"

"The duke and I were not on friendly terms."

Had no one warned Sebastian not to volunteer information? He was digging himself a rather large hole.

"What do you mean?"

"He did not wish to see me."

"While you were in London?"

"No. sir. Never."

"Never?"

"Yes, sir."

"Why?"

"He did not approve of my parents' marriage. Ergo, I was painted with the same brush."

"I . . . see." The coroner noted that as well. "Now these lodgings at Portchester Place, do they belong to you?"

"No. They belong to my uncle, Lord Percy. He'd offered them to me if I ever visited London."

"Very well. Now, Mister Dalrymple, if we could discuss the evening of May 31st. Where were you, specifically between the hours of ten and midnight."

"I can't say."

Another uproar, even louder than the one before caused the coroner to employ his gavel. Only when the noise died down, did he ask, "You can't say, or you won't say?"

"I can't say. A friend asked me to supper. We went to a gentleman's club off Piccadilly called Cherubs. We arrived there a little after eight."

The coroner raised a brow. Clearly, he knew about the club. "Go on."

"That's all I remember, sir. One minute I was dining with my friend, and the next . . ."

"What's his name?"

"Thomas Hodgkins. He works for one of the committees at Parliament. Foreign Affairs, I believe. I was enjoying supper with him. Nothing fancy. Beef and potatoes. He'd sprung for a bottle of claret. And . . . and . . ." He stroked trembling fingers across his brow.

"Well, sir."

"Next thing I knew it was morning. I woke up under a tree at Hyde Park."

Mad whispering rippled through the crowd.

"What did you do then?"

"I went home to Portchester Place, but the police were outside so I headed to Worthington House. They know me there."

In the end, the coroner's ruling surprised no one. He concluded the duke had been murdered by person or persons unknown and asked Scotland Yard to investigate. Sebastian was arrested the next day.

CHAPTER ELEVEN

SANCTUARY

*A*FTER SEBASTIAN'S ARREST, Margaret, Mother, and I descended into deep melancholy. Mother's upset had been so great, she'd cancelled our at-home, something she'd never done. I would have kicked up my heels if I weren't so despondent. Father was furious, as he was convinced Sebastian was innocent. I understood Mother's and Margaret's feelings on the subject, but Father's? He'd resented Sebastian's intrusion into our lives. But seemingly, he'd had a change of heart.

"Did he hate his grandfather?" Father asked while we were at breakfast the next day. "Yes, he probably did. The man was downright beastly to him. But this murder seems premeditated, and, more than that, planned by a cold, calculating mind. Someone sent the duke a note which drew him into that garden to be murdered with a dagger emblazoned with his ducal crest. A dagger conveniently left behind. Sebastian might be brilliant in his field, but he doesn't strike me as a cold-blooded killer. The lad just doesn't have it in him. Besides if he'd killed his grandfather, he certainly wouldn't leave the weapon behind. He'd figured a way to retrieve it." Pausing for a moment, he suddenly glanced up. "I'd just like to know where this friend of his is."

"Thomas Hodgkins?" I asked.

"The papers say he's disappeared." He scoffed. "Not bloody likely."

"Edward, dear, language," Mother reminded him.

"Apologies, my dearest. But this entire affair is so fantastical. The note, the garden, the dagger. It's the work of a devious mind. Brilliant, really, when you think about it. It would have taken methodical planning to accomplish it, and nerves of steel to carry it out. And somehow Hodgkins was part of it." He tossed a piece of sausage to Sir Winston, who'd been patiently waiting by his side for a treat.

It spoke volumes to the level of Mother's distress she didn't protest.

A knock sounded on the dining room door, a second before a footman entered. He approached Carlton and whispered something to him.

"Anything wrong?" Father asked.

I sincerely hoped it wasn't more bad news. We had enough of that already.

"Forgive the interruption, sir, but a young lady has come calling."

"A young lady?" Mother asked. "Did she provide a name?"

"Miss Lily Dalrymple. Simmons showed her to the—"

Margaret, Mother, and I flew out of our chairs.

—drawing room," Carlton finished as we were halfway out the door.

She stood trembling in the center of the room, tall, svelte, with mounds of blond hair. Her blue eyes, so like Sebastian's, glimmered with trepidation. The poor thing was petrified.

A realization that was not lost on Mother as she curtsied. "Lady Lily." As the granddaughter of a duke, Lily was entitled to be addressed in such manner. "I'm Mrs. Worthington."

"Thank you for seeing me, Mrs. Worthington. But please don't call me that," Sebastian's sister spoke in a tremulous tone. "Lily will do."

"If that's what you wish, dear," Mother said. "Won't you take a seat?"

"Yes, thank you." Lily settled on the closest furnishing, a blue settee which splendidly complimented her beauty. While everything about her person screamed proper lady of quality, her garments did not. The simple gown she wore, patched and mended in places, appeared styled for a younger person and not someone of marriageable age. Not only that, but the ivory silk purse she carried was frayed at the edges. It seemed the duke had spent as little money on her as he did on Sebastian.

"Would you like some tea? Or sustenance?" Mother always did everything that was good and proper. I firmly believed if the world were coming to an end, she would offer guests Earl Grey, scones, and seed cake while they waited for extinction.

"Oh, no. I couldn't." Lily shook her head, sending her curls bouncing. "I'm too upset to eat. But I thank you all the same."

"Very well." Mother sat on one of the upholstered chairs across from Lily and motioned us to do the same on the divan closest to us. I understood her message. No sense overwhelming Sebastian's sister with our presence by remaining on our feet.

Mother folded her hands on her lap. "What can we do for you, Lily?"

Anxiety made itself known on Lily's face. What on earth did she fear? "I've come to beg for sanctuary."

"Sanctuary?"

"If I may be allowed to explain?" Lily asked. She was worrying the straps of her purse so much, I was afraid they'd break.

"Of course, my dear."

Releasing a nervous breath, Lily settled more fully into the settee. It was only then I realized, she'd been sitting on the edge, as if she expected to be sent packing. She need not have worried. Mother would never deny refuge to Sebastian's sister. "My brother wrote of your kindness to him. That's how we communicate. Through letters. Grandfather forbade everything else."

"How distressing not to be able to see your brother and speak to him."

"Yes," Lily wiped a tear that rolled down her face. "It was, rather. But I accepted it. What else could I do? The duke was my guardian." She sighed. "But now—" Her breath hitched.

"Things have changed," Mother completed her thought.

"They have. I believed I would finally be able to see Sebastian. But now that he's been arrested . . ."

"We believe he's innocent, Lily," Mother rushed to say.

"Yes, he is. I may not have seen him for several years, but his correspondence speaks of a kind heart and a generous spirit. He would never do such a thing." She finished with more emotion than we'd seen in her.

"We agree," Mother said, pointing to Margaret and me.

"But then as I was determining my future course" —a fire suddenly burned in her eyes— "my odious cousin arrived at Wynchcombe House demanding I marry Viscount Tottingham. Immediately, if you please." She scoffed. "He gave me a day to prepare for the wedding and said he would return today with the viscount and a minister."

"You do not wish to marry the viscount?" Mother inquired. Silly to ask, but it needed to be confirmed.

"No!" That heartfelt denial left none of us in doubt as to how she felt. "I apologize. I shouldn't have yelled."

I would have screamed from the rafters myself if such a demand were made of me.

Mother moved to the settee next to Lily and held her hand. "I understand, my dear."

More tears flowed from Lily which she promptly brushed off. "He's old and horrid and . . . and . . . he smells."

I shuddered. A young woman married to a man three times her age. The thought was not to be borne. "Of course, you shouldn't marry him."

"Absolutely," Margaret seconded.

"You need not worry about that anymore, my dear," Mother assured her. "You're safe here with us, and you can stay as long as you wish."

"Oh," Lily exclaimed. If there were tears before it was nothing to the deluge that erupted. "You are just as kind as Sebastian said." From deep in her purse, she retrieved a handkerchief to mop up the waterworks.

"Dear Sebastian." Mother patiently waited for Lily's storm to pass. Once it had descended into mere sniffles, she came to her feet. "If you'll excuse me, I'll go arrange for your room."

"Oh." The forlorn look in Lily's eyes was enough to break your heart.

Mother patted her hand. "I won't be gone long. I promise. In the meantime, Margaret and Kitty will keep you company."

Lily raised pleading eyes to Mother. "Thank you. My maid, Hester, came with me. I couldn't leave her behind. Will you be able to accommodate her as well?"

"Of course. I'll have Mrs. Simpson, our housekeeper, arrange for it all."

"You're so kind, Mrs. Worthington."

"We love Sebastian, my dear. How could we fail to provide shelter for his sister?"

Mother sailed out of her room on her mission, leaving an unsettled Lily behind.

With one thought in mind, Margaret and I rose from the divan and joined her on the settee.

"Mother will take care of everything," Margaret said. "You'll see."

"Absolutely," I echoed Margaret's sentiments. "She's the best."

Lily's gaze bounced from Margaret to me and back again. "I'm sorry. But do you think you could tell me your names? I'm not sure who is who."

How rude were we? "I'm Kitty, and this is Margaret, my *older* sister."

"Sebastian's Margaret." She gazed in awe at my sibling. "How lovely you are. My brother has written many fine things about you."

Margaret's cheeks bloomed pink. "He has?"

"Oh, yes. For the last two years, it's been "Margaret this" or "Megs that.""

"Really?" I interjected. "Please do tell."

"Don't you dare, Lily," Margaret objected while darting a fulminating glance toward me. "Kitty is being her usual obnoxious self."

"Oh, you two are so droll." Lily's laughter rang out. And wouldn't you know it? It tinkled. Like bells. Of course, it did. She was perfection itself. How that old grandfather of hers could even think about marrying her to a smelly old viscount was beyond me.

She was still laughing when Mother walked back into the room, shortly followed by two footmen carrying trays stacked with cakes, pastries, porcelain cups and plates, and pots of lovely coffee and tea.

"Forgive me, Lily, but I really do think you need sustenance after the ordeal you've been through."

"Oh, gracious, Mrs. Worthington," Lily said, a bright smile now in place. "Now that I've unburdened myself, I do believe I'm famished."

"Well, there you are." Mother sat across from Lily once more while the footmen laid out the food on the table between us. Silence reigned while we fortified ourselves with the delicious offerings. But once our appetites had been satisfied, we prodded Lily on.

"Did you always reside with your grandfather, Lily dear?" Mother asked. We already knew, as we'd learned about Lily's history from Lady Emma. But it would be better to hear it from Lily herself.

"Oh, no. For the first three years of my life, I lived with my parents. In Edinburgh. Along with Sebastian, of course. But when I was three . . . they passed."

"How very sad to lose your parents at such a young age. You must miss them."

"I do, especially my mother. She always smelled of lilies. Her favorite perfume. That's why she named me Lily." She put down her cup. "It was then I went to live at Wynchcombe Castle. The family seat in Hampshire. It was built by one of the early dukes to guard England against an attack from the sea."

"A big change for you," I said.

"Yes, it was. It was lonely at first, away from everyone I loved."

"How awful that must have been for you." I pressed her hand for comfort. Having been born into a loud, boisterous family, I couldn't begin to imagine the pain she must have endured.

"It was rather, but soon I was given into the care of a nanny. She was lovely. Used to rock me to sleep every night.

When I turned six, a governess was hired to educate me. She taught me letters and numbers, and eventually the classics, geography, history. When I grew older, dance, pianoforte, and drawing instructors were employed to teach me those arts."

"You received a proper education then," Mother said.

"I did. Some would have thought it a solitary existence; but I had my books to keep me company and the freedom to roam our land. During growing season, I watched the workers till the fields and harvest the crops. We grow cereals, you know. Wheat and such."

"You share a love of nature with your brother, then."

"Yes." She smiled. "That's one thing we have in common."

"Was your grandfather there as well?"

She shook her head. "He spent most of his time in London as he preferred town life. But he'd arrive in late autumn and remain through the winter. I almost never saw him when he was in residence at Wynchcombe Castle. He requested I be kept away. He didn't want to be reminded of my existence, you see."

Mother made some sort of sound; but other than that, she didn't say a word.

"In March, he would return to the city where he remained while Parliament was in session."

"So how did you come to be in London?"

"Well, two years ago when I turned eighteen, my uncle— Lord Percy—arrived. At first, I thought it was one of his usual jaunts. You see, he'd made himself responsible for me. Every three months, he would visit to ensure I was getting the care and education due a granddaughter of a duke. His words. I was grateful for it. If it weren't for him, I would have probably grown up a wild child, entirely unkempt and igno- rant. But this visit was different. He informed me the duke wanted me in London as I was to be introduced to town life.

I took it to mean a social season." She laughed a self-deprecating laugh. "Silly me. The duke had no such thought in mind. He was looking to marry me off."

"Goodness." Mother said. "He wouldn't arrange a season for you?"

"No. When I dared ask him about it, he told me I wasn't worth the expense. He'd already wasted enough money on me. The upshot of it was I spent all my time cooped up at Wynchcombe House in my set of rooms. I only joined him at supper when there was a candidate for my hand. For a year and a half, none would do. The duke was looking for someone with a title and a very large purse, you see. He found both in Viscount Tottingham."

"How did you find out he'd been chosen?" I asked.

"The duke called me down to the library. An odd choice, I thought, for he was not one to frequent that room. I arrived to find him and Viscount Tottingham drinking brandy and smoking cigars. Without much ado, he informed me I was engaged to the viscount, and the announcement had been sent to the papers. That was about a week ago. In a panic, I wrote Sebastian to let him know. He tried to gain entrance to Wynchcombe House, but he was denied. Yesterday, I received another note from him. It contained but a few words. 'Seek sanctuary at Worthington House.' He included directions and funds for a taxicab."

"And so, you decided to come here."

"Yes, but first I had to get away. I informed Hester, my maid, last night. She's a good and faithful servant, having been with me since I was ten. I knew I could trust her. We packed my things as silently as we could. This morning before dawn we took the servants' stairs to the kitchen and exited through that door. It was too early to come to you, so we hid in the bushes. When the sun rose, we made our way to the street and hailed a cab."

"What an adventure you've had, my dear. But now you're here, safe and sound, and here you'll stay."

"Thank you."

"Well," Mother said, coming to her feet. "Now that we've had a nice coze, why don't I show you to your room. Your maid is already there arranging your things. If you need anything, anything at all, you are to ring."

Lily stood as well. "Can Margaret and Kitty join us?"

"Of course. But you're exhausted, my dear. After they've answered your questions, you are to rest. Is that clear, you two?" The latter was addressed to Margaret and me.

"Yes, Mother," Margaret and I said in unison.

Woe befall the child who went against Mother's wishes.

CHAPTER TWELVE

A DEBUT FOR LILY

"*Y*OU MUST LOOK INTO THE DUKE'S MURDER, Kitty," Margaret demanded. "Look at what you did for Ned. If it hadn't been for you, heaven knows what would have happened to him."

"Who's Ned?" Lily asked, her gaze bouncing between Margaret and me.

"Our brother. If Kitty hadn't investigated a death he was embroiled in, he would have been charged with murder and most likely been found guilty. There was that much evidence against him."

"Goodness!" Lily exclaimed.

We'd been at this for the last half hour. Ostensibly, we'd accompanied Lily to her room to help her settle in. But soon after her things had been comfortably arranged, the discussion turned to the duke's murder. Before long, Margaret was demanding I investigate it.

I was astounded she was asking me to do this for the

circumstances were not remotely the same. "That was different, Margaret. Not only do I know Ned, but I was on the train when the murder occurred. I know nothing" —less than nothing if the truth be told— "about the Duke of Wynchcombe."

"That shouldn't prove a hindrance," Lily said. "Obviously, I'm familiar with him since he was my grandfather. I'd be happy to share what I know."

"But—excuse me for saying so, Lily—you're not very well acquainted with his friends, never mind his enemies." After seeing the duke's behavior at the ball, and hearing Lady Emma's accounting of him, I firmly believed there were some who wished him ill. "You yourself said you only joined him for supper when he invited a likely candidate for your hand."

"I may not be as familiar with him as you wish, but the Wynchcombe House staff certainly is. Mister Temple, the butler for one, and Mister Farthington, the duke's valet. Oh, and grandfather's private secretary, Mister Nevins. Between them, they must know a great deal. And then there's Uncle Percy. He's been very kind to me. I'm sure he's eager to discover who murdered his father for he cannot possibly believe it was Sebastian."

Maybe the servants would be willing to talk. After all, those who'd been employed at Wynchcombe Castle had spread tales of his perfidy far and wide. But that had been many years ago. Would his London retainers feel the same way? "Do you think the staff will talk to me? I have no authority to pry into the duke's affairs."

"I'm sure it can be arranged," Lily said with a smile. "My brother is now the Duke of Wynchcombe. They would want to be in his good graces."

"But what if they're loyal to your grandfather? Our staff certainly is. If someone were to question Carlton about anyone in our family, he would send off that person with a flea in his ear."

She folded her hands on her lap. "Grandfather was thoroughly disliked by the staff. Now and again, I'd catch a conversation between disgruntled servants about some disagreeable thing he'd done. I believe they will spill the beans fast enough."

Going by the way he'd treated Sebastian, I could very well believe he'd been a downright tyrant to them. "The duke did seem to be an unpleasant individual."

"He was. Goodness knows he caused Sebastian and me enough heartache. And we were his kin."

Unfortunately, neither Margaret nor Lily had involved themselves in a murder investigation, so they had no idea what that entailed. Interviewing suspects would take a prodigious amount of time, never mind sifting through the information to get at the truth. I couldn't see how it would work. "Even if the staff is willing to talk to me, there are bound to be more than a few suspects. How on earth am I to investigate them all?"

"We'll help. All of us," Margaret stated.

I gazed at her askance. "Who exactly are all of us?"

"Me for one. And I'm sure Ned will want to help as well. After all, he knows what it's like to be suspected of a crime he did not commit."

"And, of course, you can count on me," Lily said. "For starters, I can get you access to the Wynchcombe House staff so you can talk to them."

Her statement took me right back to my previous concern. "Are you sure? After all, you had to sneak out of the place."

"I didn't want them to get into trouble, so I sneaked out for their benefit, as much as mine. If anybody, like my odious cousin, asked, they could honestly say they had no idea where or when I'd gone."

"Lords Marlowe and Newcastle helped with Ned's investigation as well, didn't they?" Margaret enquired.

The fact she knew that surprised me. "How on earth do you know that?"

"Mother. She was very forthcoming. She wrote me letters and letters about what you were doing." Margaret pressed my hand. "She was very proud of you. As fond as she is of Sebastian, I'm sure she will approve this investigation. So you see, you'll have plenty of assistance." She was like Mother in that respect for there wasn't an obstacle Mother encountered that she couldn't overcome.

But there was one major difference between the two cases. "You're failing to consider a very important fact. Inspector Crawford oversaw Rose Trevvyan's murder investigation. I was able to discuss issues with him which helped clarify my thinking. Not that he ever shared any information with me," I was quick to add. "But he's not supervising this enquiry. How will I handle the Scotland Yard side of things?"

"Actually," Margaret opined after mulling it over, "it's better that he's not the one leading the investigation. This way, he can provide his opinion without running afoul of Scotland Yard protocol."

I scoffed. "I doubt it. The man is obsessed with following the rules. More than likely, there is some benighted regulation or other about offering an opinion in someone else's ongoing inquiry."

"If there is, we'll figure something out. So, what do you say? I'm in." Margaret put her hand in the space between us. "One for All, and All for One."

The motto of the musketeers. It was something she, Emily, and I used to do when we dreamed up a scheme to do something naughty, like sneaking sweets from the kitchen before supper time. We'd made a perfect team. Margaret would plan it, Emily would fine tune it, and I, being the smallest and least likely to get caught, carried it out. Although we were found out more often than not, we all took responsibility for the crime, and suffered the same punishment—going to bed without dessert.

"Me too." A grinning Lily got into the spirit of things and placed her hand on top of Margaret's.

I hesitated, for this was a gargantuan task.

"Kitty, it's for Sebastian," Margaret said. "We're the only hope he has."

"He has a solicitor," I protested.

"Who doesn't know him as well as we do."

"Please, Kitty," Lily begged, her big, blue eyes shimmering with emotion.

Unable to deny them any longer, I put my hand on top of theirs. In unison, we yelled, "One for All, and All for One!"

We were giggling as Mother walked into the room. She was not pleased. "Lily is supposed to be resting."

"Oh, Mrs. Worthington, I don't need to rest," Lily said brightly. "I'd rather chat with Margaret and Kitty. You see, I've never had any sisters. But now I feel I do."

How could Mother say no to that?

* * *

THE NEXT MORNING, Lily and I settled into her bedroom, eager to plan the visit to Wynchcombe House. Margaret had been unable to join us as she was meeting with Sebastian's solicitor to determine what progress he'd made.

We'd barely started discussing our strategy when Mother knocked on the door. "Mind if I interrupt?"

"Of course not, Mrs. Worthington," Lily said with a smile.

"Thank you, dear. I just wanted to know when we could expect the rest of your wardrobe?"

Lily's complexion grew pink. She was clearly flustered by the question. "I'm afraid this is the extent of it, Mrs. Worthington. Three day dresses, one gown to attend the duke's supper parties, and a dark one for everything in between."

Mother's shocked countenance reflected my thoughts.

"But what about gowns to wear in the afternoon and for tea. Or a ball?"

"I never attended, nor was I ever invited to one. My grandfather preferred I remain confined—"

Jailed, I thought.

"—at Wynchcombe House. Since he wished me wedded as soon as possible, he didn't see a need to order a new wardrobe for me. He flat out told me my new husband could bear that expense."

Mother's expression revealed exactly how she felt about the duke, but being the lady she was, she kept the opinion to herself. "That's fine, dear. For the time being, we'll make do. I dare say you and Margaret are like enough in size we should be able to alter one of her gowns for you. But you'll need more clothes for the season. I'll contact Angelique's. She's our modiste, highly sought after, and see when she can fit you in."

Lily appeared shocked. "But I couldn't possible attend social events, Mrs. Worthington, not with the death of my grandfather and my brother in prison."

Mother gazed at her with understanding. "That sentiment does you credit, my dear. But I've consulted Lady Kingsley about this issue. Yes, you will need to seclude yourself from society, but only for three weeks. You'll need crepe if you wish. But honestly the period is so short, we might as well skip to half-mourning. You'll look divine in lavender."

Lily offered a small smile. "That's my favorite color. Do you really think I should? Someone may think it not entirely appropriate, and I might be criticized."

"Well, if someone dares to do such a thing, I'll refer them to Lady Kingsley. She's one of the best-known arbiters of etiquette. And she has informed me three weeks is the correct period of mourning. By that time, the matter of your grandfather's unfortunate demise should be resolved, and the correct person apprehended. And, of course, dear Sebastian will be freed. Time enough for you to enjoy the rest of the season. We should start on your wardrobe right away."

But Lily was not quite convinced. "Would you mind terribly, Mrs. Worthington, if I took some time to think it over? I would not want to rush into anything."

Mother patted Lily's hands. "Of course not, dear. Take all the time you need."

But I could see Mother was crestfallen. And I understood why. Lily reminded Mother of Emily, my dear sister who'd succumbed to the Spanish influenza several years ago. They differed in looks, for Lily's blond curls and blue eyes did not in the least resemble Emily's dark coloring, but their personalities were the same, sweet as can be. And, of course, Mother wanted to do right by Lily, as well. It was horrible she'd been practically entombed her whole life— first in a cold, drafty castle and then that great mausoleum of a house—with hardly any social interaction, except for the servants and her maid. She called to mind a chrysalis still in the cocoon, ready to become a butterfly, spread her wings, and fly. We would move heaven and earth to see she did just that.

After Mother excused herself for she had a great deal to do, I sat next to Lily. "It's all a bit much, isn't it?"

"Yes," she said. "I would hate to go against your mother's wishes, but I don't feel three weeks is enough. Three months feels right, though, with another three months of half mourning."

"You'll miss the entire season then." I was disappointed for her. With her beauty, never mind her title, she would most surely shine.

A small smile trembled across her lips. "Can't miss what I've never known."

"Mother will respect your wishes, whatever you decide, but please allow her to organize a wardrobe for you. It will keep her busy while we investigate the murder of your grandfather."

She glanced at me with surprise. "You think so?"

"I know so. There's nothing she loves more than to shop for new clothes."

Her face tinged with pink. "But I . . . the expense."

"Oh, piffle. We have more than enough. Besides, it will keep Mother happy, and there's no price you can put on that, can you?"

"Well, if you think that's best."

"I do."

And so it was arranged. Lily would accompany Mother to Angelique's leaving Margaret and me free to investigate the duke's murder.

CHAPTER THIRTEEN

WYNCHCOMBE HOUSE

*L*ILY HAD SENT A NOTE, so we were expected at Wynchcombe House the next day. Lily and I, along with Hester, Lily's maid, drove up in the Rolls my family had gifted me on my birthday. I could have driven it, but Mother insisted on having Neville act as our chauffeur.

"A young lady doesn't motor herself to a duke's house. It just isn't done, Kitty."

Since it was easier to agree than argue, I acceded to her wishes.

Set in a grand landscaped setting, Wynchcombe House was an imposing presence even among all the other great houses of Mayfair. A Georgian mansion built by one of the earlier dukes, it stood three stories high with wings flaring out on each side and a myriad of large windows lining its front. The knocker had been removed from the front door, so it was evident the house was in mourning.

Given the hostile reception Sebastian had endured, I half

expected we would suffer the same treatment, but thankfully, I was wrong. As soon as the Rolls pulled up to the entrance, the butler I recognized from the inquest swung open the door. Clearly, he'd been expecting us.

Within the stately residence, black cloth draped every furnishing as was the custom when there was a death in the house. From the little I was able to discern, the furniture, with its gilded details, heavy moldings, and twisted and elaborate motifs, appeared to be from the baroque period. A mirror to the commanding, arrogant persona of the duke.

After walking for what seemed like miles, we were shown to an austerely decorated drawing room where the butler Temple soon oversaw the service of an elaborate spread consisting of tea, scones, assorted cakes and pastries, all presented on delicate porcelain cups and plates. Going by a pattern I recognized as centuries old, the china must have been handed down through generations. The message was clear. We were being welcomed in style.

"Thank you, Temple. This is very generous of you," Lily said, once everything was laid out in front of us.

"Our pleasure, Lady Lily. There's nothing we wouldn't do for you. I speak for the entire staff when I say we are entirely at your service." His elegant bow was one you'd show to someone of high rank, not a granddaughter who'd been hidden away in a dark corner of the house. "How may I serve you, milady?"

Lily and I had agreed she would lead the conversation at the start, for the servants were familiar with her. But once the discussion progressed, I would become more involved.

"Miss Worthington and I are here to enquire about, well, grandfather. We are especially curious about the events that transpired on his last day and night."

"Anything I can answer, I'll be glad to do," Temple said. His open countenance demonstrated he was speaking the truth. I breathed easier knowing he would not impede the investigation.

"Mister Temple, I know this goes against convention, but do you think you could possibly sit?" Lily asked. "It's rather uncomfortable to stare up at you."

"Why, it's no trouble at all, milady." With this, he perched on one of the dark leather chairs across from us, his back ramrod straight.

"Would you like some tea?" Lily asked.

"No, thank you, milady."

"Very well." She folded her hands on her lap. "Could you take us through the duke's last day and night?"

As surreptitiously as I could, I retrieved notebook and pencil from my purse. Temple noted it, but he didn't object.

"Thursday morning, his Grace met with his man of business, Mister Tellman, in the city."

"Forgive me for interrupting," I said, "but did he normally visit rather than have the gentleman come to him?"

"He preferred to perform those tasks at the city office as the duke believed it afforded them more privacy. That way no one would know the matters they discussed."

"I see. Please proceed."

He inclined his head. "After the meeting, he attended a luncheon with Lord Gresham at his gentlemen's club."

"Which one?"

"White's. He returned to Wynchcombe House around four. He liked to rest before his evening's activities. Mister Farthington can tell you more about that if you wish."

Lily and I exchanged a look. We would need to interview the valet.

"We would," Lily said. "Can you ask him to join us, please?"

"Of course."

He came to his feet and tugged the bell pull. When a

footman responded to the summons, Temple asked him to have Mister Farthington come to the drawing room. While we waited, Lily and I enjoyed the tea and scones. It took but a short time for the valet to step into the room. I hadn't known what to expect in the duke's man, but he surprised me, nonetheless. In his forties, immaculately dressed, with a touch of gray at the temples, he was the epitome of a valet. After the introductions, he availed himself of one of the leather chairs across from us.

"Mister Farthington, we are here to enquire about the duke's last day and night." I filled him in on what Temple had relayed to us before asking him about the duke's evening. "We understand the duke returned to the house around four after a luncheon with Lord Gresham."

"He did." His melodious words were spoken in the King's English. Not only did he look the part of a proper gentleman's gentleman, but he spoke it as well.

"Do you know the nature of his meeting with Lord Gresham?"

He bristled at my question. "I would never enquire as to His Grace's activities, Miss."

"Mister Farthington," Lily stated in a tone that brooked no opposition, "we are trying to determine who murdered my grandfather, for it most certainly was not my brother. Your cooperation would be appreciated." She gazed directly at him in a no-nonsense manner.

Inwardly, I smiled for the soft-spoken mouse who'd appeared at our door a mere two days ago was no more. The chrysalis had morphed into the butterfly, and an assertive one at that, she'd been always meant to be.

"I beg your pardon, Lady Lily. I did not mean to offend." He cleared his throat. "His Grace enjoyed weekly luncheons with Lord Gresham at which time they discussed topics of interest to them."

"What sort of topics?" I asked.

"Those that were of mutual benefit."

If he thought for one moment that answer would satisfy me, he was wrong. "Such as?"

He heaved out a sigh. "His Grace was heavily involved in the legislative aspects of the House of Lords. My understanding was that Lord Gresham acted as his right-hand man —drumming up votes, gathering support either for or against legislation."

"Any particular legislation his grace favored or disapproved at the moment?"

He cleared his throat again. "His Grace was particularly opposed to extending suffrage to more women. He'd been vehemently opposed to them getting the vote in the first place."

Just as I thought. He'd probably plotted with Lord Gresham not only to block legislation enfranchising more women but, more than likely, supported the employment of rabble rousers to break up our rally. I made an emphatic note of that and double underscored it.

"What happened after he returned home?" I asked.

"He usually rested in midafternoon for two hours. He would then rise, bathe, and dress. That evening he did just that. Afterward, he requested a supper tray be brought to his rooms."

"Did he do that often?"

"Yes, unless, of course, he was entertaining at home."

"How often did he entertain at home?"

"He rarely did, but after Lady Lily arrived, he did it more frequently."

"Why do you think that was?"

His glance took in Lily, who returned it with a nod. Interpreting that as assent, he continued, "He was eager to find a husband for her, so he invited likely candidates to supper."

Just as Lily had explained.

"But that evening he was not holding a supper party."

"No. He'd been invited to an evening of card playing."

"Where did he go that evening?"

"Viscount Tottingham's."

Lily made a noise of disgust but didn't say a word. She didn't have to. Her expression spoke volumes for her.

"Did his grace attend many social events?" I needed to get as full an understanding of the duke as I could.

"Very few balls. But he did attend the Duke of Torrance's, a friend of long acquaintance. He much preferred an evening of playing cards."

"How often did he do that?"

"Four, five times a week."

"That many?"

"He was very good at it." He hitched up his chin and offered a brief smile. "He still had all his faculties, you see."

"When did he usually return home?"

"Close to midnight. But he never made it home that night." His tone changed into something resembling sadness. He'd been fond of the old duke. Probably one of the few.

"If I may explain, Miss Worthington," Temple interrupted.

"Of course." Having been at the inquest, I knew what he was going to relate. Still, I was eager to hear him tell the tale for I had questions for him.

"An envelope was delivered for the duke earlier that evening. It had the word urgent printed across it and underlined."

"Who delivered it?"

Temple brushed his fingers across his brow. "I don't know. The envelope had to have been dropped through the letter box on the front door while the staff was enjoying their supper."

I asked the question that the coroner did not ask. "Could

someone within the house have placed that envelope in the entrance hall?"

He thought about it for a moment. "I don't see how. The entire staff was below, enjoying their supper in the servants' dining hall."

"There was nobody else in the house?"

"No. Well, except for Mister Nevins, his Grace's personal secretary, and he would have no need to deliver correspondence in such a manner."

Unless he wished to make it appear as if the envelope had been dropped through the letter box.

"Is the front door locked, Mister Temple?"

"At all times, Miss Worthington. That's an order straight from his Grace. He didn't trust what he termed the riff raff."

"You have no idea where the envelope came from or what time it arrived?" Lily asked.

"No, Lady Lily, we don't."

"What did you do with the envelope?" He repeated the same facts he'd testified at the inquest. Given the urgent note on the envelope, he'd taken a taxi to Viscount Tottingham's and delivered the envelope straight into the duke's hands.

"What happened when his grace read the note?"

"He cursed, begging your pardon, Miss, and exclaimed, 'Damn impudence.' He then asked me to hail him a taxi."

"Why would he do that when his car and his chauffeur were waiting outside for him?"

"The only reason I can think of is he didn't want the chauffeur to know where he was going."

The same thing he'd testified at the inquest.

"I hailed a taxi for him, of course. And that's the last I saw of His Grace."

"How did you find out about his death?"

"An inspector from Scotland Yard came by. It was close to

two. He asked many questions, of myself, of the staff, but we couldn't tell him any more than I am telling you."

"You didn't know who the duke went to meet?"

"No. His Grace didn't say."

"What happened to the note?"

"He took it with him along with the envelope."

It was well and truly lost, for it had not been found among the duke's possessions. The murderer had to have taken it. "Did the envelope have any distinguishing features?"

"It was made of quality linen, and it had a watermark."

"Do you recall what it was?"

He thought about it for longer than it should have taken him. "No, sorry. I did not."

He was lying. He'd seen something but wasn't talking.

"A shame, but it can't be helped. If you do remember later, please let us know."

"I will, Miss."

"Well, that's about all the questions I have. Do you have any, Lily?"

"No. I believe you've covered what we needed to know." She addressed the butler and the valet. "Thank you, Mister Temple, Mister Farthington. You've helped a great deal. Your assistance may clear my brother."

"We sincerely hope for that as well, milady," Temple said. "We wish to serve him to our very best ability."

And there it was, the reason why they'd been so accommodating. They hoped to remain employed. Well, at least Temple did. I wasn't entirely certain about Mister Farthington.

"Is the duke's private secretary available? We'd like a word with him, as well."

"Certainly, milady. I will enquire." Temple bowed before making his way out of his room.

Mister Farthington rose as well. "Unless there is anything

else, milady."

"Actually, I have one more question. It's of a rather delicate nature, I'm afraid."

The valet raised a brow but didn't say a word.

I posed my enquiry in the least offending manner possible. "Did His Grace have a particular lady friend?"

"No." Mister Farthington," said, with feeling. "He didn't care for women as a general rule. He found they" —he sniffed — "didn't quite measure up."

In other words, the duke was a misogynist at heart. I suspected the valet was as well. "What will you do now that the duke no longer needs your services?" I asked.

The question took him by surprise. "Go on as before. The new duke will need guidance in matters of dressing. I will make my expertise available to him."

"Thank you, Mister Farthington. You've been very helpful," Lily said.

"My pleasure, milady."

After he'd gone, Lily and I exchanged smiles. "I know," she said. "But Sebastian will need him since he'll be required to attend formal and official functions as a duke. The opening of Parliament for one, the occasional ball for another."

"He'll be much in demand at social events, unmarried as he is."

"Ahhh," Lily said, but before she could say anything else, Temple returned with a man at his heels. Neither short nor tall, balding, wearing a pince-nez on his very short nose and stooped like he spent every day poring over ledgers. It could only be the duke's private secretary.

"Mister Nevins, you remember Lady Lily," Temple said.

"How do you, milady." Mister Nevins bowed. The poor man appeared extremely nervous, twitching, and perspiring quite heavily.

"Won't you take a seat?" Lily said. "Miss Worthington and

I have some things we'd like to discuss with you."

He wiped his brow with a balled-up handkerchief. "I'm afraid I can't."

"Why not?" Lily asked.

"If you would permit me to explain, milady."

"Of course," she said.

"I'm the duke's private secretary."

"Yes, we know," I said, hoping to hurry him along.

"As such, I handled matters between the duke and other gentlemen. Because many of them were confidential in nature, I would only be able to discuss them with the new duke."

Lily and I glanced at each other. He objected talking to us because we were women. The cheek of the man! Well, he was not going to get away with that.

"As you very well know, the duke is presently not available. He has authorized us to investigate all matters related to the former duke, including those that fall within your purview."

"I beg your pardon." Another mop up of the brow. "I'm not making myself clear. I would be glad to discuss the matters with the new duke, or his representatives."

"That's us," Lily said.

He heaved a sigh and closed his eyes. "But you see, Lady Lily, I'm not sure of who the new duke will be."

"I don't understand," Lily said. "My brother, Sebastian, is the new duke."

"My apologies, but it is my understanding that is not assured."

"What do you mean?" I asked.

"Lord Henry is challenging the succession. He believes— and pardon me for saying such a thing, milady—he believes your brother was not born of a legitimate marriage. If true, he cannot become the Duke of Wynchcombe."

CHAPTER FOURTEEN

A CHALLENGE TO THE SUCCESSION

*A*FTER THAT CALAMITOUS BIT OF NEWS was dropped on our laps, there really was nothing more to say. With as much composure as we could muster, we thanked Mister Nevins and made our way out. By mutual assent, Lily and I deferred any discussion about what we'd learned until we reached home. It wasn't that I didn't trust Neville. I did. But if somehow word got out, I could honestly say I'd never discussed the revelations from Wynchcombe House in his presence.

Although I managed to remain calm, Lily was another matter. She was visibly shaking by the time we arrived at Worthington House. So much so, I rushed her into the drawing room to keep anyone from noticing her emotional state.

As soon as we stepped into the room, she yanked off her kid gloves and stuffed them into her silk purse. "I can't believe Henry is challenging Sebastian's succession to the title. That worm."

"I agree." For several minutes, I allowed her to vent her spleen while I furiously cogitated about what could be done.

"What grounds does he have to do such a thing?" Like her brother before her, she paced the drawing room, more agitated than I'd seen her before. "Grandfather acknowledged Sebastian as his heir a long time ago. Henry can't possibly believe he'll succeed."

"He's probably hoping to gain something from challenging it."

Lily stopped pacing and faced me. "Such as?"

"Time."

"For what?"

Yesterday while we were planning our strategy for Wynchcombe House, she'd shared the unsavory details of Lord Henry's life, most particularly his addiction to cards. "You mentioned he's a prodigious gambler who rarely wins, and that he regularly applied to your grandfather to pay off his debts."

"And grandfather paid them time and again for he did not wish a scandal attached to the Wynchcombe name. Apparently, a gentleman always pays his debts, never mind Henry is no gentleman."

"But now with the duke's death, he has no hope of obtaining funds to satisfy them. The longer he keeps the succession in question, the longer he has to come up with the money." I came to my feet. "Father needs to know what we discovered so he can investigate the matter. And it cannot be delayed. I need to telephone him."

Seeing how the issue was of such delicacy, I opted to make the call from Father's office rather than use the telephone in the hallway where anybody could listen in on a conversation. Sacrosanct as his study was, it needed to be done, even if I was invading his private sanctuary.

After I shared what we'd learned at the duke's residence, he brought Ned into the conversation. But there was so much to reveal, the discussion became somewhat convoluted. And then it became downright impossible when an urgent matter arose at the office that Father needed to handle. So, in the end he asked Ned to look into it and report what he discovered to us tonight.

After the call ended, I turned to Lily. "Well, that's one less thing to worry about at the moment."

"It is?"

"Oh, yes. Ned will have an answer by supper time." We might not like what he had to say, but he would have something to share.

Since we still needed to discuss what we'd discovered, we adjourned to Lily's room. On our way, we ran into a clearly distraught Margaret.

"What's wrong?" I asked her once we were in the bedroom with the door firmly shut.

"They won't let me see him," Margaret said.

Him being Sebastian, of course. It had been only three days since his arrest, but to her it had been agony. After all, they'd been practically inseparable since they arrived in London. Rather than accompany us to Wynchcombe House, she'd set off for the gaol where they were keeping Sebastian to try and gain an audience with him. But it appeared her trip had been unsuccessful.

"Why not?"

"I'm neither family, nor a member of his solicitor's office," she said.

"But did you tell them—"

"I tried everything, Kitty," she cried out. "I'm so worried about him. You know how much he treasures the outdoors.

Being cooped up, such as he is, must be affecting his wellbeing."

It was difficult to see my usually unflappable sister become well, flappable. But it only proved the strength of her feelings toward Sebastian. Wishing to provide comfort, I pressed her hands. "We'll bring it up tonight when we discuss things with Father and Ned. See if something can be done."

Her eyes grew wide with alarm. "What do you mean? What happened?"

We filled her in on what we'd discovered at Wynchcombe House, ending with the news of the challenge.

"But how could Lord Henry do such a thing?" Margaret asked. "The duke acknowledged Sebastian as his heir years ago."

"That's exactly what I said," Lily exclaimed.

Heavens! They were both beside themselves.

Mother would know how to deal with their overwrought state. Unfortunately, she was not available as she was at a meeting of the Ladies Benevolent Society. Well, there was no help for it, I would need to do what I could. So, I asked myself, what would Mother do? The answer came quite quickly. "Should we order some tea?"

Margaret's gaze told me she understood what I was trying to achieve. "Yes, please do."

Lily simply nodded which only went to show what a good egg she was. She'd already drunk enough tea at Wynchcombe to float the entire British navy.

In a short time, Betsy, my sprite of a maid, arrived with a tray laden not only with tea but seed cake and scones.

"Thank you, Betsy," I said.

"You're welcome, Miss," she said, after putting down the tray.

"Betsy accompanied me to the jail since I needed a chaperone," Margaret said. "I'm so glad you were there."

Betsy flushed with pleasure at the praise. "Oh, Miss, it was nothing."

More than likely, she probably enjoyed the adventure as she had a fascination with Scotland Yard and constabularies. Now she could add a jail to her list. At the first opportunity, I would ask her to share what she'd discovered. She had a way about her that encouraged those in charge to let down their guards, and she was smart enough to learn a thing or two.

We took time to enjoy the tea and scones, but once they'd worked their magic, Margaret asked, "The Wynchcombe staff opened up to you without any problems?"

"The butler, Temple, was very accommodating," I said. "Mister Farthington less so until Lily reminded him who she was and what we were trying to accomplish." I pressed her hand. "I was so proud of you today."

Her face turned pink. "Thank you, but I only did what I had to do."

"Well, you did it magnificently. Was the staff always friendly toward you?"

"I never dealt with Mister Farthington since he was the duke's man, but Temple and the other servants were kindness itself. If the duke was not in sight, that is. If he was present, they turned glacial as the duke preferred formality in all things."

"Regardless of their motives, I'm glad they shared their knowledge with us," I said. "Well, except for Mister Nevins. And, as soon as we resolve the issue of Sebastian's legitimacy, he should open up."

But as it turned out, the answer was not that simple.

* * *

THAT EVENING we gathered before supper in the drawing room eager to hear what Ned had to say. He'd spent the afternoon making telephone calls and obtaining an expert's advice about hereditary titles and successions. Unfortunately, the news was not good.

"Do you mean to tell us that that worm may have a valid argument?" I asked.

"He does, but only for the time being. You see, the Duke of Wynchcombe never formally acknowledged Sebastian as his heir. Apparently, it was a casual arrangement between Sebastian's maternal grandfather and the duke."

"So Lord Henry may take this case to court and win?" Father asked. "That's outrageous!" He'd been so busy with his urgent office matter he hadn't had a chance to hear from Ned until now.

"Well, first of all, it would not be up to him," Ned explained, "but his father, Lord Percy, to challenge the succession, as he would then be the heir. And from what I learned this afternoon, Lord Henry is arguing for him to do just that. Lord Percy may accede to his son's wishes for the sake of stopping the argument. Apparently, he abhors conflicts."

No wonder. With a father like the Duke of Wynchcombe, Lord Percy probably found it easier to agree with the duke than challenge him. It'd been clear at the Torrance ball that the duke didn't listen to him. "So what's to be done?" I asked.

"We have to obtain irrefutable proof that Sebastian's parents were married legally, and that Sebastian was born of their union. In other words, we'll need marriage and birth records. I can't imagine Sebastian having them in his possession. We'll need to travel to Scotland to obtain them. Do you know anything about them, Lily?" Ned asked her.

"No. I was only three at the time my parents died." Her newly found vibrance was missing. "And, of course, I never had a chance to discuss anything with Sebastian since we were kept apart." She'd kept quiet until now. Not a surprise. She'd spent years being ignored.

"You need not worry, Lily. We'll get it done." Ned must have noticed her despair, and, kind person that he was, sought to reassure her.

"Will we?" Hope shown in her eyes.

"Yes. You have my word on that."

Having addressed her fears, he turned back to us. "I've asked Sebastian's solicitor to visit him in the morning and see if he can shed any light on the subject, as well as obtain his authorization for me to pursue the matter. Regardless of what Sebastian remembers, we'll need to obtain the legal documents. Once I have Sebastian's power of attorney in hand, I'll travel to Scotland to obtain the documentation. Upon my return, it would only be a matter of putting the papers before the Chancery Court for Sebastian to be declared the true heir." His no-nonsense manner spoke volumes. Whatever needed to be done, he would take care of it.

"Oh," Lily said, biting her lip.

"What's wrong, Lily dear?" Mother asked.

Lily took to worrying the monogrammed handkerchief she held in her hands. "We're being such a lot of trouble. And here your entire family is helping us out." She waved a hand at me. "Kitty could be enjoying her season without having to engage in this investigation, and Margaret would have time to dedicate to her causes. Mister Worthington and your son, well, they have a business to run. And you, Mrs. Worthington, you have your charities to manage. I'm so sorry we're being so much bother."

"Why it's no bother at all, dear," Mother said. "We couldn't live with ourselves if we allowed Sebastian, and you, to suffer through these difficulties by yourselves."

"And don't worry about my season," I piped in. "I'd rather

be doing a bit of sleuthing, than attend another insipid event. Honestly, it's no bother."

"And as for the business," Father added, "it's doing fine. We suffered a minor hiccup after the protest. But it didn't last. This murder has taken precedence in the public's mind—"

"Edward!" Mother cautioned.

"Yes, well," he cleared his throat. "No need to worry about Worthington & Son, Lily."

Margaret joined Lily at the settee and took her hand. "And as for me, you know how much Sebastian means to me. I would do anything to help him."

"Yes, I do know. He and I are so lucky to have you, all of you, on our side."

"Well, then, that puts paid to any apologies. They're not needed. Shall we proceed to dinner?" Mother glanced fondly at all assembled. "I love it when my family is gathered around me. Well, except for Richard, of course."

"Richard? Who's that?" Lily asked, taking Father's proffered arm.

"My second son," Mother said, curling her hand around Father's other elbow. "He's in Egypt. Fancies himself an archeologist. Apparently, he's so busy playing in the sand and digging up ancient pharaohs, he can't find time to write his mother."

"Oh, Ma'am, you are so droll." Lily laughed, her somber mood forgotten. Goodness, she had a mercurial spirit. It would take time but eventually she would find her center.

Margaret and I followed behind with Ned as our escort.

"She really is quite lovely," Ned said. "Isn't she?"

"Quite," I said. Mother would be in alt if she'd heard that praise.

CHAPTER FIFTEEN

VISCOUNT TOTTINGHAM

"*I* DEMAND TO SEE MY FIANCÉE" Viscount Tottingham bellowed. He'd presented himself at Worthington House at the unseemly hour of eight in the morning.

Awakened by Betsy with the news that this personage had arrived, I'd rushed through my morning ablutions, determined to greet him before Mother could. But alas, I was too late. She was already in the drawing room.

"I do apologize, milord," Mother said, "your unexpected arrival caught us off guard. Lady Lily has been notified of your presence. She'll make her appearance shortly."

"And who are you?" he blared out.

The rudeness of the man!

Rather than take umbrage, Mother responded with all politeness. "I do beg your pardon. I should have introduced myself. I'm Mrs. Worthington," she turned to me, "and this is my daughter—"

"I don't give a damn who she is."

Bristling in outrage, Mother stood up to her five four. "Milord, this is a Christian household. We do not tolerate such language in our home."

"If I may, milord," the fashionable gentleman standing next to the viscount said. He was exquisitely dressed in a suit which could only have come from Savile Row. "Perhaps it would be best to take a softer approach. Much more is gained through honey than vinegar."

Viscount Tottingham's indignant gaze snapped to him. "Do you dare criticize me, Lord Henry?"

"No, sir, I'm not, only pointing out a strategy more likely to succeed. I did not wish to offend," he said, offering a slight bow.

This was Lord Henry? The worm who was challenging Sebastian's succession to the title? Should have known. Blond and blue-eyed, he bore the same coloring of the other Dalrymple men. However, where Sebastian was trim and fit, Lord Henry suffered from a slight paunch, and his face bore the lines of dissipation. Too much drink would be my guess.

"Forgive us for the early arrival, Mrs. Worthington," he said. "You are correct in your assessment. We should have alerted you. As you can see, Viscount Tottingham is eager to claim his bride. He's arranged to marry today. Why, the minister is awaiting us right now at the church ready to perform the ceremony."

Lily arrived with Margaret; their arms entwined around each other's waist. Rushing to join them, I embraced Lily from her other side. All for one and one for all.

"And here she is. Lady Lily," Lord Henry bowed, "how lovely you look, cousin." He held a monocle to his left eye. "Is that a new dress?"

Leave it to the tulip of fashion to notice her new gown. Well, new to her. Margaret had gifted dresses to Lily before

Angelique could style a new wardrobe for her. The poor girl could not go around wearing the same old dreary clothes day in and day out.

"Why are you here, Henry?" Lily asked, her lip curling with disdain. Not Lord Henry, only his surname.

"Why, cousin, Viscount Tottingham is here to claim you as his bride." A smile that thought to charm formed across his lips. It failed miserably.

"I never consented to this marriage," Lily exclaimed.

I pressed her waist in support. Good for her.

"Nobody asked your opinion, gel," Viscount Tottingham spit out. "I made a deal with the duke. We signed papers. Monies were exchanged. You are mine, from your topmost curl down to your toes," he said, approaching her.

He didn't get far. Margaret and I stepped in front of Lily, barring his way.

Mother apparently had enough of the viscount for she walked toward the bell pull and tugged it. Carlton must have been right outside the door because he appeared instantly, along with two of our burliest footmen.

"Carlton, please show the viscount and Lord Henry to the door. I believe their visit is done."

"I'm not leaving without Lady Lily," Viscount Tottingham blustered. "I paid for her, damn it."

"If you'll come this way, milord," Carlton said, polite to his core.

The viscount continued to rant while the footmen, along with Carlton, escorted him toward the door. But once he arrived there, he turned. "This is not the end of it. By God, I'll set the law on you. Let's see where you stand then." And then, with one final huff, he was gone.

Lord Henry, who'd leisurely trailed in his wake, turned, and bowed, "Ladies," before making his own way out.

Once they were out of the room, Lily tottered to the

settee on shaking legs. "Thank you, Mrs. Worthington, Margaret, Kitty."

Carlton returned. "The" —he sniffed— "gentlemen have left the house, ma'am."

"Thank you, Carlton. We'll partake of breakfast in the dining room in a half hour or so, but could you bring us some tea now, please."

—and coffee," I piped up.

"Yes, and coffee."

"Of course, ma'am."

"Well, that was—"

"Horrid," Lily said. "It was horrid."

"Yes, it was," I said. "Well, at least Lord Henry was polite."

Her lip curled up in a sneer. "Oh, yes, in public, Lord Henry is all smiles and bows. In private, it's another matter. He used to pinch me when he visited Wynchcombe Castle with Lord Percy. And one time he" —she shuddered— "he tried to kiss me in a most improper way. My governess caught him out and sent him packing. I hate him."

"With good reason," Margaret said.

Carlton returned with the tea and coffee service which he placed on a table. To my joy, muffins were included. Soon we were reviving ourselves with the beverages and munching away on the delicious treat.

"He'll be back, you know," Lily said, after consuming two of the muffins. "Somehow, he'll get a magistrate to rule in his favor, and he'll return to force me into this horrible marriage." She trembled.

"Well, then, dear," Mother said in as calm a tone as I've ever heard from her, "in that case, you won't be here."

Lily's countenance turned pale. "Wh-what do you mean?"

Poor thing probably thought we were going to toss her out on the street. As if we would ever do such a thing.

"I've been thinking. Ned could use your help in Scotland.

After all, you are Sebastian's sister. If a problem arises, you'll be able to claim kinship with him."

Lily's eyes widened. "Travel all the way to Scotland with your son?" The thought would be shocking to her. Not only had she just met him, but a young, unmarried woman did not hop on a train with a bachelor. Not if she wanted to preserve her reputation.

"Well, of course, you'll need a chaperone." Mother's gaze turned pensive. "Maybe I can arrange—"

"I'll go. I'll be the chaperone," Margaret offered.

"Are you sure, dear? It'll be a long trip, and your shoulder hasn't quite healed."

"My shoulder is fine, Mother. And no one could possibly object to my accompanying my brother, along with my friend. Kitty traveled with him all the way from Switzerland."

I shuddered. "Please don't remind me about that awful trip." A woman had been murdered right in front of me.

"Well, we'll make sure nobody gets killed on The Flying Scotsman," Margaret said. "What do you say, Lily?"

"I've never been aboard a train," she said softly.

What else hadn't this young woman enjoyed in her life?

Smiling, Margaret hugged her. "We'll have a great time. You'll see."

Because of the urgency of Lily's situation, plans were made to leave the very next day. Ned had needed little convincing. After being informed of Viscount Tottingham's demand, he was downright outraged. The following day he arrived bright and early, escorted Lily and Margaret to the Rolls, and all three headed for Paddington train station. We'd thought the trip would be but a few days, but unfortunately it took longer than that.

CHAPTER SIXTEEN

KITTY VISITS LORD PERCY

*B*EFORE LILY DEPARTED FOR SCOTLAND, I'd asked her to pen a letter of introduction to Lord Percy. I had many questions for him, first and foremost whether he felt the same way as his son about Sebastian's succession to the title. His response arrived quickly, and our meeting was set for the next day.

With Betsy as my chaperone, I set out dressed in one of my finest day frocks, an azure dark purple chiffon, with a matching cloche hat and gloves. Mother once again insisted on Neville at the wheel. I was beginning to think she didn't wish me to drive. And all because of a tiny accident with a lorry on Piccadilly which had *not* been my fault.

Upon my arrival, I was shown to Lord Percy's study. A surprise, for guests are usually received in the drawing room. He was seated at a secretary desk next to a massive bookcase which took up most of the wall. An impressive array of tomes filled the shelves.

While the furnishings at Wynchcombe House were of the baroque period, Lord Percy's belonged to the Queen Anne style. Smaller, lighter, and infinitely more comfortable with their cushioned seats and wing-back chairs.

As soon as I stepped into the room, he stood and bowed. "Miss Worthington."

Blond, tall, and blue-eyed as he was, I was once again struck by the close resemblance to Sebastian, as well as Lord Henry. Although in Lord Percy's case, he wore his age well, for his face did not carry the lines of dissipation so evident on his son's face.

I curtsied and offered my condolences. "I'm so sorry for your loss." It needed to be said, if only for politeness' sake.

"Thank you, my dear. The thought does you credit." A sad sort of smile lined his lips. Even though the duke had treated him abominably, he'd loved his father.

"I appreciate you taking the time out of your schedule to see me. I know how busy you must be." At the very least, he had to be planning his father's funeral, for such a noble aristocrat would need to be sent off with pomp and circumstance.

"It's my pleasure." He pointed to a delicate armchair next to a round table. "Would you like to take a seat? I've ordered tea."

"You didn't have to, but I thank you nonetheless." What would an uncomfortable situation be without tea to ease the way?

After settling into the chair across from me, he asked, "How is Lily? I'm surprised she didn't accompany you."

"She's not feeling well. She offers her regrets." I wasn't about to volunteer she'd left for Scotland. Not without knowing how he felt about the succession and Lily's guardianship. For all I knew, he could be planning to make a bid for it and would frown on his niece being removed from his reach.

A look of concern drifted over his face. "Nothing serious, I hope."

"A temporary megrim, that's all."

We continued chatting about Lily and inconsequential things like that old chestnut, the weather, until a servant appeared with the tea service.

But once we refreshed ourselves, he wasted no time. "What may I do for you, Miss Worthington?" He folded his hands on the table and leaned slightly toward me in a gesture that seemed to offer encouragement. Time would tell whether the gesture was a true reflection of him or a ruse.

Nothing like the present to test him. "A few days ago, Lord Henry visited us at Worthington House, along with Viscount Tottingham. Without prior notice, I might add. He used the excuse the viscount was eager to claim his supposed fiancée, Lady Lily."

"Ah, yes. Henry told me about it." A small, rueful smile lit upon his lips. "I apologize, my dear. He shouldn't have inconvenienced your family. That was ill-suited of him."

"You don't agree that Lily should marry the viscount, then?"

"Indeed, no. I tried to talk my father out of it. But he would not be moved from his position." He opened his hands and shrugged. "There was nothing I could do. He was her guardian."

"Does the guardianship now fall to you?"

"No, it does not. It falls to Sebastian. He is her brother, after all."

"So, you will not press Lily to marry the viscount?"

Once more, he leaned toward me, his gaze fixed with resolve. "I will not. As I have no authority over her, my opinion is of no value whatsoever." Lord Percy seemed to be one of those persons who went through life trying to cause as little a stir as possible.

"But your son —"

For a moment, he looked down as if with regret. "Henry has long followed his own path without counsel from me." His gaze found me once more. "I tried to steer him to the right course. Unfortunately, he inherited my father's firmness of mind and refuses to be guided by me."

"I understand he's challenging Sebastian's succession to the title."

If lips could frown, his did. "A misguided attempt, for Sebastian is the true heir. He is the Duke of Wynchcombe."

"So, you do not support your son's endeavors in that regard?"

"Indeed not. The Dukes of Wynchcombe have inherited the title through centuries without a single challenge to the succession. For Henry to even think of doing such a thing, well, it offends my every sensibility."

I studied him while he sipped his tea. "You seem to take great pride in the title."

"I do. It is the one thing my father and I had in common." He paused. "I hope you don't think I'm being unfeeling when it comes to the way I speak of him."

I gazed at him with sympathy. To have withstood the vileness of his father through so many years had to have taken a toll on him. It was a wonder he possessed the manners of a gentleman. "From what I understand, he was a difficult man."

"Yes, he was. Intractable in his beliefs. Once he set his mind on something, he wouldn't veer from it. No matter what arguments I offered him. He'd taken it into his head Lily should marry Viscount Tottingham. And by God, he'd carry through with it, no matter what I said."

"Do you wonder who killed him, Lord Percy?" I asked, as gently as I could.

He leaned back into his chair while he pondered my question. "I don't wonder someone did," he finally said. "The question is who? It wasn't Sebastian. The boy does not have it in him."

"That's what my father says. Do you have any idea who could have done it?"

His face took on a haunted look. "My father was feared by many, Miss Worthington. He enjoyed exerting power over everyone who met him, from the lowliest servant to a high-ranking member of the nobility. That's what gave him the greatest joy."

"What about you, Lord Percy? Did you fear him?" I watched him carefully for his answer would reveal much about him.

"No." He emitted a self-deprecating laugh. "I never did. You see, in his own strange way, he loved me."

If the way his father treated him was 'love,' I wanted no part of it. But then, I knew the meaning of true love for my family showered me with it every single day. His father probably never had.

"But to answer your question, Miss Worthington, I'd look at those who owed him money. Father was an adept gambler who won most of the time."

"Really?" I knew, of course, from remarks the duke's valet had made. But I wanted to discover Lord Percy's thoughts on the subject.

"Yes. I've watched many match wits with him and bet vast amounts of money. Few win. Many lose. Maybe someone found it difficult to pay back the debt. And sought his death as a way out."

"How much money are we talking about?"

"I wouldn't know, my dear. Mister Nevins would, though. As my father's personal secretary, he kept track of that information."

No wonder Mister Nevins would not open his books to me for they would contain not only the amounts owed but the names of those indebted to the duke.

"Unfortunately, Mister Nevins refused to share the information because of your son's challenge to the succession." I paused before I made my next point. "We'll get it in the end, though. We have right on our side." I couldn't tell him Ned was traveling to Scotland to obtain the documentation needed to verify Sebastian's right to the title. I didn't trust him not to share the information with his son, and God only knew what Lord Henry would do.

He glanced at his wristwatch. "Anything else, my dear. I'm afraid I have a prior appointment."

"One more thing." I hesitated for he would think my request as curiosity at best and macabre at worst. "May I see your dagger? The one like the one that . . ." I couldn't complete the thought.

His brow wrinkled. "Whatever for?" he asked, not unkindly.

"I'm curious about its markings. But I understand if you'd rather not."

"No. It's not that. I just . . . I would hate for your sensibilities to be offended. It is a rather fearsome weapon."

"I won't be offended."

"I'll go fetch it then." He returned a few minutes later with the dagger in his hand. As described in the inquest, it was long with a narrow blade and pointed end.

"It's a rather excellent example of a medieval weapon, don't you think?" He said, presenting it to me.

Even though I'd believed it wouldn't affect me, I shivered. "I wouldn't know, milord, as I'm not a connoisseur of such things."

"Ah, but I am. I was very proud the day my father gave it to me as recognition I was his son. The spare, if you will," he offered with a smile. Lord Percy seemed perfectly comfortable with that role. "Would you like to hold it?"

"If you don't mind."

"Be careful. It's very sharp." He carefully handed it to me, hilt first.

I was surprised to find how heavy it was. Somehow, I'd thought it'd be lighter. The family's crest, as revealed at the inquest, was carved into the hilt. But something that also made the dagger memorable, and yet had not been mentioned, was engraved on the blade—*Audaces fortuna juvat.*

"What do those words mean?" I'd never taken to Latin in my studies, much preferring live languages to dead.

"Fortune favors the brave. The first duke adopted it as his motto. He fought alongside Henry V, during the Hundred Years' War, gaining the monarch's favor during the Battle of Agincourt. As a reward, he was awarded the dukedom by his son, Henry VI."

How curious. "Why the son, and not Henry V himself?"

"He became ill during a battle and died of dysentery. Cleanliness was not a high priority during those times."

"How sad." I refocused on the weapon. "Were both daggers identical?"

"Yes, they were cast from the same mold."

"And there were no more?"

"No. Once the two were cast, the mold was broken as Father wished no others to be made. The pieces were sent to him as proof. But that's enough talk about weapons and such." He took the dagger back and rested it on the table before turning back to me. "Would you like a tour of the house?"

I gazed at him with surprise. "But you have an appointment."

He shrugged. "It will keep."

The meeting must not have been important. "In that case, I would love one."

His eyes twinkled with mirth. "I'd like to show you my pride and joy."

Whatever could it be? "Of course, milord."

He guided me through the house, which, compared to Wynchcombe House, was more modest in size. Still, its priceless furnishings spoke of vast wealth. It took but a few minutes to reach our destination—a door fastened with a padlock hanging from a chain. Without any fanfare, he retrieved a key from inside his jacket and sprung the lock. "Here we are."

Stepping inside, I gazed around in wonder. "A conservatory." The room, with its lush array of plants and blooms, bore a strong resemblance to the one we had at home. Smelled like it as well. I was surprised, to say the least, for I'd expected an armory filled with weapons. "How lovely!"

"Growing up at Wynchcombe Castle, there was little for young boys to do to entertain ourselves. My brother and I found delight in the outdoors. When Sebastian's grandfather, our master gardener, noticed my curiosity, he fostered it. I learned to grow things from him."

An impish grin flittered across my lips. "One would think it was your brother's inquisitiveness he would have encouraged."

"He was eight years older than me. His interests lay with the gardener's daughter."

I smiled. "I see."

"But I got the green thumb." He led me through the room showing off all his plants. When he paused by a beautiful blooming one, I reached out to touch it. But he stopped me before I could. "Forgive me, my dear. It's quite deadly. Must only be handled with gloves."

I hastily withdrew my hand. I'd taken off my gloves while I'd sipped the tea.

"You see, my dear, I have quite a collection of deadly flora. That's why I keep the room locked. No one comes into this room but me."

I shuddered as I stared at the purple-bloomed flower labeled *Aconitum*. "Beautiful but deadly."

A strange light blazed in his eyes. "Indeed."

CHAPTER SEVENTEEN

KITTY INVESTIGATES LORD HENRY

*M*Y INTERLUDE WITH LORD PERCY, although strange at the end, had been fruitful for I'd discovered an avenue of investigation to pursue. But until Ned and company returned with the documents to prove Sebastian's right to the title, that aspect was temporarily at a lull. Mister Nevins would not allow access to the duke's financial affairs until Sebastian was officially named the next Duke of Wynchcombe.

Since time was of the essence, I decided to investigate Lord Henry's whereabouts the night of the murder. One of the papers reported he'd spent the night at some gambling club. But was that the truth? After all, as I'd learned during the investigation into Rose Trevvyan's death, newspaper reports couldn't always be trusted. I would need to find out and do it quickly.

Drawing on my acquaintance with Lord Newcastle, I asked him to discover the name of the establishment Lord

Henry had patronized. It took him but half a day to get back to me. The place was not one a proper gentleman favored, he wrote, but a gambling hell located in St. Giles, the worst part of town.

He cautioned me against visiting the place and advised waiting until Ned returned from Scotland. He would be better suited for that task. He apologized for not being able to take on that endeavor himself, but he was currently under the weather and was not able to perform at his best.

I sighed. In the last month, he'd become too fond of the bottle. The reason was not difficult to surmise. He was in love with Lady Wakefield, whose husband abused her on a regular basis. Ever since Lord Newcastle's altercation with the earl over the scandalous treatment of his wife, Newcastle had been either absent from social events, or worse, shown up intoxicated. Unfortunately, there was no way out of his particular hell. Marriage among the nobility was not easily put aside, not even when the lord in question used his wife as a punching bag.

Since I couldn't rely on him for help and Ned's date of return was unknown, I opted to investigate on my own. I contacted Dickie Collins, one of my sources from my previous investigation. If anybody would know somebody who worked at that gambling hell, it would be him. Thankfully, he came through with the information the very next day. Not only did he provide the name of a hostess who was willing to talk to me, but escorts who'd guide me through the streets of that stew. Impossibly, they were both named Giorgio. Cousins from Sicily, they were temporarily unemployed and having a hard time making ends meet. Since both were married with children, they were desperate for earned coin. I wrote back to Dickie, arranging our adventure for the following night when for once I had no scheduled social event on my calendar.

On evenings free of responsibilities, my family retired early to catch up on sleep. Tonight, being one of those nights, I waited until after ten before taking the servants' stairs to the kitchen and sneaking out the back of the house. I then made my way to the mews where the two Giorgios were waiting for me.

Dark-haired and dressed in tradesmen's clothes, they were easy to spot as I'd asked them to wear red kerchiefs around their necks.

Not knowing any other way to address them, I simply said, "Giorgio?"

"Si." They both answered. The one with the impressive mustache which covered the lower half of his face, pointed to his chest. "Giorgio the Fierce."

The other one bowed. Showing quite a charming smile, he said, "Giorgio the Bello" and winked at me.

Goodness! They were a sight to behold. "Pleased to meet you." Not knowing how much English they understood, I simply said, "I need a taxi."

"Si, signorina," Giorgio the Fierce said. "There." He pointed to the end of the mews where the proper street ran. I nodded in agreement.

Once we reached the corner, it took no time for one to come along. The fierce one let out a whistle of prodigious proportions, and the cab rolled to a stop next to us.

Usually it was only a matter of climbing into the vehicle. But when I tried to do so, I found the door was locked.

"Where yer going?" the driver asked.

"The Silver Slipper at Seven Dials," I responded.

"Oi don't go into that area. More than me life is worth." He looked me up and down. "You sure you want to go there, Miss? You look like quality."

I bristled at his remark for I'd worked hard to dress the part. I'd sent Betsy to a rag shop to pick out some clothes.

She'd returned with a skirt and a blouse that reeked of onions and gin; plus a raggedy old hat the shop owner had thrown in for free. Maybe I should've rubbed some dirt on my face.

But right now, I had a bigger problem. If the cabbie wouldn't drive us to St. Giles, my entire plan was ruined. But maybe he would compromise. "Can you drop us off close to there?"

He sniffed. "Best oi can do is Covent Garden."

I had no idea if that was near where we needed to go, so I turned to Giorgio the Fierce. "Will that work?"

"*Si.*"

He was a man of few words, the fierce one.

"Shew me your money first," the cab driver demanded.

Betsy had warned me against carrying too many coins, so I'd packed but a few of them into a purse I'd slung around my neck. Fishing into it, I drew out a pound. "Will this do?"

He tried to grab it, but I held it back from him. "Not until we arrive at Covent Garden."

"Foin." He reached toward the back of the cab and unlocked the door. "Climb in."

As soon as the two Giorgios and I scampered into the rear, with me sandwiched between them, the conveyance rumbled off. There was little traffic that night, so it took the driver no time to get us to our destination.

After I paid, he said, "Be careful, Miss. Eyes on the back of your 'ead, mind you."

"Yes. Thank you."

The two Giorgios organized themselves, one in front of me and the other in back. The farther we traveled, the dirtier, and smellier, the area became, and the seedier the people appeared. A woman leaning against a lamppost, yelled something to the Giorgios. When both Giorgios ignored her, she raised her skirt to display her wares. *Heavens!* Right out in the open? In front of God and everyone? Blushing fiercely, I turned away from the sight and stepped up my pace.

The next street was little better as a fight had broken out between two men. When one drew a knife, Giorgio the Fierce pushed me into a dark alley while the other Giorgio kept a lookout. Once the hollering stopped, he nodded to be on our way. Thankfully, we didn't have to go much farther. The Silver Slipper was located at the next corner at the infamous Seven Dials intersection where seven roads met.

As instructed by Dickie, I rapped on the door with two slow knocks and three fast ones. A man with a shirt half open to the waist yanked open the door. He smelled of liquor and filth. I doubted he'd seen the inside of a bathtub in quite some time. Running a slow gaze over me, he flashed a smile that was missing several teeth. "Ain't you a sight for sore eyes."

Ignoring the leer, I said, "I'm looking for Maisie. I have an urgent message for her."

"Do you, lovey?" He stepped down to the street and reached out for me. But the Giorgios put a stop to that.

"No touch," Giorgio the Fierce said, a scowl on his face.

The man spit in their direction. "Wait here."

I nodded as I thought it would be best to keep silent.

A woman soon emerged from the smoky gloom of the place. "Wot you want?"

"Are you Maisie?"

"Yeah."

"Dickie sent me."

"Oi." She glanced over her shoulder, but the bouncer had disappeared into the depths. She pointed to me. "You come in. They stay outside. Their kind ain't welcome 'ere."

"I'm sorry," I said, turning to the Giorgios.

"You not out in five minutes. I come for you, *si*?" Giorgio the Fierce said.

139

"*Si.*"

Just like the man before her, Maisie spit on the ground at the two Giorgios' feet. "In here." She nodded toward a small alcove, the size of my clothes chest.

"Dickie tell you 'ow much?"

"Five pounds?"

Her lip curled. "It's ten now because of the Italians."

"I'm sorry. I only brought a few coins."

She stuck out her hand. "Give it."

I retrieved my purse and started to draw out the money, but she snatched it from me and emptied the contents into her hand. Five pounds spilled out. The rest was in another purse my very wise maid had sewn to my skirt.

She spit on the floor. "Wot you want to know?"

"Lord Henry Dalrymple. Was he here the evening of May 31st?"

She sniffed. "Wot if he was?"

"I need to know. Please. It's important."

"That was more than a week ago."

"Yes. A Thursday."

"'E was 'ere. That was the noight someone cut Mary. Can't use 'er 'and no more."

"Maisie!" A male voice called out from deep in the gloom. "Where you at, girl?"

Alarm rolled over her face. "Blimey. 'E's back. Ye got to go. Now."

"Wait. What time did he leave?"

"Early before supper. 'Said 'e 'ad an appointment."

They served supper in this place? "What time is it served?"

"Ten." She nodded toward the voice. "'E feeds them to keep 'em 'ere. So 'e can take their blunt."

"Maisie! If yer flappin' your jaws, Oi'll skin ye alive. Maisie."

Pounding footsteps grew closer, and her alarm turned into panic. She pushed me out and slammed the door shut.

Thankfully, the two Giorgios were waiting outside for me. I'd never been so glad to see other human beings in my life.

"Go now?" Giorgio the Bello asked, a look of fear about him.

I nodded. The atmosphere of the Silver Slipper, with its underlying threat of violence, rattled me, so I didn't need his urging to walk as fast as I could. Unfortunately, we were not fast enough. We'd barely walked twenty meters before we ran into a full-blown fight. At least a dozen men, each one nastier than the next, were trading blows and not only with fists, but bottles, sticks, rocks. As we attempted to skirt the fighters, more men converged upon us, pushing us into the melee.

The two Giorgios did their best to protect me. But it was an all-out brawl. Not shy about protecting myself, I barely got off a kick before I was knocked to the ground. Knowing that was the worst place to be in a fight, I struggled to rise. But no sooner had I gained my feet than someone stumbled backwards and took me down with him. The air whooshed out of my lungs as his weight bore down on me. When breathing became impossible, panic set in. I couldn't die, not this way. How would someone explain it to Mother?

And then, somehow, miraculously, help came in the form of uniformed policemen. Blowing whistles, drawing cudgels, they jumped into the fray. Someone fired a pistol, and a man fell next to me. More officers soon drew near. Outnumbered, the brutes scattered into the shadows, leaving only me, the man crushing me, and the wounded one in the dirt.

Someone pushed off the body on top of me, and I was finally able to draw one deep breath. An officer with a kind face held out a hand and helped me to my feet. "Are you all right?"

"Yes, I think so." I ran my hand over my parts. Thankfully, nothing felt broken. I'd only suffered bumps and bruises. I glanced around to see if I spotted the Giorgios, but they were gone, probably fled along with those who started the fight. I didn't blame them. They couldn't afford to be arrested by the police for there would be no one to support their children. I would have to contact Dickie to get their fee to them.

Another officer approached, one whose face I recognized. "You'll need to come with us to file a report," he said.

"I'll be glad to do so, Constable Peters."

His eyes widened with surprise. "Miss Worthington?"

"Inspector Crawford's Miss Worthington?" Another officer piped up, a lilt to his voice. "All the saints preserve us. You're in for it now, Miss."

I bristled at the insinuation I was Inspector Crawford's anything. "What do you mean?"

"We'd been asked to be on the lookout for you, Miss," Constable Peters explained. "You do have a knack for getting into trouble."

"I'm not in trouble." All evidence to the contrary.

"Yes, Miss. All the same we better head to the constabulary. This is not a healthy place to conduct a conversation."

Now with that, I had to agree.

CHAPTER EIGHTEEN

INSPECTOR CRAWFORD ESCORTS KITTY HOME

"ARE YOU HURT?" Inspector Crawford's dark gaze scrutinized me. Half an hour after Constable Peters telephoned him, he'd arrived at the station perfectly turned out in a dark two-piece suit. I, on the other hand, looked like a dog's dinner and smelled worse.

I shrugged. "Mostly scrapes, nothing serious."

"That's good to hear. Come, I'll take you home."

I wasn't about to turn down the offer. With any luck, I'd be able to sneak into my bedroom with no one the wiser about my escapade.

In no time at all, I was escorted to a police vehicle. Climbing in the back next to me, Inspector Crawford gave the driver my address.

"What were you doing in St. Giles?" he asked staring right ahead once the motorcar was speeding its way to Worthington House.

"I heard about a gambling hell Henry Dalrymple

favored. The Silver Slipper. Supposedly, that's where he was the night the duke was murdered. I found out he was only there part of the time. He left before ten. Said he had an appointment." I faced him full on. "He did it. I know he did it."

A muscle ticked in his jaw. "Did you go by yourself?" He kept his gaze pinned on the road ahead as if that was the most important thing to him.

"No. I asked a friend to recommend an escort. He came through with two men who know the area well."

Rather than praise me for taking steps to ensure my safety, he said, "This friend. Was it Dickie Collins?"

Should have known he'd figure it out. He knew Dickie Collins helped me investigate Rose Trevvyan's background. So it was logical I'd ask him for help once more. But I was not about to answer Inspector Crawford's question. Dickie had a family to feed. Last thing I wanted was for him to get into trouble.

"I'll find out eventually. You might as well tell me now."

I turned away. "Sorry. I don't squeal."

"You were attacked after you left The Silver Slipper?"

I swiveled toward him once more. "I wasn't attacked, Inspector Crawford. A skirmish had broken out on the street, and we got caught up in it."

"What did these two men, these so-called escorts, do to protect you?" There was a snarl to his lips.

"They fought off the men, giving as good as they got. But then a gang of ruffians emerged out of nowhere. Before I knew it, I was knocked down. That's when I lost track of the two Giorgios."

"The two Giorgios. Italian cousins from Sicily, I believe."

Drats! Now he knew their names. I should not have allowed myself to be goaded by him.

I hated to do it, but I turned supplicant on their behalf.

"You are not going to haul them to Scotland Yard, are you? They were only trying to help."

"They put you in danger; and when the going got rough, they abandoned you," he snapped out.

"You can't throw them in jail. They have families who depend on them," I snapped right back.

The volley of words and accusations continued. "Maybe you should have thought about that before you decided to go on this mad escapade."

"The Giorgios shouldn't pay for my lack of judgment."

"You entrusted your safety to men you don't know."

"They were vouched for, Inspector."

"St. Giles is a dangerous place, Miss Worthington."

"Yes, thank you. I discovered that tonight."

"Did you? Did you really?" His piercing gaze found me in the dark. A hot light of fury blazed in his eyes.

It was only then I realized how angry he was. He'd held on to his ire while he interrogated me, but now it was spilling out in full force.

Astonished, for I'd never seen him like this, I turned silent. It would not do to add more fuel to his rage.

He took a deep breath, let it out slowly. "St. Giles was my beat back when I was a foot police officer."

That explained his outburst. He knew from personal experience how vile that area could be. His anger sprung from concern. Over me. Seeking to turn the conversation into less volatile territory, I asked, "Is that where you met Lord Rutledge?" He'd saved the aristocrat from a gang who'd assaulted him. Although Lord Rutledge had come away with only minor injuries, Inspector Crawford had been hurt seriously enough to be out of commission for six months. To show his gratitude, the aristocrat had paid for Inspector Crawford's education at Oxford and, subsequently, become his mentor.

"Yes." Seemingly under control once more, he gazed at me, the unruly anger gone. In a much calmer tone, he asked, "Do you know what would have happened to you if the police hadn't intervened?"

"I would have been seriously hurt."

"It would have been a lot worse than that, Miss Worthington. Some of those men are part of a gang of white slavers. If they had cottoned on to who you are, they would have tossed you into one of the ships docked at the Thames and transported you to a place where the color of your skin and your virtue would be valued higher than rubies."

I'd heard from Margaret such gangs existed, but I'd never thought . . . That was the problem. I hadn't thought. I'd put myself in peril without giving my safety the consideration it deserved. "I'm . . . sorry."

"Did you even once think about the consequences? And what that would do to your family? To your mother?"

It didn't bear thinking. Mother would not survive the loss of another child.

"Next time you get a hankering to put yourself in peril, you might want to think twice. Or better yet, call me."

I hitched up my chin. "So you could talk me out of it?"

"No. So I could protect you. That's my job, after all." He gazed softly at me. "I'm serious. Call me." He retrieved a business card and a pencil from within his jacket. On the back, he jotted down something. "My telephone numbers. Scotland Yard's on the front. My home's on the back."

In the dim light of a passing street light, I caught what he'd written. It was more than his telephone numbers. "Is this your address?"

"Yes."

"Off Eaton Square?"

He nodded.

Only people of means could afford the townhouses that

bordered Eaton Square. So once more I wondered about the state of his finances. Time and again, I'd seen how he dressed. His clothes were made of the finest materials and fashioned by superb workmanship. A policeman's salary could not support such a wardrobe, much less a home at that address. I ached to find out how he could afford such things. But it would be downright rude to ask.

"Maybe I'll drop in one day for tea," I joked.

"If you wish. Call first. I might be otherwise engaged."

I blushed. I honest-to-goodness blushed.

His lips twitched.

"You beast."

He turned to gaze at me. Full mirth shown in his eyes. But before I had a chance to say something, the vehicle came to a stop.

"We're here, sir," the driver said.

After Inspector Crawford ordered the driver to wait for him, we trekked up the driveway that led to the house. Oval in shape, it contained a water fountain in the center featuring a mermaid cavorting with a dolphin. I'd always thought it was rather naughty. My family, however, did not share the same belief.

"How did you exit your house?" he asked, breaking the silence.

"The tradesman's entrance in the back of the house." I pointed to the third-floor window where a light flickered. "Betsy, my maid, is waiting up for me. She would have unlocked the back door so I could slip in."

With no moon out, the path that skirted the house was dark, so I took his hand to lead the way. That was the reason I told myself. In any case, he didn't reject my gesture, but remained comfortably in my hold. His hand was warm, much warmer than mine, but then he was better dressed against the cold. He smelled of that same masculine cologne

I'd noticed before. Amazing he'd taken time to throw some on before he left Eaton Square. But then, maybe, he hadn't been at Eaton Square. Maybe he'd been at a different address with someone else. I shook off the thought that bordered on jealousy as we rounded the house. A few more steps found us at the back door. Sadly, the handle did not give. Carlton must have secured the door.

"It's locked," I said, turning back to him.

Fighting off a smile, he gazed down at me. "You could always knock on your front door. Somebody will let you in. You do live here, after all."

"Absolutely. That would alert the entire household, including my mother and father, that I was gallivanting around London, in this ragpicker outfit. Surely, they wouldn't object. After all, I'd have an honest-to-goodness Scotland Yard Detective Inspector there to—how did you put it—protect me. How very droll of you, Inspector."

He'd quirked a brow during my speech. "Are you done? Because I do have another suggestion. One that won't end in you getting into trouble."

I waved a hand. "Suggest away."

Without saying another word, he removed a leather pouch from his jacket and retrieved a couple of tools. After barely a minute's work, he'd sprung the lock.

"Do they teach you that in police school?"

"No. That I learned from a thief." He swung open the door to reveal a darkened kitchen. Sir Winston, sprawled on his bed, gazed up sleepy-eyed. When he saw it was me, he returned to his slumbers.

"Fine guard dog, you are," Inspector Crawford chided him. "Somebody breaks into your house, and you barely blink."

"He recognized me, Inspector. That's why he didn't bark." I advanced into the room to a spot where illumination could be found. When I turned back with the unlit candle, I bumped into him. "Whum."

He put his hands on my shoulders to steady me. It wasn't the first time he'd touched me. We'd danced the waltz at my birthday ball. But this was the first time we were alone in the dark.

"I bumped into you first time we met. Remember?"

"I remember everything about you, Catherine," his deep voice responded.

His thumbs rubbed my shoulders, setting me ablaze. "Why do you call me that?"

"Because it's your name."

"But everyone calls me Kitty."

"That's a young girl's name. You're a fully grown woman."

Everything in me grew liquid. Seconds ticked by while we stood barely an inch apart gazing at each other in the gloom with only a Bassett Hound to chaperone. I wished. Never mind what I wished.

"Can you find your way?" he finally asked, breaking the mood.

"Of course, it's my home."

After one more searing gaze, he walked away, stepped through the open door, and turned back. "Lock it behind me."

Temporarily having lost the power of speech, I could only nod.

"Good night, Catherine."

"Good night. Robert," I whispered into the night, but he was already gone.

CHAPTER NINETEEN

NED RETURNS WITH THE DOCUMENTS

*N*O ONE WAS THE WISER about my escapade, except for Betsy, of course. Faithful servant that she was she'd kept vigil, drifting on and off to sleep, while she waited up for me. I didn't share the full extent of my adventure as I felt it'd be too much for her. She would only worry that much more during my next outing. And, given the information I'd discovered, there would be another. But I did share my findings. We agreed that the nephew was a strong suspect for the murder even if the inspector did not share the same belief.

To the family's great joy, Ned, Lily, and Margaret returned the next day with the documents proving Sebastian's legitimacy. Within hours, Ned handed them to the solicitor who would set the process in motion to declare Sebastian the twelfth Duke of Wynchcombe. Once that was accomplished, Wynchcombe House, the other properties, as well as all the funds attached to the title would be placed under his husbandry. Sebastian would no longer be a pauper but quite wealthy, something that would relieve his mind as he now would be able to provide for Lily.

A day later, the issue of the ducal succession was resolved in an emergency hearing as that decision bore upon the location of the trial. Now that Sebastian had been declared a peer, he would be tried in the House of Lords.

This concerned me.

Since many of its members tended to vote conservative and Sebastian had liberal leanings, I feared they would allow their political beliefs to influence their verdict. After all, if Sebastian were to be found guilty, the title would descend to his uncle, Lord Percy, whose politics leaned conservative from what I'd learned. Thus, it was even more imperative to discover the murderer before the trial could be held.

With the issue of the succession resolved, I made an appointment with the duke's private secretary, and Ned set a time to talk with the duke's man of business. Since Sebastian had ordered them to share with us what they knew, neither could withhold information. Between Ned and me, we would get to the bottom of the former duke's financial dealings.

Ned had no trouble with the duke's man of business since he was eager to keep Sebastian's patronage. The private secretary, however, proved a harder nut to crack.

"Mister Nevins, you have not only the duke's permission but his command to divulge this information to me. Why do you object?" I'd provided him with a copy of the decision which named Sebastian the Duke of Wynchcombe and asked him to make himself available so I could examine the books. His reply signaled he was willing to comply with my request, but upon my arrival, he'd balked.

"Most of the items are of a private nature. I don't feel it proper to reveal it to anyone, and most especially not to a lady of your tender years."

"Then share those items that are not personal." I could fashion a way up from that.

"I'm afraid most of it is."

He was trying to shield the duke's transactions by classifying them as 'personal.' That simply would not do. "Very well, Mister Nevins, if that's the way you feel about it. Should I ask the duke's legal counsel to bring you before a judge so you can explain the nature of these private items?"

He ran a finger around the inside of his starched collar as dots of perspiration popped up on his brow. "No . . . well . . . I don't know."

"If you don't stop this shilly-shallying, I will do just that." He'd thought me a young lady who'd be easily cowed. But I was no such thing. "What will it be?"

"Well, I guess as long as the new duke allows it?" he offered tentatively.

"He demands it, Mister Nevins, as you can plainly see from the notarized letter I've handed you. Now, open the books and let's see what's so confidential you don't wish to discuss it."

"Well, the duke, the former duke I should say, gambled."

"So I've been told."

"He was amazingly gifted when it came to cards, especially whist. Other gentlemen who were not as adept at the game lost quite heavily to him."

"How unfortunate." For myself, I couldn't see betting a fortune on the turn of a card. But certainly, there were many gentlemen who did. Some of them were so addicted to the game, they'd bankrupted themselves. "And it was your responsibility to keep track of his winnings?"

"Yes, exactly." His tension eased when he perceived I

understood his role. "You see, Miss Worthington, some possessed sufficient resources to immediately satisfy their debts. But if a gentleman proved unable to do so, the former duke provided them with an extension of time. I kept accurate records of these transactions." He pointed to the ledgers that rested on his desk. They were similar in appearance to those I'd seen in Father's office used to keep track of investment funds.

"For how long?"

"Indefinitely."

"Well, that was generous of him." Wouldn't have expected it of the old duke.

"Not really, Miss Worthington. You see, he collected interest on the debt."

"Interest? How much?"

"Three percent."

"Per annum?"

"Per month."

"That seems excessive." And possibly illegal. I'd need to consult with Ned for he would know what was allowed under the law.

Mister Nevins, however, sniffed at my suggestion. "The duke received no complaints. They'd rather pay three percent on the principal every month than have the entire sum demanded of them. Some chose to pay as they did not owe large amounts. Others, however, would not have been able to settle their debts in their lifetimes."

"They owed that much?"

"Oh, yes."

What a horrid situation. From what I've learned of the duke, he probably enjoyed watching those who owed him twist in the wind. "And you kept those accounts for him?"

He nodded.

"May I see them, please?"

His hand clenched the top ledger. "Miss Worthington, the gentlemen whose names appear in these accounts would not like their debts known."

I speared him with a hard stare. "I assure you, Mister Nevins, I will keep that information in the strictest of confidences and will share it only with my brother Ned."

He hesitated.

"Of course, if you're reluctant we can always adjourn to a judge's chambers and see what he has to say."

He breathed out a sigh. Retrieving a pince-nez from the depths of his jacket, he secured it to the bridge of his nose. "Very well. Let's repair to the table as there is more space there."

Once we'd settled around the mahogany table, he opened one of the ledgers. The first entry went back twenty years. A debt of 20,000 pounds which remained largely unpaid.

I gazed up in astonishment. "Do I have this right? The original debt was for 20,000 pounds?"

"Yes."

"But the person now owes 35,000? How can that be?"

"This particular gentleman has fallen behind several times, so the interest is added to the original debt."

Good heavens!

"Will he ever pay it off?"

"He won't have to."

"Why not?"

"The gambling voucher exchanged between the duke and everyone who lost to him contained very specific language. It forgave the debt in case of the duke's death."

I waved a hand at the ledger. "And this applies to every one of these amounts?"

"Yes. The duke planned it this way." He removed his pince-nez to polish the lenses and then perched them back on his nose. "You see, he did not want his heir to inherit the benefits of his winnings."

In other words, he didn't want Sebastian to get that money. As if Sebastian would even consider collecting on those gambling debts. He would have forgiven them on his own.

"If I may ask, Mister Nevins, how many 'gentlemen' are affected?"

"Oh, roughly a hundred. The duke, the former duke, enjoyed gambling, you see," he offered with a tight smile.

"And what is the sum of all those debts?"

"Over a million pounds."

"Goodness!" I gasped at the vast sum. "What is the average amount owed?"

"Ummm." He tapped an index finger against his lower lip while he pondered the question. "Probably 10,000 pounds."

"Who owed the most?"

"That would be Lord Gresham." He flipped to Lord Gresham's page. "Over 100,000 as you can see."

Perusing the amounts, I noted he'd made payments, but other amounts had been added as well. "He kept gambling, even though he owed a fortune?"

"Sadly, he finds it difficult to stop. He always thought the next turn of the card would give him a winning hand." His lugubrious gaze landed on me. "It never did."

Glancing at the figures, I found some notations which did not coincide with the gambling debts. "These credits that appear in a different column. Were those amounts not paid in cash?"

"Occasionally, the former duke would ask me to credit certain amounts to Lord Gresham to reduce his debt. He always termed them 'for services rendered'."

"What kind of services?"

He bristled at my question. "Miss Worthington, as the

duke's personal secretary, I was not in a position to make such an enquiry, only to do as he asked."

'His not to reason why, his but to do or die' to paraphrase Lord Tennyson. "Very well. I'll need a list of all the gentlemen on these books and the amounts owed. Can you get it to me by tomorrow?"

He hesitated.

"I assure you, Mister Nevins, you have nothing to worry about. The papers will be kept firmly locked in my desk." I came to my feet and started to take my leave, but then a thought occurred to me. "Oh, one more question. What about Lord Henry? Did he owe the duke money?"

He scoffed. "The duke never played cards with his grandson. He wasn't adept enough at the game."

"How would the duke know if he never played with him?"

"Lord Henry's gambling debts. Time and again, he applied to his grandfather for loans to pay them off. The duke paid them in the past, but recently he cut off Lord Henry. Told him he wouldn't give him one more shilling. He'd need to get himself out of the hole he'd dug for himself."

Well, that was certainly news. "Lord Henry had to be furious."

"Oh, he was more than furious, Miss Worthington. He threatened the duke. Told him he'd make him pay."

"The duke must have been alarmed."

"Just the opposite. He laughed. Told Lord Henry that he was too much of a weakling to carry out the threat." Mister Nevins sneered. "The former duke did not have a high opinion of Lord Henry."

So, not only was Lord Henry desperate for money, but his grandfather had impugned his honor. One could easily see how he would seek revenge. But was the duke's assessment of his grandson correct? Did Lord Henry lack the gumption to thrust a dagger into his grandfather's heart? It would take someone with a lot of hate to do that.

"Why didn't Lord Henry appeal to his father for money?"

"Lord Percy has none to give. He receives a small quarterly allowance for incidentals, but everything else is paid from the duke's accounts, including his clothing and even the very food he eats."

"What about his home?"

"Owned by the duke."

"And the Portchester Place address?"

"Likewise."

"But Lord Percy has access to it." He'd provided it to Sebastian while he was in town.

He turned a bright shade of red. "Lord Percy uses it for entertainment of a private nature."

In other words, he kept a mistress there. "And the duke allowed it?"

"By necessity, such activities have to be conducted away from Lord Percy's personal residence. It was an understanding between them."

I bid him goodbye but left the door open for my return. After perusing the papers he would send to me, I was sure I'd have more questions. The Rolls and Neville were waiting for me outside Wynchcombe House. As the motorcar rolled down the driveway, I ruminated over what I'd discovered. Several things had become clear. I'd known Lord Henry had a great deal of gambling debt for which he regularly appealed to the duke to pay, but the duke's refusal to settle any more was new. That was most certainly a motive to kill him and put the blame on his cousin. If Sebastian were found guilty, Lord Percy would inherit the title. As one who abhorred conflict, he would accede to his son's wishes and pay off his gambling debts.

But Lord Henry was not the only suspect. The so-called

gentlemen who owed the duke money had a motive as well for their debts would be deemed paid upon the duke's death. But there were a hundred of them. The question then became who would owe such a large sum he'd want to kill the duke?

CHAPTER TWENTY

ANOTHER BODY IS DISCOVERED

*B*ETSY WOKE ME the next morning with the news of a note from Scotland Yard. "The police officer who delivered it said it was urgent, Miss."

I'd spent the night tossing and turning with dreams of somebody chasing me with a bloody dagger. An omen or a manifestation of my fears? Regardless, it meant a restless sleep. I dreaded reading the message, but there was no help for it. I ripped open the envelope to find Inspector Crawford's scrawl. He'd been in a hurry when he wrote the note.

Miss Worthington,

Body found in the Thames. Preliminarily identified as Thomas Hodgkins. I've been asked to investigate.

Your Humble Servant,

Inspector Robert Crawford

Metropolitan Police

The sense of foreboding in my dreams had materialized. Thomas Hodgkins' death could only make matters worse for dead bodies don't talk. Without his testimony, we couldn't verify Sebastian's account of the night the duke was killed. Just as important, my discussions with Inspector Crawford would need to cease since Sebastian would feature prominently in both investigations.

"Anything wrong, Miss?" Betsy must have noticed my distress.

As I climbed from my bed, I shared the note contents with her.

She glanced wide-eyed at me. "Blimey, Miss. Is that the gentleman Mister Dalrymple had supper with?"

"I'm afraid so." I shivered. Either the morning was cooler than usual, or my body was reacting adversely to the news.

"Here, Miss." Betsy held out my wrap. "Should I draw you a warm bath?"

I glanced gratefully at her for she always looked out for my wellbeing. "No, thank you, Betsy. I'll bathe later. Right now, I need to tell Margaret the news and telephone Ned to let him know." We already had so much to do. And now we had this to investigate as well. I didn't know how we would get it all done.

Once I'd dressed, I headed to the library where a footman told me Margaret was to be found. More than likely with her nose stuck in some legal journal. After being denied access to Sebastian by the prison governor—only family or a member of the solicitor's office was allowed to see him—she'd taken to studying criminal law in the hope of qualifying as a solicitor's assistant. An uphill climb to be sure, but it kept her occupied. Besides, something she discovered might very well help with the investigation.

I found her staring into the distance, an open book in front of her. She appeared to have been crying.

"What's wrong, dearest?"

"Oh, Kitty." Her breath hitched, and a sob broke through.

Things were dire indeed. Five years ago, when our sister Emily died from the Spanish Influenza, Margaret hadn't broken down once. Just the contrary. She'd been the rock we'd clung to when Mother had fallen apart. So, if she was this distraught, her emotional wellbeing was rocky to say the least.

Putting my arms around her, I led her to a leather divan and rang for tea and scones.

"Now tell me all about it," I said.

"I received a note from Sebastian this morning. He's being so brave and trying to stay positive. But he's so alone, Kitty. Cooped up in a small room as he is and allowed to exercise for only an hour a day is fraying his nerves. And now with the weather as blustery as it's been, he hasn't been allowed out. You know how much he loves the outdoors and nature. I'm afraid of what this is doing to him." Tears welled in her eyes. "We have to get him out of there."

I squeezed her hand. "We will."

A footman arrived with our petit dejeuner. After helping ourselves, I took on the dreaded task of sharing the bad news. I hated to do it, seeing the state she was in, but it had to be done. "I received a message from Inspector Crawford." I handed her the note.

"Thomas Hodgkins is dead? That's awful. That poor man."

I wasn't so sure we should feel sorry for the gentleman for I suspected he'd been part of some scheme to embroil Sebastian in the duke's murder. We spent a good while discussing the possible repercussions of his death. But half an hour later we had to stop when Mother and Lily returned all atwitter from the modiste.

"They were waiting for us right outside Angelique's. The cheek of them," Mother huffed red-faced.

"Who?" I asked.

"Those newspaper men. Ruffians, that's what they are." Her voice softened. "We'd just enjoyed a lovely session with Angelique. She personally attended to Lily."

Of course, Angelique did. She knew the value of a duke's sister wearing her clothes. It would be gilding the lily for every article of clothing showed to advantage on Sebastian's sister.

"We ordered three day dresses," Mother continued, "the most darling afternoon frocks, as well as evening and ball gowns for dear Lily to wear after she emerges from mourning." Her tone grew rough again. "And then those hoodlums ruined everything. They pounced on us as soon as we stepped from the shop."

"Oh, no."

"They crowded around us, blocking our way. The camera men jostled each other to snap a photograph of Lily. Poor girl didn't know what to do." She huffed out an angry breath. "But Cummings did."

Cummings. Mother's lady's maid. A fierce dragon when it came to protecting Mother. "What did she do?"

"She brandished her umbrella and beat them back. By God, she did. Thankfully, Neville caught on to what was up and pulled the Rolls right up to the kerb. Knocked them back, he did. Those ruffians had to scramble not to get run down."

"Brava, Cummings, and bravo, Neville," I said. We honestly had the best staff in London. They'd fight tooth and nail for every one of us.

"Shall I order more tea, Mother?" Margaret asked. "A restorative refreshment might be just what you need."

"Yes, thank you, dear."

While they enjoyed tea and scones, we caught them up on the Hodgkins news. In the middle of that discussion, I received another note from Inspector Crawford. What now?

The investigation into Thomas Hodgkins' death has been reassigned to Inspector Bolton. The inquest will be held tomorrow at the Westminster coroner's court.

Your Humble Servant,

Robert Crawford

London Metropolitan Police

"What does that mean?" Lily asked.

"Inspector Bolton is the lead investigator in the duke's murder," I explained. "So, an assumption can be made that the two deaths are connected. Or at least Scotland Yard thinks they are."

"Would that affect Sebastian?"

I exchanged a look with Margaret. She'd caught on to the meaning. "I believe so. They're looking at him for both deaths," I said.

All her grief forgotten, a fiery Margaret turned to me. "We need to attend the inquest."

"We can't all go," I said. "The press is too fascinated with Lily for her to make an appearance. And those reporters are fully aware of your connection to Sebastian. If either of you showed up, the inquest would become a circus. It will have to be me."

"The newspaper reporters know you as well, Kitty," Margaret reminded me. "How do you intend to evade their notice?"

"Wear mourning clothes. Won't be the first time I've disguised myself."

"Well, if you can wear such clothing, so can we," Margaret asserted.

"Three women all dressed in mourning black, sitting next to each other? The reporters will cotton on to that in a flash. No, Margaret. It can only be me. I'll ask Inspector Crawford to find me an inconspicuous spot from where I can watch."

Neither Margaret nor Lily was pleased about my suggestion for them to stay away, but they understood my reasoning was correct.

The inquest was just as bad as I feared. After the coroner established where and when the body of Thomas Hodgkins had been found, he called the medical examiner to the stand.

"Have you had an opportunity to examine the body?"

"I have. A male in his twenties. He drowned, but he'd also suffered trauma to the back of his head."

"How do you know he drowned?"

"There was water in his lungs, your honor."

From my perch in the gallery, I had a bird's eye view of the courtroom, so it was easy to see the coroner make a note of that.

"Very well, continue," he said.

"The body had been in the water for some time. My guess would be between ten days and two weeks."

"Were you able to ascertain whether he fell in or was pushed?"

"No, sir, I was not. All I can say for certain is that the cause of death was drowning."

After the medical examiner finished his testimony, Inspector Bolton was called to the stand.

Once the preliminaries were gotten out of the way, the coroner asked, "How did you identify the body, sir?"

"By his fingerprints, as well as a ring he wore."

"The medical examiner testified he drowned. Do you believe he fell into the river or was pushed?"

"I don't see how he could have hit himself in the back of the head, your honor. So I do not believe he died by misadventure. I think someone struck him. Mister Hodgkins was then either tossed or fell into the Thames."

"Any idea—"

"If I may, your honor," Inspector Bolton interjected. The coroner did not appear too pleased by the interruption.

"We'd been looking for Mister Hodgkins in connection with the death of the Duke of Wynchcombe. In that investigation, his grandson, Sebastian Dalrymple, claimed he had supper with the deceased. When prompted for more details, he couldn't recall the rest of the evening."

A murmur rippled through the crowd.

"And where is Mister Dalrymple now?"

"In custody of the police, your honor, charged with the murder of the Duke of Wynchcombe."

A roar erupted, but it was quickly silenced by the coroner's gavel.

I was glad I'd insisted on Lily and Margaret remaining home. They couldn't have heard that statement, never mind the crowd's outburst, without becoming severely distraught. The papers would have had a field day reporting their reactions.

"Are you implying that Sebastian Dalrymple had something to do with Mister Hodgkins' death?"

"Not at the moment, sir. An investigation must be thoroughly conducted first. But he seems to have been the last person to have seen Mister Hodgkins alive."

Well, if that didn't put the last nail in Sebastian's coffin. The newspaper reporters wasted no time rushing out of the courtroom. They had an afternoon edition deadline to meet, after all.

But the testimony that firmly pointed the finger to Sebastian was that of the last witness—a Mister Bertie Sutton. After being duly sworn in, he was asked to report on his connection to the matter in question.

"Well, sir, about two weeks ago, I saw something by the river."

"What did you see?"

"A tall gentleman tossing a large something into the Thames."

"Where?"

"Underneath Westminster Bridge, sir. He dragged this thing and rolled it right into the water. It made a big splash, it did."

"What did you think it was?"

"No idea. I wasn't exactly clear-headed that evening."

"What do you mean?"

"I'd had a bit of a row with the missus and had gone off for a pint or two at the pub."

"What was it? A pint or two?"

Mr. Sutton cleared his throat. "It may have been more than that, your worship."

"How many?"

"Six."

The crowd burst into laughter.

The coroner employed his gavel again. Once the gallery settled down, he turned back to the witness. "Describe the person you saw, if you will."

"He was tall, yellow-haired. No hat on him. Clean clothes. Dressed like a toff, he was."

"How far away were you?"

"About ten meters, I would say. He was right under a lamppost. That's how come I saw him so clearly, even through the rain."

"Why didn't you come forward earlier?"

"Well, sir. I had no idea, no idea whatsoever, it was a body he'd tossed over. But then yesterday my missus pointed out the story in the paper. That's when I realized what I'd seen. I came to the police right quick."

After that testimony, the verdict was a certainty. "Murder by person or persons unknown." Well, at least Sebastian wouldn't have to be arrested again. They would just tack on another murder charge. After Inspector Bolton's 'proper investigation' that was.

When I reported the proceedings back home, Margaret was beside herself. "There's too much to consider. We can't investigate this as well as the duke's murder by ourselves. We need help."

"Lords Marlowe and Newcastle assisted with the Rose Trevvyan investigation," I said. "Maybe they'd be willing to do it again. Lady Emma has also volunteered. With her knowledge of the nobility, she'll be able to discover information not readily available to us. And Ned, of course. With the addition of the three of us, that should hopefully prove sufficient."

"You can gather here in the library for there's more than enough space," Mother said. "We'll order a nice repast as well. It wouldn't do for our guests to go hungry while planning things."

"Thank you, Mother," Margaret kissed her cheek.

Lily and I echoed Margaret's sentiments.

Margaret put her hand out. "What do you say, ladies? One for All, and All for One." With Lily giggling, she and I placed our hands on top of hers.

"The Three Musketeers' motto," Mother exclaimed. "How apropos."

The three of us gazed expectantly at her. "Join us," Margaret said.

She gazed at us confused. "But there were only three."

"You forget D'Artagnan," Margaret reminded her. "The fourth Musketeer."

Pinking up with excitement, Mother laughed and dropped her hand on top of ours.

And then all four of us cried out the motto and tossed our arms in the air.

CHAPTER TWENTY-ONE

COUNCIL OF WAR

*M*ARGARET POINTED OUT Oxford had pots of committees of this and seminars of that, but unless they were stamped with a name, nothing ever got done. And even then, some suffered from lack of participation. Determined not to fail, we decided to name our effort. After much back and forth, Margaret, Lily, and I settled on 'The Unofficial Investigation into the Duke of Wynchcombe's Murder,' a mouthful to be sure, but one which clearly set out its purpose.

We would need to write an announcement of the committee's formation which would include an invitation to attend its initial meeting. Again, much wrangling was involved. In the end, Lily and I assigned the task to Margaret (because she shouted the loudest). It took her but an hour to draft the language which I offer in its entirety below (my comments in parentheses).

Margaret and Catherine Worthington

(Margaret insisted on her name coming first as she was the oldest),

and Lady Lily Dalrymple

(of course, dear Lily's courtesy title had to be included. No one caviled at that),

would like you to attend the initial meeting of the 'Investigation into the Duke of Wynchcombe's Murder,' to be held at Worthington House, 4 Grosvenor Square, Mayfair

(I reminded Margaret all the invitees knew where we lived but she argued it was proper etiquette to include our address)

from two o'clock until four in the afternoon on Tuesday, June 18.

(As the meeting was of prime importance, Mother cancelled our at-home day. A notice was placed in all the society papers to that respect. Do I need to mention my joy?)

Refreshments will be served.

(Margaret insisted on adding that last bit. I reminded her that the Worthingtons always provided superb fare at any event we held. Therefore, such mention was not necessary. Needless to say, she won that particular argument, as she has always known best.)

With only minor changes, the final copy was completed and delivered by a footman to all our invitees.

Unfortunately, the meeting could not take place on June 18 as both Ned and Lord Newcastle were engaged that afternoon. By necessity, we rescheduled it for the next day.

On Wednesday, we rose early to review the items we needed to discuss, and then, after an early luncheon, we retired to our rooms to don our finest gowns. Margaret and I were particularly excited to see Lily's, for her afternoon dresses had only just been delivered that morning.

She chose a sky-blue chiffon with a low waistline band which displayed her height and coloring to advantage. Of course, she looked quite beautiful in it. For once, she was dressed in a gown that was appropriate for her age and station in life.

Lady Emma was the first guest to arrive, sporting a new burgundy frock with a pleated skirt which suited her no end. We all fell in love with the style and vowed to order similar ones. In different colors, of course, for we would not wish to compete. Lord Newcastle appeared next, a little worse for the wear. While his clothing was clean and pressed, his complexion was pale and listless. I would need to drop a hint in Ned's ear to take Newcastle in hand for he couldn't continue like this. Ned and Lord Marlowe arrived almost simultaneously. Ned dressed in his usual grey, three-piece business suit, while Lord Marlowe wore a dark blue suit with a Savile Row flair, a boutonniere in his lapel.

Ned, of course, knew Lily, for he'd not only traveled with her to Scotland, but afterwards had dined several times at home. Whereas before Lily's arrival he'd joined us on Wednesdays, he now attended Tuesdays and Fridays as well.

Lord Marlowe, on the other hand, had never met Lily. It was fair to say he was bowled over, as his eyes widened as soon as they lit on her. "Lady Lily, what a pleasure to meet you. I've heard much about you."

As he bowed over her hand, Lily blushed that pretty shade of rose which came so naturally to her. "The pleasure is all mine, milord."

Not to be bested by a peer of the realm, Ned, ever so subtly, nudged him aside, "Lady Lily, how very good to see you again."

Looking up at him through her lashes, Lily offered a shy smile. "Mister Worthington."

Lord Marlowe seemingly objected to the way his place had been usurped, as he not-so-gently bumped Ned away.

Margaret and I glanced at each other with dismay.

Neither of us had anticipated this male skirmish over Sebastian's sister. We would have to proceed with care as we didn't want the meeting thrown off track before it even got started.

Although we'd put careful thought into the seating arrangements, we changed them on the spot, placing the combatants as far away as possible from each other. While at first it seemed awkward, they accepted our suggestion with grace. Or at least without objection.

Aside from that minor kerfuffle, the mood was convivial as everyone was eager to participate. Because so many avenues needed to be explored, we would need to keep careful track of everyone's assignments. As Margaret had informed us she was best suited for that task, we appointed her our secretary.

To catch everyone up, Margaret and I spent half an hour discussing what we'd learned about the duke, his gambling activities, the debts owed him, his skinflint ways. While reviewing the documents Mister Nevins sent me, I'd been shocked to learn he'd paid minuscule wages to his staff, certainly a lot less than he could afford. His reasoning had been clear. He simply didn't wish to lay out more funds than was necessary to keep a houseful of servants.

We also spent some time discussing Lord Henry's gambling habits and his whereabouts the night of the murder. While he'd spent the early part of the evening at The Silver Slipper, he'd left early for an appointment. We would need to find out where he'd gone.

As the afternoon progressed, several avenues of investigation emerged. Everyone agreed that the nephew looked a likely candidate for the murderer. But we would need to discover more information about him, specifically his whereabouts after he left The Silver Slipper.

Thomas Hodgkins' death was too much of a coincidence. Could he have been friends with Lord Henry? Had they plotted to do Sebastian mischief? And what exactly had caused Sebastian to lose his memory? A drug seemed the likely agent, probably introduced through either the food or wine he'd enjoyed at Cherubs. The waiter would have to be interrogated. Ergo, a visit to the gentlemen's club would be necessary.

We also needed to know if Sebastian's memory had returned.

The march's rabble rousers also looked suspicious. Although a connection to the duke's murder was not apparent on the surface, it coincided a little too neatly with his death. Since Sebastian discovered they had been employed to disrupt the rally, we would need to find out whose coffers had paid for them. Was it the duke's or someone else's?

Once all the points of interest had been clearly laid out, we drew up a chart to assign the tasks. The easiest was Lily's. She would bear the responsibility of visiting Sebastian at the prison to discover if he'd regained his memory. As Sebastian's closest relative, she wouldn't be denied access to him. Of course, she readily agreed to do it, but felt nervous about it, for she hadn't seen him since she was three.

"I'll escort you," Ned volunteered. "You can hardly visit a prison on your own. It's not the most pleasant of places."

"Or I can help," Lord Marlowe offered. "I haven't yet been assigned a task."

"Oh, but you'll be too busy, milord," I interjected. Last thing I wished was to have the two of them argue over who would accompany Lily to the gaol.

"Doing what, may I ask?" he challenged, arching an arrogant brow.

"You'll need to look into who paid the agitators to disrupt the women's march. You're eminently suited to investigate that issue since you're a member of the House of Lords.

Something Ned is not." Hopefully, that bone tossed in his direction would mollify him.

"Are you implying a peer was responsible for causing that riot?"

"Sebastian suspected his grandfather was behind it, but you might discover it was someone else. More than likely, an aristocrat who resents more women getting the vote."

"But what, pray tell, does that have to do with the duke's murder?" After being denied the pleasure of escorting Lily to jail, Lord Marlowe was not giving in with grace.

"I don't know, milord. It may well have nothing to do with it. But it all happened the same day. There might be a connection, and it's something we need to investigate."

"Very well," he said in a disgruntled tone.

Heavens! He was in a state. He shouldn't resent Ned's close connection to Lily. It was Ned's kind spirit that prompted his offer. He probably realized how daunting a prison visit would be for her. She'd grown up so cloistered any outing proved a challenge, especially if the newspapers got wind of it. Having experienced his name being dragged through the mud during the Rose Trevvyan murder investigation, he would know best how to protect her. But it would not do to alienate Lord Marlowe for we truly needed his help. At some point, I would take him aside and explain things to him.

"What would you like me to do, Miss Worthington?" Lord Newcastle asked, shifting the focus from Lord Marlowe's churlish mood.

Grateful for his intervention, I smiled at him. "I need you to go to Cherubs and question the waiter who served Sebastian and Mister Hodgkins. Specifically, you'll want to find out what they ate and drank. Hopefully, he will remember. And see what you can discover about Lord Henry's whereabouts the night of the murder." Hopefully, such useful occupations would keep him away from the bottle.

Lady Emma cleared her throat. "What about me, Kitty?"

"I want you and Margaret to put your heads together and discover what you can about Thomas Hodgkins. At the very least, we need his vital information. Find out about his Oxford days. Your brother may be able to help with that since they probably were there at the same time. Is Mister Hodgkins the kind of fellow who would embroil himself in something unsavory? Could he be bought? That kind of thing."

"And what will you do?" Margaret asked.

"I intend to delve deeper into the duke's past which means a visit to the Duchess of Torrance is in order. She's known him for a long time." I took a deep breath. "Do we all understand our assignments?"

Everyone signaled they did.

"Wellesley could have used you as an aide-de-camp." Lord Newcastle said, flashing a ghost of his former carefree smile.

Wellesley, the Duke of Wellington's family name. "Doubt it. I faint at the sight of blood."

CHAPTER TWENTY-TWO

LORD RUTLEDGE'S SUPPER PARTY

"*M*AY I JOIN YOU, MISS WORTHINGTON?" Inspector Crawford asked. In the past, he'd eschewed most of Lord Rutledge's invitations. I was glad his mentor had finally prevailed upon him to attend tonight's supper.

"Of course." I was seated on a lushly upholstered dark velvet settee in the drawing room where the ladies had adjourned, leaving the gentlemen to their port and cigars. Since I didn't care much for gossip, I'd engaged in only the briefest of conversations before drifting to the somewhat secluded seat to await the male contingent. Since I desired a private conversation with Inspector Crawford to discuss the case, I was happy he'd sought me out. "How very nice to see you again."

"The pleasure is all mine." He joined me on the settee, proper distance observed, of course. Any closer would give the tabbies much too much to talk about. "No more . . . escapades, I gather."

"None. I did promise I'd call if I saw the need to investigate something outside the norm."

"Excellent. I can now sleep better at night." His grin told me he was only half serious. Just as well. I doubted my activities kept him awake.

Glancing toward where the other guests were gathered, I noted they were not close enough to overhear our conversation. "I'm glad you're here. I need to consult you on a few things."

"Oh?"

"I discovered Henry Dalrymple was always asking the duke for money to settle his gambling debts. But, according to the former duke's private secretary, Mister Nevins, the duke had recently cut him off. Told him he wouldn't pay another shilling and threatened to end his allowance. Doesn't that add weight to my argument that Lord Henry was the murderer?"

He leaned back against the settee. "Miss Worthington, you tend to create a theory and then try to fit the facts to it, totally ignoring other possibilities as you did with the Rose Trevvyan case. One doesn't identify a murderer *before* one gathers information and sees where that leads."

He was right. It was exactly what I'd done before. Still, I couldn't help but feel that my method had worked. I'd bumbled my way through that case gathering as many facts as I could. And then, I'd applied that knowledge to identify the murderer. But I'd done it with his help. He hadn't revealed confidential information, but he'd asked questions which helped me get the right result.

Problem was, since he was not in charge of the investigation, he would not be privy to the evidence. So, he wouldn't be able to hint I was on the wrong path. And worse than that,

I was rapidly coming to the conclusion Scotland Yard was not doing its job. "It's a shame you're not leading this inquiry. If you were, I would trust it to be conducted the proper way. Inspector Bolton seems to have concluded that Sebastian is the murderer. I don't believe he suspects anyone else."

He took a moment before he spoke. "Inspector Bolton is an experienced detective. You don't know what or who he's investigating. You'll have to trust his approach."

"That's the problem. I don't know. With you, at least I knew where you were headed."

"Be glad I'm not. If I were, I couldn't engage in this discussion with you."

"Margaret said the same thing." Still, it would be good to get his opinion. "So how would you go about investigating the murder?"

He remained silent while the servant refreshed our coffee service. He took his with neither sugar nor cream. I, on the other hand, had a sweet tooth.

"I would look at the Duke of Wynchcombe," he said, after taking a sip. "Who was he? What were his passions, his hates, his friends, his enemies?"

"I'm doing exactly that. He was a proud, arrogant man with few acquaintances, and even fewer friends. He loved lording it over his peers. Anyone who wasn't a duke, he barely engaged. As far as I can tell, gambling was his only passion. He was quite good at it, in fact. Many gentlemen owed him money."

He tilted his head to the side. "How do you know this?"

"His private secretary. Once Sebastian was properly acknowledged as the new duke, he opened up the duke's personal accounts. I can't name names, as I've promised to keep them confidential. But quite a number owed him money, some rather large amounts. But the most inter-esting fact I discovered was this. Once the duke died, all the debts were deemed settled. He arranged it that way so Sebastian could never collect. Wouldn't that make a prime motive for someone with a large debt to put a period to his existence?"

He smiled. "It would indeed. What about the duke's business dealings?"

"Ned is looking into those. I should know more in the coming days."

"What about his"—he cleared his throat—"his personal entanglements."

"Women, you mean?"

"Yes."

"There were none. He seemed to have a strong dislike of females. Hated them, if you asked me."

"Hated women? How did you determine that?"

"From his valet, Mister Farthington. He flat out said the duke didn't care much for women as they didn't 'measure up.'"

"That doesn't come naturally. Most men like women, if only to satisfy their physical needs."

My face heated up.

He shook his head. "Beg your pardon. I shouldn't have mentioned such a thing."

"Oh, please, Inspector Crawford—"

"Robert," he murmured.

"Inspector Crawford," I insisted, for it would not do to call him by his first name in public. The tabbies would have a field day. "Please don't mind my blushes. If I'm to make serious inroads into this investigation, I must be able to discuss the more lurid side of things."

"All right. What about his duchess?"

"She died when the youngest son—Lord Percy—was seven. From what I've learned, the duke treated her abominably. He didn't even allow her to travel on her own. He regarded his granddaughter, Lily, with the same lack of respect."

"I understand she's staying with you now." Not hard to understand how he knew. The gossip rags. Unable to access Sebastian since he was in jail, they had now focused on her, hounding her existence every time she left the house.

"Yes. She appeared at our home the day after Sebastian was taken into custody. Her cousin, Lord Henry, had demanded she marry Viscount Tottingham which was the last thing she wanted to do. Her grandfather affianced her to that horrid man without even consulting with her. Why would she wish to marry him? He is three times her age and has a paunch to boot."

His lips quirked. "Not a prime specimen of the male species then."

"Far from it." There were worlds of difference between the viscount's physique and the inspector's. The gentleman seated next to me was dressed in evening attire which suited his tall, fit body like it had been tailor-made for him. Which it probably had. The weave of the cloth and the workman-ship clearly branded it as bespoke from a fashionable estab-lishment.

He rested his cup on the small table in front of us and curled his arm on the backrest of the settee. His fingers dangled so close to my bare shoulder he could almost touch me. Almost.

Taking a deep breath, I continued. "Anyhow, the duke kept Lily at Wynchcombe Castle until two years ago when Lord Percy convinced him to bring her to town so she could make an advantageous marriage. That horrid man only allowed her to walk the grounds and take the occasional foray into Hyde Park. She was practically entombed in the house. She hasn't even had a season!"

"Oh, the horror of it." He mock-shuddered.

I glanced up at him through my eyelashes. "Most young ladies of noble birth have one. That's how they catch a husband." This time it was my turn to shudder.

"But not you?"

"Heavens, no. Last thing I wish is to be tied down to a marriage where all I do is birth babies."

He turned serious. "There are ways to prevent that."

"None foolproof, as I've learned from my sister Margaret."

An inscrutable look rolled over his face. "I . . . see."

"She has intellectual, not practical, knowledge of the subject, Inspector. But back to the investigation. Do we agree that there might be something there in his hatred of women?"

"I don't see how if he hasn't had a liaison in many years. Plus, the fatal thrust that killed him, no common woman could have accomplished."

"What do you mean?"

It was his turn to peruse the company. What he found must have satisfied him because he picked up a spoon from the coffee service and leaned closer to me. "Let's say this is the dagger."

I nodded.

"If you'll recall from the description at the inquest, the weapon used to kill the duke had a long, narrow blade, mostly pointed but with sharpened edges, the sort of blade that existed in medieval times."

A twin to the one Lord Percy had shown me.

"It was used to parry, but it could also deliver a deep wound."

"How would it do that?"

"The small width of the blade allowed it to penetrate between the ribs without having to be turned sideways. And because it had sharp edges, a saw and sweep motion, from side to side, could do massive internal damage, like so." He pushed the spoon to his chest and mimicked a lateral motion.

Suddenly feeling faint, I took a sip of the now cold coffee. "And that's what happened in this case?"

"Yes. The medical examiner also concluded the thrust came from the left."

"So, it had to be a left-handed man?"

"Or someone ambidextrous."

That didn't help Sebastian as he was left-handed.

"In the duke's case, the dagger was thrust between the fourth and fifth ribs with such strength it pierced right through the chest wall into the left ventricle of his heart. The saw-and-sweep motion was then employed to destroy a massive amount of tissue."

"The medical examiner testified no blood had been spilled." I swallowed back the nausea that suddenly arose. "How can that be?"

"The dagger was left in the body, so relatively little blood would have escaped. The fluid would have filled the pericardium, squeezing the heart to such a degree it could not expand. The flow of blood to the body would have stopped at that point. The duke would have become unconscious within fifteen minutes, and death would have occurred a few more after that." Concern rolled over his face. "Was I too graphic? You've grown rather pale."

"I'm fine." I wasn't, but I knew I would be. All I needed was a little time to get back my bearings.

"Should I fetch some smelling salts? Perhaps your mother has some." He started to rise, but I stopped him before he could stand.

"Don't you dare. I'm not as missish as all that."

"Very well." He offered another jesting smile after settling back into the settee. He'd been teasing me, the beast.

"Should I have fresh coffee brought? Or tea?" He pointed toward the service. At least he was serious about that.

"No, thank you. If I were to drink any more of either, I wouldn't sleep a wink tonight."

For the next few seconds, he watched me closely while I regained my composure.

Once I finally did, I asked, "In your opinion, no woman could have killed the duke?"

"It's not totally out of the question, of course. But most gently reared ladies do not possess the strength to make that thrust. Why do you ask? Do you have someone in mind?"

"No. It's just a point of inquiry, that's all."

He fixed me with a steady stare. "Miss Worthington, you may devise as many theories as you wish, but one incontrovertible fact remains. The duke was killed with a dagger which presumably belonged to his grandson. As far as I can tell, you must prove that is not so."

"How am I supposed to achieve that?"

"Find another dagger." He leaned toward me and lowered his voice. "I've looked into it myself."

I leaned right back. "Have you?"

"Unofficially, of course. Don't want to ruffle any feathers at Scotland Yard."

"Of course not."

"As you said, the duke was a proud sort of man. He believed in the superiority of his title. Usually, there are certain traditions families as old as his conduct. Something like holding a May ball every year or sending their male children to Eton. But my guess is those daggers did not spring from the brow of this particular duke."

"You think it was a tradition?"

"Yes, and a long held one at that. As I mentioned before, that style of dagger was very popular in medieval times. The dukedom goes back to that time, awarded to a commander who fought alongside a king. For all we know, such a dagger may have been employed in the assistance of the monarch himself. If that is so—"

"One of the dukes, maybe the first duke himself, may have started the tradition of awarding a dagger to his son. And that means the duke himself would have been given a dagger by his father."

His eyes shone brightly. "Exactly. Now the question becomes, if such a dagger exists, who had possession of it? Could it have been used to kill the duke?"

I laughed. "Oh, Inspector Crawford, I could kiss you."

I thought he'd see the jest and laugh along. But he became rather serious and intent as his gaze traveled beyond me to the company a few feet away. "That would not be wise."

"No. You're right." Talk about setting the tabbies' tongues wagging. It would make their day. "Just a slip of the tongue."

He barked out a laugh. "Oh, Catherine."

As I realized the extreme faux pas I'd made, my face heated up. I had no personal knowledge of kissing, but I'd learned plenty from my fellow students at the Swiss finishing school I'd attended.

"Kitty, dear." Mother. She'd approached so silently, I hadn't noted her presence. Or maybe I had been too fascinated by the Inspector to notice.

Inspector Crawford instantly came to his feet. "Mrs. Worthington."

"Inspector Crawford." She acknowledged him before turning to me. "Are you ready to leave, dear? It's been rather a long day."

"Of course, Mother." I stood as well.

"I wish you a good evening, sir." She turned and walked away, trusting me to follow behind.

"Thank you for shedding so much light on the investigation. Moving forward, I will take what you've said into account."

His brow furrowed. "You will take care, won't you?"

"Don't worry. I don't intend to put myself in peril again. At least not if I can help it."

"If there's any chance of that, contact me. You have my telephone numbers." His gaze bounced toward Mother who'd finished saying her goodbyes to Lord Rutledge and was waiting patiently for me. "You better go. Your mother awaits."

"Goodnight, Inspector." I held out my hand.

He kissed it before straightening up. "Good night." And then more softly. "Miss Worthington."

CHAPTER TWENTY-THREE

KITTY TALKS TO THE DUCHESS OF TORRANCE

"*T*HANK YOU FOR SEEING ME, YOUR GRACE."
I'd sent round a note to the Duchess of Torrance
requesting an audience. She would have been right to deny a
meeting for she was barely acquainted with me. But I'd
mentioned the Ladies Benevolent Society, hinting that it was
connected to that worthy endeavor. Since she'd been a
generous benefactress for many years, she'd graciously
granted my request.

Upon my arrival, I was shown to the drawing room
where she was seated on a richly upholstered cerulean settee.
Bright blue eyes shone brightly from a face that spoke of a
well-lived life while a halo of abundant white hair, artfully
arranged, gave her the appearance of a benevolent being. Age
had most definitely not withered her.

The early Georgian period furnishings sprinkled about
the room—sculptured, richly carved, upholstered, and gilded

—weren't designed so much to welcome as to impress. They were not my cup of tea.

"Rather horrid, isn't it?" she said, smiling.

"I beg your pardon," I said, my gaze returning to her.

"The furniture. Your expression gave you away."

"Did it?" Heat rose on my face.

"Do not be embarrassed, my dear. I happen to agree with you. But what can one do?" She shrugged. "It's been here for over a hundred years, and here it shall stay."

"Of course. I didn't mean." I curtsied. "Your Grace." I was repeating myself.

A crinkle of a smile lit upon her lips. "Please take a seat, Miss Worthington." She pointed to the settee across from her. Except for its cream color, it matched the opulence of the one she occupied.

I rushed to comply before I made a further cake of myself. "Thank you for seeing me." *Heavens!* I'd already said that.

Thankfully, she ignored my twittering. "You're quite welcome, my dear. I've asked tea to be brought around. Unless you prefer something else?"

"Tea is fine, thank you. But you did not have to trouble yourself."

"Nonsense. It's the least I could do. Is it still chilly out?"

Grateful for a topic which took the focus off me, I replied, "A bit, yes."

We continued making inane remarks about the weather— but then it wouldn't be England if we didn't—until the tea service arrived. She allowed several minutes for us to refresh ourselves before she broke the silence. "Now what do you wish to discuss? I assume it's not about the Ladies Benevolent Society," she said, with a twinkle in her eye. Her intellect matched her beauty.

"How did you know?"

"If it were, your mother would have visited, not you. She's an excellent steward of that charity."

"Thank you. I'll let her know." I cleared my throat and jumped in. "I wanted to discuss the Duke of Wynchcombe."

"Ahhh. I thought so." She placed her cup on the small table in front of her and looked off into the distance as if she was gathering her thoughts. "I knew him for quite a long time as his wife was a dear friend of mine. Even though she was a year or two older, we made our debut together. There was a delay in her family in bringing her out. A death in the family, I believe. So, we ended up coming out the same year."

"When was that?"

"Let me think." She glanced toward the ceiling as if somehow the answer was to be found there. "Must have been 1872." She let out a soft laugh. "More years than I care to count."

"Was that when she met the Duke of Wynchcombe?"

"Officially, yes. But there had been much back and forth between him and Sophie's family prior to her debut. I should say Lady Sophie as she was the daughter of a Marquis. He was looking for a bride of good stock who would provide him the heirs he needed to continue the Wynchcombe line, and Sophie fit the bill. She was barely out when she found herself attached to the duke." Her gaze snapped back to me. "The family was eager for the match, you see."

"But she wasn't?"

"No, she was not. Having lived a rather sheltered existence, she was eager to taste life before she wed." She issued a barely audible sigh. "But it was not to be. By the end of the season, she found herself married to the duke."

"Forgive me if I'm stepping out of line, but it seems you didn't approve of him."

She stiffened, seemingly in outrage, but, as her words bore out, not directed at me. "He was a hard man to like. The continuation of his line was the only thing that interested him. He gave no thought to the fact Sophie was innocent of life." She clenched her teeth. "He treated her abominably."

I sensed a retreat was in order lest she become too emotional and imbue her narrative with more opinion than facts. "Did you marry at the same time?"

"Oh, no, my dear." The dark cloud seemed to lift from her. "Torrance and I didn't meet until my third season. He was away on some mad adventure to travel the world. When he returned, well, it was over for me. He was the most handsome man I'd ever seen. To my good fortune, I caught his interest. A surprise for there were younger and more beautiful debutantes that season. He feted me with flowers and chocolates and declared himself a slave to my eyes. Can you believe it?" The twinkle in her eye was back.

"Yes, I can. You're quite beautiful."

She laughed as she touched her hair. "My hair has gone white, and the lines of time mark my face."

"Even so, you wear your age very well indeed."

A small lift of her lips. "What a flatterer you are, my dear."

Since she'd regained her good mood, I deemed it a good time to return to the object of my visit. "Was the Duke of Wynchcombe always difficult?"

"Yes. He was rather." A frown. "I blamed it in part to his upbringing. You see, although he had a loving father, his mother wanted nothing to do with him."

Well, that explained his attitude toward Sebastian and Lily. He didn't want anything to do with them, either.

"As soon as he was old enough she enrolled him at Eton and then forgot all about him. She was a social animal who invested her time in one grand event after another. Her house parties were legendary—masked balls, spring fetes, autumn celebrations. Extravagant affairs from what I've heard. No expense was spared. And, of course, anyone who was anyone attended for that was the place to be seen. In the meantime, Thropplethorpe was exiled at school, coming home only for the winter holidays and summers."

"Thropplethorpe. That's the title Sebastian inherited."

Her brow rose slightly. "You call him by his first name?"

"He insists."

"He's nothing like his grandfather then."

"No, he's not." Sebastian possessed a kind and loving heart, so different from his grandfather's.

"Thank heaven for that."

"There were no other children from that marriage?"

She scoffed. "His father wanted another child, but the duchess apparently shut the door on that endeavor. Literally."

"How do you know?"

"Servants. They know everything. Thropplethorpe's father consoled himself by taking in his nephew. The younger brother he adored fathered a little boy of his own. When the brother died an early death, the duke took in his son. And that seemed to solve the issue of more children. He was happy, his nephew was happy. Even the duchess was happy since she was not imposed upon to do her marital duty." She suddenly stopped and gazed at me, an apology in her eyes. "I beg your pardon, Miss Worthington. I should not be discussing such a thing with you."

"Oh, please, do not mind me. I'm not the least missish."

"Very well, if you insist."

"I do. Please go on."

She sipped her tea before continuing. "Well, everyone was happy. Except for Thropplethorpe, that is. He hated his cousin with every fiber of his being. Pure envy if you ask me. When his father died and he inherited the title, he tossed his cousin out on his ear and told him to fend for himself.

Thankfully, the duke had provided for his nephew, and he was able to live comfortably."

"Well, that's good." It was time to draw the narrative back to Sophie for that would get me closer to the truth about the duke. "What happened after the duke married Lady Sophie?"

"She did her duty. In short order, a child was born. Thankfully, a boy. They named him Thomas. As soon as the succession was assured, the duke returned to London. He didn't care much for Wynchcombe Castle, you see, and spent most of the year in the city, including every spring and summer. Sophie was left to fend for herself and her newborn with only the servants for company. Can you imagine such a thing?"

As Mother never discussed the subject, the only knowledge I'd gained of childbirth was from Margaret's pamphlet, *The Yoke of Womanhood*. And that publication did not discuss the process, only the woman's burden for bearing many children. But I could very well imagine how an inexperienced young woman would feel with no one to provide aid. "She must have been fearful."

"She was. I visited as soon as I could, provided whatever aid I could. But after a fortnight, my parents called me back to town as the season was about to start."

"I'm sure she appreciated your visit. You were able to provide her with a friendly face, if only for a little while."

"Yes, I was that. I left somewhat at ease, though. Her maid had proven herself invaluable in the subject of post-confinement care. A fiercely loyal creature who'd come with Sophie to the marriage, she made sure Sophie got everything she needed and the babe, too. I don't know what Sophie would have done without her."

Her account reminded me of my own faithful maid, Betsy. I don't know what I would do without her either. "Did the duke return at some point?"

"Not until that autumn. That pattern remained the same for the rest of their marriage. But then something happened that changed the rhythm of their lives. When Thomas was seven, the duke's cousin returned to Wynchcombe Castle."

That surprised me, to say the least. "Why would he do such a thing after the duke had exiled him?"

"He'd joined the Inniskilling Dragoons, a cavalry regiment in the British Army, which was being sent to fight in the Boer War. He didn't wish to go off to an armed conflict without saying goodbye to his only living relative. Or so Sophie explained in her letters."

"She wrote to you?"

"Often, my dear. I still have them. I treasure them to this day."

"Was the duke there?"

"No, he wasn't." She pierced me with a look I found hard to interpret. "Sophie was happy that summer. Happier than I'd ever known her to be. She wrote me many letters telling me it was so. But her happiness would not last. As soon as the duke got word of his cousin's presence, he made his way to Wynchcombe Castle. Sophie and the cousin had just returned from a ride in the estate. I can just imagine how she looked, glowing with happiness as she gazed at the man with whom she'd fallen in love. Well, the duke dragged his cousin to the ground and beat him with a horse whip, bloodied him by Sophie's account. And then the duke threw him out and told him if he ever returned, he would kill him."

"Oh, my."

"He left, of course. Not much else he could do."

"What happened to him?"

"He was killed in a skirmish during the First Boer War."

"How sad."

"Yes, it was."

"When was this?"

"The winter of 1881."

A knock on the door interrupted our conversation shortly followed by the Duke of Torrance's entrance. Lord Percy trailed in his wake.

"Randolph," the Duchess murmured.

"My dear." The duke kissed her cheek. The loving exchange told me more than words ever could they truly cared for one another.

"You remember Catherine Worthington, Mildred Worthington's daughter?" The duchess pointed toward me. "She was at attendance at our ball."

His gaze narrowed as he looked at me. "I'm sorry. I don't. My memory is not what it was, my dear," he said by way of apology.

"I promised Mrs. Worthington the name of a possible benefactor to the Ladies Benevolent Society. With every-thing going on, I forgot all about it. Miss Worthington is here to obtain the name and address."

Well, that was news to me since Mother had forgotten to tell me.

"We are much alike in that respect, then, my dear." He flicked her cheek before turning to the gentleman who remained in his shadow. "I hope you don't mind. But I invited Lord Percy for supper."

"No, of course not. Lord Percy is more than welcome." Her smile seemed a bit strained. Didn't she like the gentleman or did she have another objection to him?

Whatever the reason, it did not affect Lord Percy's greeting for he bowed and kissed the air above her hand. "You are the very kindest of ladies, ma'am."

"May I introduce Miss Worthington, Lord Percy?" the duchess said by way of response.

"We've already met, dear lady. Miss Worthington was kind enough to offer her condolences in person." When he strolled toward me, I was once more struck by the close resemblance between him and Sebastian. But then all the Dalrymple men appeared much alike.

All smiles, he bowed and kissed my hand with the same obeisance he'd shown to the duchess. "How are you, my dear?"

"I'm doing well, thank you." I couldn't help but like him. He'd inherited all the grace his father had lacked.

"And your family?"

"Everyone is enjoying good health." Freeing my hand from his grasp, I came to my feet. "I will take my leave, your Grace. You have a supper to attend to, and I've taken enough of your time."

"I enjoyed our conversation, my dear. Let me write that name and address for your mother." Having said that, she walked toward an escritoire at the side of the room and quickly wrote something on a sheet of paper which she tucked into an envelope and handed to me.

With so much to think about, I forgot all about the note until the next day when I handed it to Mother during breakfast.

"How very odd," she said after opening the envelope.

"What's odd?"

"This can't possibly be the name of a contributor."

"No?"

"It's somebody named Edith Clemson in a place called Headbourne Worthy in Hampshire."

"Wynchcombe Castle is located near there," Lily exclaimed.

"Did the duchess mention anything about this person?" Mother asked.

"No. But we were interrupted by the duke's arrival. Lord Percy was with him. Maybe the duchess didn't wish to mention it in front of them." I considered the matter while I helped myself to a plate of food from the sideboard. Once I'd joined them at the table, I said, "I think that name and address were meant for me."

"Whyever so?" Mother asked.

"Call it a hunch." I took a bite of the shirred eggs. "I'll need to determine who she is so I can talk to her. Obviously, that's what the duchess wants me to do."

"Travel to Hampshire?" Mother's brows rose in dismay. "You'd have to take the train." Mother was not a fan of railroads. As far as she was concerned, they traveled too fast and belched out too much filthy smoke.

"Yes, and I know just who will escort me."

Mother frowned. "No, Kitty. I will not allow it."

Lily's confused gaze bounced between Mother and me. "Who would accompany Kitty?"

"Inspector Crawford would be my guess," Margaret said, biting into a muffin.

"I forbid it," Mother said. "You can't gallivant around England in the company of a bachelor unrelated to you."

"Betsy can chaperone, Mother. We can go and return the same day. I'll travel heavily veiled so no one will recognize me."

"You don't know who this Edith person is."

"I will send her a telegram. I'll inform her the Duchess of Torrance referred me to her, and I'd like to discuss something with her."

"But who could she be?" Margaret asked.

"Maybe someone from the Wynchcombe London staff would recognize the name," Lily suggested.

"I don't need to ask them. I believe I know who she is."

"Who?" Mother asked.

"The Duchess of Wynchcombe's maid." And more than likely, the keeper of her secrets.

CHAPTER TWENTY-FOUR

KITTY VISITS THE DUCHESS'S MAID

*T*HAT SAME DAY, I sent a telegram to the name and address the Duchess of Torrance had provided. And then I waited for a return letter since I doubted Edith Clemson could afford a telegram. The cost would be downright prohibitive to someone of limited means.

But that was not the only issue which needed to be resolved. I also needed an escort for I couldn't travel alone. Since Inspector Crawford had volunteered his assistance if I went on another jaunt, I wrote him asking for his help. His return note was succinct and to the point. He was available to accompany me on Thursday.

Now the question became whether I would receive word from the duchess's maid in time to arrange that trip. Thankfully, her letter came in the post that same afternoon. She was available to meet any day this week. Much relieved, I called Inspector Crawford who informed me an early train would deliver us from Waterloo Station to Winchester in two hours' time. From there, we could organize a taxicab to drive us to the village of Headbourne Worthy where Miss Clemson lived.

Only then did I go in search of Mother for I would need her final blessing for the trip. I found her in her personal parlor planning the next fundraising event for the Ladies Benevolent Society. For the past several months, she'd shouldered that heavy burden by her lonesome. Lady Ainsley, who shared leadership responsibilities with Mother, was in Europe, allegedly recuperating from an illness. In recent days, though, she'd been spotted at the Paris Worth Salon. A strange place to regain your health. But I suppose shopping for a new wardrobe might prove therapeutic for her after what she'd gone through. I could only hope she returned soon for Mother had enough to deal with now.

"May I interrupt?" I asked Mother.

"Of course, dear," she said, looking up. She was working on a seating chart for a fundraising supper.

"I received a return letter from Edith Clemson. She's available to meet any day this week. I'd like to visit her tomorrow."

Sighing, she laid down her pen. "Is this something you must do, Kitty?"

I folded my hands in front of me. "It is vital to the investigation, Mother."

"How so?"

"I believe the solution to this murder lies in things that happened long ago."

"How could something that occurred in the past bear on the present?"

"'Old sins cast long shadows,' as the proverb goes." I thought I was being clever, but all I got was a raised brow in return. No, cleverness wouldn't work in this instance. Logic would. "We need this information, Mother. Either I'm right, and we act on it; or I'm proven wrong, and we discount it altogether."

She pondered on it for a minute and finally nodded. "Very well. I imagine you've discussed it with Inspector Crawford?"

"I have. We leave tomorrow from Waterloo Station and will return in the afternoon. You'll hardly know I'm gone." I tried to make a joke out of it, but she refused to smile.

"Take Betsy with you. And don't forget your veil. We wouldn't want you to be recognized."

"I will, and I won't. Thank you, Mother." I kissed her cheek before sailing out with a spring in my step.

The next day at the appointed hour, Inspector Crawford presented himself at our house in a taxicab. Dressed in a dark blue suit and a Homburg hat, he was the epitome of a proper gentleman. Not that he'd ever been anything else.

Mother, Margaret, Lily, and I met him in the drawing room, for Mother would not allow us to go on our way before she'd had her say.

"I'm entrusting my daughter's safety into your keeping, Inspector." As if that wasn't enough, Mother fixed him with a hard stare. "I'll have your word as a gentleman nothing untoward will happen."

He bowed his head. "You have it, ma'am. I give you my most solemn oath."

Seemingly satisfied, she nodded. "I'll hold you to that, Inspector."

Since time was not to be wasted, I quickly bid goodbye to them, and we, along with Betsy, went on our way.

Not wishing to be recognized, I'd worn the ubiquitous black veil of so many times before which obscured my features while still allowed me to see. Waterloo Station was its usual beehive of activity, but since Inspector Crawford had arranged for the train tickets, it took us no time at all to board the train. Betsy tried to make herself invisible as we sat next to each other in the private train compartment Inspector Crawford had reserved.

When she excused herself to visit the lavatory, Inspector Crawford remarked, "She's quite faithful to you, isn't she?"

"Yes, she is. I don't know what I would do without her."

He'd tossed his hat on the seat next to him. Strange that he seemed more approachable this way. "What do you hope to discover today?"

"I've been given to understand the Duchess of Wynch-combe confided a great deal in her. She may hold secrets that the duke would not wish be made public."

"Who told you this?"

Glancing down, I stated, "I can't say."

"Can't or won't."

I gazed at him directly. "What's the difference? The result is the same."

Betsy returned, stopping the awkward conversation. The rest of the trip I maintained silence while mulling over the questions I would ask. Truth be told, I was nervous. So much rode on discovering the truth about the duchess. What if Edith Clemson wouldn't talk? What if we didn't get satisfactory answers? Well, if that happened, we would just have to figure out something else.

Upon our arrival at Winchester, it took little time to arrange for a taxi, and in no time, we arrived at Headbourne Worthy. We were greeted by Miss Clemson's niece who told us her aunt was expecting us. After I asked and was granted permission for Betsy to remain in the parlor, she led us to a bedroom where the curtains had been drawn so very little light entered the room. The white-haired figure on the bed appeared quite frail.

The niece wasted no time introducing me. "Aunt Edith, this is the lady who wrote you 'bout the duchess."

Miss Clemson waved me over. "Come closer so I can see ye. My eyes aren't what they used to be."

Assuming the request was meant for only me, I approached the bed. Inspector Crawford wisely chose to remain closer to the door.

"Who are ye?"

"As I explained in my telegram, my name is Catherine Worthington."

"Why do you want to know about the duchess?"

"Her grandson, Sebastian Dalrymple, has been arrested for the murder of the Duke of Wynchcombe."

Her sneer was clear even in the dim light. "That devil. I'm glad he's dead. He never did a good deed for anyone, least of all my mistress."

"You were close to her?"

Her voice softened. "I loved her like she was me very own."

Inspector Crawford moved closer to set a chair behind me.

Edith squinted at him. "Who's that?"

Something told me she wouldn't look favorably upon an inspector from Scotland Yard, so I answered. "A friend. I needed an escort to come see you."

She blinked and turned her gaze back to me. "How do you know the Dalrymple lad?"

"My sister is. They're . . . sweet on each other."

"And ye want to save him from the rope?" Miss Clemson didn't mince words.

"He didn't kill the duke."

"How do ye know that?" she snapped out.

"He's very sweet and kind. So is his sister. She sought shelter with us to escape her cousin's reach."

"Lord Henry Dalrymple," she spit out. "Heard about him. He's a bad 'un, he is. Reminds me of the duke." She'd heard about him all the way here. Maybe the servants in the castle talked. Lily had said he'd cornered her one day. Maybe he'd done the same to some poor servant girl.

"Won't you please tell me about the duchess?"

"My lamb." A soft smile bloomed across her lips. "She was the sweetest thing. Blonde, blue eyed, beautiful."

"So is her granddaughter."

Lost in her memories, she kept on talking as if I hadn't said a word. "Quality she was." Her voice turned rough. "Until that devil got a hold of her. Her family made her marry the duke. Overnight she went from a happy lass to a sad woman. So sad. He was not kind. All he wanted was an heir. So he visited every night until she quickened with child. Once he was assured of that, he left for London. Good riddance, I said."

Hate was too mild a word from what emanated from her.

"He returned when her birthing time came. Wanted to see his son born." She let out a wheezy laugh. "As if there was a way of knowing. Only God knew, and he wasn't talking. But it did end up being a boy. Beautiful lad with her blonde hair and light eyes. As soon as she laid eyes on him, all the love in the world flowed from her. The duke wanted nothing to do with the rearing. Only that there was somebody to carry on his name. Satisfied of that, he left."

"Did he ever return?"

"Hunting season and winter holidays. He hated Wynchcombe Castle. Didn't stay a day more than he had to. As soon as spring came, he was gone. No one missed him." She cackled again. "Year to year, it was the same. Until the summer the young master turned seven, and the duke's cousin came calling. He was bound for the military and wanted to say goodbye to his only relative, the duke. They'd grown up together, you see."

Of course, I'd heard the story from the Duchess of

Torrance, but hers had been filtered through her friend's eyes. Miss Clemson would have a more intimate view of what had happened. "Did they?"

"Oh, yes. His uncle, the old duke, had loved him like a son. A kind man he was. His wife was another matter. A right old tartar, she was. Loved only herself. She gave him one son and no more. She locked her door against him. If he minded, nobody knew. But he was happy with his son. He had a big heart and when his brother passed leaving his son an orphan, he had the boy come live with him. Showed him the same love he'd showered on his son. Of course, the devil became jealous of all the attention his father gave to his cousin."

"What was the cousin's name?"

"Lord Trenton. My mistress called him 'Trent.' They carried on that summer like children. Picnicking by the water, horse riding. He was the father master Thomas never had. Everyone was happy to see the mistress and the young master so happy." Her voice roughened again. "But then the devil returned. At the end of the summer. Before his time. He'd heard from a neighbor about his cousin. He couldn't find them when he arrived. They weren't at the house. The mistress, master Thomas, and Lord Trenton had gone for a ride in the estate. So he waited for an hour for them to return. When they did, he yanked Lord Trenton right off his horse and horsewhipped him in front of the entire stable staff. Bloodied him, he did. Told him never to return. If he did, he'd kill him."

"What did Lord Trenton do?"

"He left. What choice did he have?"

"How horribly sad."

"But the devil wasn't done. For seven years, he'd ignored my lamb, but no more. He demanded his rights then and there. She submitted. And eight months later, Master Percy was born."

"He was early."

"Oh, no, Miss." Her eyes shown with glee. "He was born right on time."

"What do you mean?"

"Lord Trenton fathered Lord Percy, not the duke."

Heavens! I wasn't expecting that. "Did the duke know?"

"If he suspected, he never said a word."

"What happened to Lord Trenton?"

"He went off to the Boer War and was killed in an assault. When word came of Lord Trenton's death, something inside my mistress died that day. But she had two boys to raise and refused to give in to despair. She lived another seven years. But then, one winter, her spirit finally gave out." Tears rolled down her cheeks.

"I'm so sorry."

With a shaky hand, she wiped the moisture from her face. "When she knew the end was near, she asked everyone to leave her bedroom. Everyone but me. Once we were alone, she handed me a box and a key. Inside were the letters she and Lord Trenton had written to each other. She'd told him that Percy was his son. "If he was hurt, she didn't want him to die without knowing a part of him lived on. He thanked her for that knowledge."

The significance of what she'd just revealed was immense. If Percy was not the duke's son, then he was illegitimate and could never inherit the title. Was this what the duke did not wish to come to light? "Where are those letters?"

"She had me send them to her brother, the Earl of Clarendon. They were my protection, you see, for she feared for my life. Once she died, she knew the duke would come after me for I knew too much. So, I sent them with her note. The day we buried my lamb, I walked into the duke's study and told him what I'd done. If one hair on my head was harmed, the person holding the letters would release them, and the whole world would know he'd been cuckolded. He cursed me, raised his stick against me, but by God I didn't cower. I stood up to the devil. And then I took my carpet bag and left. I've been living here with my family ever since. That was thirty-five odd years ago."

"Does the Earl of Clarendon have the letters still?" I had to somehow get a hold of them.

"Got a letter six weeks back telling me he'd died. I don't know who has them now. It doesn't matter. I'm dying."

No wonder she'd been so forthcoming. She probably didn't wish to leave this earth without someone knowing the truth. "I'm so sorry. Can nothing be done?"

A slight shake of her head. "A mass in my belly. Too far gone."

"Oh."

"Your kindness does you credit, child. But there's nothing to fret about. I'm looking forward to joining my mistress in heaven." She moaned, and her niece burst in like a shot carrying a glass of water and a brown bottle. She'd probably been listening at the door. "Time for your medicine, Aunt Edith."

While she attended to her aunt, I whispered to Inspector Crawford. "We have to locate that correspondence."

"Even if you were to find them," he whispered back, "you still have the matter of the dagger to contend with."

"What's that?" Miss Clemson must have heard our murmurs.

"You must rest, Aunt," the niece said.

Miss Clemson waved her back. "Stop fussing at me. I'll be gone soon enough." Turning to us, she asked, "What dagger?"

"The Duke of Wynchcombe was murdered with a dagger that had the Wynchcombe crest on it. He'd had two crafted and gave one to each son. Lord Percy is in possession of one. The other was inherited by Sebastian Dalrymple upon his father's death. Since there are only two, Scotland Yard believes it was Sebastian's dagger that killed the duke."

A holy fire shone in her eyes. "You're wrong. There are more than two. Every Duke of Wynchcombe since the inception of the title has presented a dagger to each son. When they die, the dagger is buried with them. The devil's father had two commissioned."

"But he only had one son."

"He gave one to his son and the other to his nephew, Trenton. There are two more."

CHAPTER TWENTY-FIVE

A CONVERSATION ON THE TRAIN

"*W*E NEED TO TALK IN PRIVATE," Inspector Crawford stated on the way back to the Winchester train station after we ended our discussion with Edith Clemson and collected Betsy on the way out.

"Yes."

"And it must be done before we arrive in London. There will be no time afterward."

"I agree. But what about Betsy?" I nodded in her direction. She'd climbed into the taxicab's front row seat and was chatting with the driver.

"I'll arrange for a private compartment for both your maid and us. With your approval, of course."

It was the best solution for we couldn't discuss what we'd learned within her hearing. The issue of Lord Percy's legitimacy was too delicate to talk about in front of her. "You have it. But how will you go about it?" If a person held a first class ticket, he could sit anywhere he wished.

An impish sort of smile flit across his lips. "I'm a Detective Inspector with the Metropolitan Police. I'll make a special request."

"I'm impressed, Inspector." I grinned.

"Don't be." He shook his head. "I shouldn't be doing this."

"Who'll know? I certainly won't tell." He was bending the rules for the investigation. There was hope for him yet.

When we arrived at the train station, he headed toward the ticket window to arrange for two private compartments. Once he'd done so, I took Betsy aside and explained the situation. As always, she accepted it with her usual sunny disposition.

"A compartment all to myself," she said, all smiles. "Won't that be a treat?"

"You can't whisper a word to anyone, Betsy, that the inspector and I were alone. Not your aunt, nor Neville, and most especially not my mother." I shuddered to think what she would say if she found out.

She turned serious; all her gaiety gone. "Oh, you need not worry, Miss Worthington. Mum's the word."

"Splendid. I knew I could count on you. We'll send a tea service your way to make up for the inconvenience." It was an out and out bribe. But honestly, it was the least I could do.

"Coo!"

After we accommodated Betsy in a compartment two away from ours, we settled into our own, drawing the shades to ensure we were not seen by anyone walking the corridor. We had two hours to discuss what we'd learned and hopefully devise a plan of action. It would not be enough, but it would have to do.

As soon as the train started rolling, I pulled the journal where I kept my case notes from my purse. "Now, where shall we start?"

"The daggers. We need to discover who has those other two."

I tossed the dratted veil aside since I had no need to hide now. "One can only assume the duke retained one. Could he have taken it with him to the rendezvous?"

"I don't see how. If he kept it at Wynchcombe House, he would have had to return home to retrieve it. But he left directly from Viscount Tottenham's house," he said. "Someone had to have known about that dagger."

"I can't imagine Lord Percy not knowing. According to Edith Clemson, it was a tradition," I said.

"Which meant he lied to Inspector Bolton when he said there were only two."

"Yes, but would Lord Percy have had access to it? Would the duke have kept it out in the open or locked up?"

"The butler did not mention seeing one at the inquest," he said.

"But he wasn't asked," I reminded him.

His eyes twinkled with appreciation. "Very good, Miss Worthington."

"Thank you, sir." I bowed my head, half in jest.

He shook his head at my antic. "In all seriousness, that was a mistake. The coroner should have asked him if he'd spotted a similar dagger at Wynchcombe House. If there was one, he'd certainly know about it since he's the butler. But let's postpone that question for the moment and address the one Trenton Dalrymple owned," he said.

"He would more than likely have taken it with him when he was sent into battle. It was a weapon, after all."

"And a reminder of someone who loved him. Yes, he would have carried it with him. The question then becomes to whom were his personal items sent after he perished? By Miss Clemson's account, he was an only child, so, more than likely, they'd been sent to the duke since he was his closest relative."

I shook my head in disagreement. "I think it was forwarded to the duchess. If you recall, Miss Clemson said the box her mistress gave her contained all the letters she'd written to Mister Dalrymple, as well as the ones she received. My guess is they sent everything, including the dagger."

"Another brilliant deduction, Miss Worthington." His lips turned upward into a laughing smile.

Was he teasing me? I squinted at him. Yes, he was. "This is serious. I don't need you pouring the butter sauce over me."

"Ahh, but what if I enjoy it?" His eyes may have been filled with mirth, but I sensed an underlying seriousness to his comment.

Whatever it was, the mood was broken when the train suddenly lurched.

It took me a moment to remember what we'd been discussing. The duchess's correspondence. The dagger given to Trenton Dalrymple. "Is there any way to find out to whom his belongings were sent?"

He nodded. "Military records are kept forever. Since we know where and when he died, it's only a matter of locating them. I'll use my Scotland Yard connections to unearth that information." He appeared unaffected by what had so briefly transpired between us, but then, it may only have been my imagination.

Eager to move on from whatever had, or had not, happened, I noted his comment in my journal.

"You carry that with you all the time, don't you?" he asked.

"Yes. I draw, make notations about people, things I observe. It's proved convenient in the past."

His gaze softened. "Yes, I know."

It'd been my drawings that had led me to figure out the murderer of Rose Trevvyan.

"The next question becomes who's in possession of the letters," I said.

"The Earl of Clarendon had sufficient time to ponder that question. He would have sent them to someone he trusted. Someone who would safeguard the information contained within."

"The Duchess of Torrance would be my guess."

"The Duchess of Torrance?" he asked. "Is that who told you about Edith Clemson?"

Too late I realized the mistake I'd made for I hadn't revealed her name to him. No help for it. I had to own up to it. "Yes."

To his credit, he didn't gloat but simply nodded.

"The Earl of Clarendon would have known she was Sophie's friend. As such, she would neither wish to besmirch her friend's reputation nor allow the question of Lord Percy's legitimacy to leak out."

"I agree she's a likely candidate."

"Do you think the duke suspected she had those letters?" I asked.

While he thought about my question, he leaned forward and propped his elbows on his knees. "It's certainly a possibility," he finally said.

"What if he did and was concerned about them? What if the Duchess of Torrance, if she does in fact have them in her possession, wrote to him about them?"

He tilted his head to the side. "Why would she do such a thing if the object was to keep anyone from finding out about them?"

"Something happened. Something that drove her not only to tell him, but to threaten him with exposure. As proud as he was about the Wynchcombe name, the duke would have moved heaven and earth to stop any information about Lord Percy's legitimacy from being released."

"That certainly is an avenue to pursue."

"But you do not think the Duchess of Torrance, if in fact it was her, is responsible for his death," I said.

He straightened out. "I don't see how it could be. She wouldn't have the strength to drive a dagger into him." He paused for a moment. "You'll need to verify she in fact has those letters before you proceed. That is vital to the investigation. And, if she does have them, you'll have to discover if she wrote to him threatening exposure. Once you have done that, you'll need to consider all the evidence before you draw a conclusion."

"Such as the nephew's gambling debts."

"Yes. Although I do not find that argument as strong," he said.

"Why ever not?" I would not allow my favorite theory to be discarded without putting up a fight. "Think of it. Lord Henry needed money to pay off his gambling debts. His grandfather would not pay. He could very well have killed the duke and put the blame on Sebastian. Once he was found guilty and hanged, Lord Percy would inherit the title, and the fortune that came with it. Lord Henry would have then been able to wheedle the money from his father."

"But he would have to depend on Scotland Yard apprehending Sebastian for the murder."

"As they have done."

"It would have been easier to continue to hound his grandfather. The old man might have given in at some point. The other plan seems too fantastical to me. Too many things had to happen."

"As they have so far."

"But how did he lure his grandfather to the garden? Very

few people had to have known about the letters. Doubt he was one of them."

"What about his father, Lord Percy?"

"Umm. A possible explanation. He could have overheard conversations as a child. He would be the one most directly affected by such revelations for they would make him illegitimate."

"Exactly."

"There's only one problem with that explanation."

"What is it?"

"He was having supper with a friend. They played chess until midnight. He'd just returned home shortly before Inspector Bolton arrived with the news of his father's death."

"I suppose the witness is reliable."

"Lord Mountford. Impeccable credentials. They've been friends since Eton."

"Oh." I dropped my head back against the seat. "I'm developing a headache."

"Shall I arrange for tea? We did promise your maid."

"Please."

We did not discuss matters while we refreshed ourselves. And then there was little time before our arrival at Waterloo. The three of us made our way through the station, the inspector and I in front, while Betsy followed behind. We were close to the entrance when disaster struck.

"Eek!" I exclaimed.

"What's wrong?" The inspector asked.

"Lady Clinton just ahead. Black hat, ostrich feathers. Full battleship mode. She's the town's biggest gossip. If she sees me." Only then did I realize I'd failed to pin my veil back on. I gazed at him in full panic mode. "Hide me." An impossible demand for there was nowhere to hide.

But the inspector was nothing if not a quick thinker. Turning me, he folded me against his body.

"What are you doing?" I whispered to his chest.

"Hiding you." He doffed his Homburg hat, leaned down, and placed it to the side of his face obscuring both of us. Hopefully, when Lady Clinton walked by, she would only see a couple in a mad embrace.

I started to turn my face to the side, but he stopped me.

"Don't. She'll pass by soon."

He smelled as usual of his intoxicating men's cologne. A man's fragrance. Nothing flowery. Everything about him was hard. His arm curled around me. The chest I was budged up against. I felt not only protected but safe.

"She's past now," he murmured.

"How do you know?"

His chest rumbled, as if he was laughing. "I looked."

Well, that would do it. I dared to glance up at him. "Maybe we should remain like this a while longer just to make sure."

"Miss Worthington. Catherine," he whispered.

I loved it when he called me by my proper first name.

"You're playing with fire."

"Am I?" I said softly, wetting my lip with my tongue.

"I swore on my honor to your mother that nothing untoward would occur."

"Oh, very well." I twisted out of his grasp and turned for the exit, leaving him to follow behind.

Neville was waiting for us in front of the station, so all that remained was to slip into the Rolls Royce. The ride was conducted in silence for I had nothing to say to the good inspector that wouldn't emerge the wrong way. While bidding goodbye, he promised to call. I promised the same. I couldn't help but feel, however, although we'd made progress, we'd ended up with more questions than before.

CHAPTER TWENTY-SIX

COUNCIL OF WAR (PART DEUX)

*T*HE DAY AFTER THE TRIP TO WINCHESTER, the investigative committee reconvened in our library for there was much to discuss. I decided against telling them what we'd discovered. Lord Percy's supposed illegitimacy was too sensitive a subject to reveal until we had substantial proof.

"Thank you for gathering again. I know how precious your time is. I met with the Duchess of Torrance early this week, and she guided me in a certain direction." After mentioning the trip, I said, "We uncovered information of a rather delicate nature which I feel at this time would be best kept to myself."

"You don't trust us." Margaret bit out. Last night she'd tried to coax the information from me. When I told her I couldn't share what I'd discovered, she'd stormed out of my room in a huff. Seemingly, she still had not calmed down.

"Of course, I do. But first of all, the facts need to be verified, and second, I don't want us to focus on those details ignoring all else." One thing I'd learned from Inspector Crawford was to examine *all* the evidence before drawing any conclusions. If I shared what we'd learned from Miss Clemson, I feared the team would only concern itself with that line of inquiry. A huge mistake, in my opinion, for much remained to investigate.

A heated conversation erupted. While some demanded I reveal what I'd learned, others were willing to wait and see. Finally, Ned stepped in to calm the waters. "If Kitty feels it's best to keep the information confidential, we should trust her to do what's right. It's not like we don't have other avenues of inquiries."

"Thank you, Ned," I said. "Why don't you start us off by reporting what you've found."

"I met with the duke's man of business who manages the Wynchcombe properties. He opened his books to me. I didn't find any unusual expenses. Everything was above board."

"That's good to know. What about Mister Nevins? Did you meet with him?"

"He proved a tougher nut to crack, for he insisted the personal matters of the duke should be kept private."

"Yes, he said the same thing to me. I had to threaten him with a visit to a judge to adjudicate the matter before he discussed the duke's gambling transactions."

"How very clever of you, Kitty," Lady Emma said. "One can never allow a man to get the upper hand. He'll ride roughshod over you if you do."

Every one of the gentlemen stared at her with surprise for she hadn't been known as a progressive thinker. But I could have told them, if they'd bothered to ask, she'd been hiding her light under a bushel. And that light had emerged as a brilliant beacon during the women's vote rally and its aftermath.

After one last questioning glance at Emma, Ned continued, "As you can imagine, there were more matters than gambling debts, such as household expenses and staff salaries. But the more interesting outlays were those made to the duke's son and grandson. Although most were what you would expect, Mister Nevins also issued personal cheques to both. Lord Percy's paled in comparison to his son's who was given amounts of five hundred and a thousand pounds on a regular basis."

"To pay off Lord Henry's gambling debts, no doubt," Lily said with a disgusted curl to her lips.

"That's what Mister Nevins intimated. But then I discovered one rather large draft in the amount of 10,000 pounds."

A murmur ran through the room. "That much?" Lily asked aghast.

"Yes. When I questioned Mister Nevins about it, he grew quite perturbed, twitching and mopping his brow. The odd thing was that the transaction did not appear in an appropriate manner in the ledger. It had been added in almost as an afterthought."

"What did he say?" I asked.

"That he didn't recall the particulars."

"Really?" Margaret asked. "Odd, if you ask me, since it was such a large amount."

"Precisely what I thought. So I took it upon myself to visit the duke's bank. Having Sebastian's power of attorney opened those doors. As it turned out, the manager recalled the transaction as the circumstances were quite unusual. Apparently, Lord Henry presented the draft in person and demanded the amount in legal tender."

"That's insane," Lord Marlowe exclaimed. He'd been lounging in his seat, but now sat right up. "Nobody walks about with that much blunt on him. It's an invitation for someone to rob you."

"Precisely. Anyhow, the bank manager told Lord Henry it would take a day to obtain the funds. An excuse he gave to verify the draft. Since he knew Mister Nevins managed that account, he called him. Mister Nevins verified it was true and correct, and Lord Henry should be provided with the funds."

"Something shady's going on with that," Lord Newcastle said, shifting in his seat.

"Yes. Unfortunately, we cannot apply to the one person who would know if he authorized such a large amount be paid to Lord Henry."

"My grandfather," Lily said. "What are you going to do?" she asked Ned.

"Obtain an expert's opinion on the signature. The draft was supposedly signed by the duke. The bank manager informed me anything larger than a thousand pounds needed his personal stamp."

"Very well. We'll have to wait on that then," I noted. "What about the nephew's gambling debts?"

"Just as we thought, they were large indeed. He owed ten thousand pounds at The Silver Slipper."

"Presumably that's why he obtained those funds to pay them off?"

"Which he did. But subsequently, he had a run of bad luck at that same establishment and lost five thousand pounds."

"You'd think he would have learned his lesson," Lily said. "But that's the problem with Henry, he always thinks he will win."

"And now he has no way to pay it off since his grandfather's passed away."

"Precisely."

"No wonder he was so desperate to place Sebastian's succession in doubt," Margaret exclaimed. "Not that it did him any good as we have now firmly established Sebastian is the true heir."

"Right," I said. "What about you, Lord Marlowe? What did you discover at the House of Lords?"

"Plenty. It turns out there's an unofficial committee, which was headed by the duke, to depress liberal notions among the lords. Anytime a progressive measure came up for a vote, they would spring into action and discourage any votes in favor of it. When they heard about the women's march, they plotted a strategy to disrupt the march. Lord Gresham was put in charge of that endeavor."

Just as I'd thought.

"How absolutely appalling," Lady Emma cried out, jumping up from her seat. "Some of the marchers were injured, including Margaret. Those so-called gentlemen should be drawn and quartered."

"I say, Lady Emma, that's a bit harsh, don't you think?" Lord Marlowe asked.

"Is it? Think about what happened, milord. We were marching peacefully, singing the suffragette anthem, proud of our sisterhood. And then those ruffians disrupted our rally. Even though we were innocent of any wrongdoing, we were dragged to the constabulary where arrest documents were compiled against us. Those of us who lead privileged lives can withstand the storm. But what about women who labor for a living? Those charges will be held against them when they seek employment or a place to live. Where's the justice in that?"

"I beg your pardon, Lady Emma. You do have a point," Lord Marlowe said, looking a bit sheepish. I was willing to bet he'd never received such a dressing down before.

"Apology accepted." With a nod, Emma returned to her seat as if nothing unusual had happened.

"There is a ray of hope, you know," Lord Marlowe continued. "Now that Wynchcombe—Lady Lily's brother, I should say—has succeeded to the title, he should be able to disband that committee. Newcastle and I have already discussed it, and we'll back him in that endeavor."

"Thank you," Lily said. "It's good to know he'll have friends at the House of Lords."

"You're most welcome, milady," Lord Marlowe responded. "If I may, there is something I wish to add."

"Of course," I said.

"In large part, Lord Gresham performed those tasks because he owed the duke a large amount of money."

"Gambling again," Lily said disgusted.

"Yes. Every time he, or any of the others agreed to something the duke demanded, their debts were reduced."

"They didn't object to the duke's bidding?" I asked amazed. I certainly would have.

"Apparently not. They were content to do so for they believed the duke would shuffle off this mortal coil soon enough. And at that time, their debts would be deemed paid."

"Do you think they would have been eager to hurry his demise along?" Not the first time that thought had occurred to me.

"From what I've learned, apparently not. They were content to pay what they could when they could. The duke, you see, was in no hurry to collect. He enjoyed having them in his power more than anything else."

"What a despicable person," Margaret exclaimed. "I beg your pardon, Lily."

"No need," Lily responded. "I quite agree with you."

Lord Newcastle, who'd been charged with talking to the Cherubs waiter, reported somebody paid the waiter to serve a particular bottle of wine to Hodgkins and Sebastian. All he could remember of the gentleman was that he was tall and blond. No help there since that matched Sebastian's coloring.

The wine had been more than likely doctored. Unfortunately, there was no way to find out. The bottle had long ago been discarded with the refuse. Nor was Sebastian any help. Lily disclosed he couldn't recall what happened after sitting down to supper.

Margaret and Lady Emma reported that Thomas Hodgkins had attended Oxford at the same time as Sebastian, but he'd forged a friendship with Lord Henry when they'd been at Eton. Apparently, Hodgkins and Lord Henry had been thick as thieves while in school. And curiously, Hodgkins had attended some Oxford university function the weekend Sebastian's rooms had been ransacked.

One question that remained unanswered was the identity of the person who'd requested the Black Rod gate be opened. It wasn't the duke, as he was surprised by the note. But it was somebody familiar with the workings of Westminster. Could it have been Hodgkins? After all, he worked in the Foreign Affairs Committee. But why would he have done such a thing? Would Lord Henry have presumed upon their friendship and asked Hodgkins to do that favor for him? He could very well have which brought us back to Lord Henry.

"Lord Newcastle, were you able to find out the whereabouts of Lord Henry the night of the duke's murder?" A long shot to be sure, for the only place we'd known he'd visited was The Silver Slipper.

"Actually, I was." His mischievous smile should have warned me I was not going to like what he was about to say. "I visited The Silver Slipper at Seven Dials, the gambling den I mentioned before, the one Lord Henry patronizes."

"Yes?" I prompted.

"They mentioned a woman visiting earlier who'd asked the same questions I did. She wanted to know how long Lord Henry was there."

"Did they?"

"They couldn't recall what she looked like, but apparently she stunk of onions and gin. Quite remarkable they remembered that since the area's famous for its repugnant stench."

I shuddered recalling the stink of that night. Although I'd asked Betsy to burn the clothes, it'd taken an entire hour in a tub laced with fragrant oils to remove the stench from my nostrils. But I was not about to allow Newcastle to get the better of me. "If we could move on, milord, to what's important."

"Of course, Miss Worthington," he said with a twinkle in his eye. "Lord Henry remained in the gambling establishment until ten o'clock. He left at that time providing the excuse of an appointment. After spreading some blunt around, I discovered he was meeting his—forgive me, ladies —mistress, a Miss Daisy Todd."

"And did he?"

"She swore on her mother's grave he was with her from a little after ten until the early hours of the morning."

"Did you believe her?"

"Not for a minute. Clearly, she's covering for him."

"Well, thank you for doing such a thorough job, Lord Newcastle."

"My pleasure, Miss Worthington."

"I believe that wraps up all our enquiries."

"What do you want us to do next, Kitty?" Margaret asked.

"Nothing for now. I need to think through what we've discussed. Once I've figured things out, I'll be in touch. Thank you so much for helping with this effort. I know, Sebastian, and Lily, as well, appreciate your assistance."

To my surprise, rather than leave, they convened into groups and continued to discuss the investigation. I did not join them for I had much to consider, and their opinions would only muddle my thoughts. I bid them adieu and left Margaret to carry on.

Once I reached my room, I slipped into my wrap and laid on my bed to think. Clearly, separate avenues of investigation had emerged. One was Lord Henry's need for money. Could he have killed his grandfather in a misguided attempt to get it? That seemed like such a long shot. And yet, events were playing out in his favor. Sebastian had been arrested. If he was found guilty and, heaven forbid, hanged, Lord Percy would become the duke. Lord Henry would have no problem getting the money from him as Lord Percy seemed eager to avoid conflict. But if the information we'd learned from the duchess' maid proved true, Lord Percy could not succeed to the dukedom because he was illegitimate, and by extension, neither could Lord Henry. That was a second matter we needed to explore.

And then there was the matter of the letters. I needed to confirm if the Duchess of Torrance held them in her possession. If she did, had she used them as a weapon against the duke? For what purpose? What could she possibly have demanded from him?

I sighed with frustration. We were caught in a maze comprised of facts, conjectures, wild guesses. I would need to figure a way through to the heart of it. When it came right down to it, there was only one person I trusted to help me make my way, Detective Inspector Robert Crawford. I would need to once more talk things over with him.

CHAPTER TWENTY-SEVEN

KITTY VISITS INSPECTOR CRAWFORD

*R*ATHER THAN WRITE INSPECTOR CRAWFORD, I made an appointment with him. There was too much to explain which could be penned in a letter. Besides, letters could go astray and end up in the wrong hands. And that would be a disaster for I was beginning to think there was something very wrong at Scotland Yard.

It'd been a month since Sebastian's arrest, and yet Inspector Bolton wasn't considering another suspect. According to newspaper reports, he was satisfied he'd gotten his man and was happy to lay the blame for the duke's death at Sebastian's feet. But he was so very wrong for Sebastian could have never done such a thing. But my opinion was not worth so much as a ha'penny. Only incontrovertible proof of his innocence would do. I would need to discover the murderer for Sebastian to be absolved of all guilt.

The night before the meeting I spent tossing and turning

in bed as I'd come to realize I was in over my head. There was simply too much evidence to wade through, too many avenues to investigate. How could I be expected to find my way through that maze to reach the truth at the center? The weight of responsibility lay heavy upon me, but it was too late to cry off. I needed to stiffen my lip and carry on.

Come morning, I glared at the funereal clothes I'd asked Betsy to lay out, the ones I'd worn so many times before. But I couldn't wear them again, not when I was as pale as a ghost. I needed something bright to cheer me up.

After a search through my wardrobe for something that fit the bill, I settled on a a red frock with a dropped waist and a flared skirt. Couldn't get cheerier than that. A black cloche hat and matching gloves completed the stylish look. Needing a bit of color on my face, I tinted my lips and cheeks with a hint of rouge. Mother would most certainly not have approved. But she wouldn't know, as she was off to one of her Ladies Benevolent Society meetings.

I stopped by the library to let Margaret know I was leaving and found her with her nose stuck to yet another legal tome.

"What are you studying?"

She peeked at me over her spectacles. "A treatise on reasonable doubt."

"How very" —boring— "interesting." I forced a cheery tone to my voice.

Her face lit up. "It is. You see, the prosecution must prove beyond a reasonable doubt that Sebastian killed his grandfather. If we can discover sufficient evidence to question his involvement, the jury will find it difficult to declare him guilty. The more proof we can unearth, the better for him."

Well, that was interesting, after all. If we found out who was in possession of those two other daggers, or merely just one, it would provide an alternate suspect. Unfortunately, even if Sebastian were ruled not guilty based on that fact alone, a cloud would still hang over his head. People would think he got away with murder. The only solution was to find his grandfather's killer.

Glancing around, I noticed her fellow musketeer was missing. "Where's Lily?" She was usually to be found near Margaret, unless she was off to the couturier's. And those trips had been temporarily halted because of the swarm of photographers that gathered as soon as word spread she'd been seen entering Angelique's.

"She's visiting Sebastian to inform him about our progress with the investigation."

"Is Ned accompanying her?"

"No. She felt she'd imposed enough on him, so she sent round a note to Lord Marlowe to see if he was available to escort her." An impish smile flitted across her lips. "And, of course, he was."

I laughed. "Clever girl."

Her mien turned serious. "You don't think she's playing one gentleman against another, do you?"

"No. I think she's spreading her wings and getting ready to fly. About time too." Poor Lily had been cooped up long enough. Her foray into the world in the escort of an aristocrat would do her no end of good. The clock on the mantel chimed the hour, sparking awareness of the time. "I better go. Else I'll be late."

She smirked. "And you wouldn't want to keep Inspector Crawford waiting."

I refused to dignify that remark with a comment. "I'll return as soon as I can." I kissed her cheek and, together with Betsy, set off for Scotland Yard.

Upon our arrival, I was once again escorted to the inspector's office, while Betsy remained in the reception area. Not a hardship, for she always thought of a trip to Scotland Yard as a lark.

As always, he came to his feet when I walked into the room. "Miss Worthington."

"Inspector Crawford. Thank you for seeing me. I know how busy you must be." I tried to infuse a bit of cheer into my greeting, but, in the mood I was in, it emerged rather flat.

At least he was splendid, even if I was not. His dark blue suit fitted, rather splendidly, his tall, athletic physique. He'd visited a barber, or maybe his valet had provided the service. Whoever had done it was an expert for it brought the sharp lines of his jaw into prominence. Not that he ever appeared anything less than perfectly groomed.

He pointed to a side table. "I've arranged for tea and seed cake as well."

Tea was fine but, as jittery as I was, food was the last thing I wanted. But I accepted his offer with grace. "How lovely."

After we'd availed ourselves of the refreshments, I summarized what I'd learned from the investigative committee.

"So there were no questionable outlay of funds?"

"Only the draft to his grandson." I fiddled with my gloves which I'd peeled off prior to eating. "And that was used to pay off his debts."

"Only for him to turn around and incur another one."

"Yes." I leaned forward eager to light on something useful. "I know you do not see Lord Henry as the murderer. But with everything's that come to pass, have you given any thought to changing your mind?"

"Too many things would have had to happen for his father to get the title. And as if we learned recently, he may very well not have a right to it."

"But Lord Henry does not know that."

"True. Still, I believe I'm right."

I pressed on. "What about Thomas Hodgkins? Any progress on that front?"

"I have not heard. And if I had, I couldn't discuss it with you."

My hand jerked, accidentally spilling tea over my gown.

He immediately came round and offered his handkerchief. "Here. You wouldn't want your lovely dress to stain."

"Thank you." Taking it from him, I mopped up as best I could. What damage remained Betsy would remove for she had a knack with such things. As I refolded the handkerchief, I noted a rather ornate 'R' surrounded by fancy flourishes on the quality cloth. Not the kind of handkerchief a detective inspector from Scotland Yard would possess. "How beautiful. The embroidery is exquisite."

"It was given to me by a friend," he offered by way of an explanation.

A friend. Had to be a lady, for a gentleman would never gift such a thing to him. My mood went from morose to despondent.

For two months, I'd been making a cake of myself over the inspector, imagining I meant something to him, when all the time there was another woman who presented him with elaborately monogrammed handkerchiefs. I stuffed the accursed linen into my purse. "I'll return it, cleaned and pressed, of course," I said, pinching my lips.

After an odd look in my direction, he reclaimed his seat behind the desk. "You need not worry about Hodgkins. At least not as far as his death is concerned."

"Why do you say that?" I asked, all business.

"Well, for one thing, there isn't enough evidence to connect him with Hodgkins' death."

"What about the witness who saw a yellow-haired man toss a body into the river?"

He dismissed my comment with a wave of his hand. "Any

half-competent barrister will be able to discredit his testimony in court."

"How?"

His lips curved into a grin. "Well, for one thing, the man was three sheets to the wind. And for another, it would have been hard to see clearly through the rain. It could have been anyone tossing something into the river. Why, it could have been Beelzebub himself, and the witness wouldn't have known the difference."

"Beelzebub does not have yellow hair," I protested.

"Seen the devil, have you?" That grin of his made an appearance, and my heart skipped a beat. Why did he have to be so charming?

"No. Of course not."

"Well, there you go. You need not fear a charge will be laid against Mister Dalrymple, at least not for that death."

"You give me cause to hope. At least in that matter." I let out a cleansing breath. "What about Trenton Dalrymple's records? Have you had a chance to look into them?"

"I have requested them from the appropriate office. Don't worry. The Army keeps excellent records. I expect word will come in the next couple of days."

"And then we'll know to whom his belongings were sent."

He nodded. "And just as importantly, an inventory of what was forwarded."

A knock on the door interrupted our conversation.

"Come," Inspector Crawford exclaimed.

A fresh-faced police officer entered with an envelope in his hand. "Begging your pardon, sir, but this only just arrived for you. It's marked urgent."

"Thank you, Constable."

The officer handed the envelope to the inspector, nodded, and left.

After one glance at the missive, Inspector Crawford gazed at me. "It's from the Records Office."

I anxiously waited for him to read what appeared to be the single sheet contained within. It took him but a minute to do so. "His possessions were sent to the Duchess of Wynchcombe. They included letters, other sundry items." His gaze bounced back to me. "And a dagger seven inches long."

I grinned. "Just as I thought. But what could have happened to the dagger? The duchess did not give it to Miss Clemson as she only owned up to the letters."

His face filled with regret. "The answer to that question may be lost in time."

"You'll keep looking, though?" When he appeared ready to deny me, I added, "Please."

"I'll do what I can."

"Thank you. That's all I ask." I pulled out my journal and glanced at the list of issues I wanted to discuss with him. "Have you given any thought to the note delivered to Wynchcombe House? Could it have been dropped in the entrance by someone who resided within?"

"Such as?"

"Mister Nevins. He has been very reluctant to share the duke's personal ledgers with Ned and me. And then there was the matter of that 10,000-pound draft which he didn't recall. Could he have somehow gotten embroiled in that?"

"We'd need proof."

"If we only had the envelope, it could be tested for fingerprints."

"But we don't. The duke took it with him, and it wasn't listed in the medical examiner's report along with the other contents found in the duke's possession. I checked."

"Did you really? Wouldn't that have gotten you into trouble? After all, it's not your case."

He shrugged. "Someone in the medical examiner's office owed me a favor."

Even so, wouldn't Inspector Crawford prefer to save the boon for one of his investigations, rather than someone else's? A question with no answer, at least for the moment.

"The question boils down to that note," he continued. "What would have sent the duke running to an appointment so late at night?"

"Knowing what we know? I'd say somebody found out Lord Percy was not his son and was threatening . . . something."

"Not money since there were no out of the ordinary withdrawals."

Another question with no answer. "And then there's the matter of the private letters between the duchess and Trenton Dalrymple? Are they in the Duchess of Torrance's possession?"

He waited for me to state the obvious.

"The longer I consider that question the more certain I am that she has them."

"Very good, Miss Worthington. You'll make an investigator yet."

I bristled at that remark. "I am an investigator."

He chuckled softly to himself.

In the end, I left with my head spinning, theories upon theories, facts with no clear path ahead. As things stood, we didn't have any evidence that clearly pointed to one person or persons. And, unfortunately, time was running out. Although the date of the trial had not been set, we expected it to be very soon.

I was so deep into my thoughts I failed to realize the swarm of reporters waiting outside Scotland Yard. And not only reporters, but photographers as well. Since I'd become a noted figure during the Rose Trevvyan case, some immediately recognized me as soon as I reached the street. Questions were hurled at me; photographs were snapped. In a panic, I hooked my arm around Betsy's and dragged her toward Westminster where I managed to hail a cab. But it proved too late. The damage was already done.

CHAPTER TWENTY-EIGHT

NEWSPAPERS EXPLODE WITH THE NEWS

*W*E WERE ENJOYING OUR USUAL FAMILY BREAKFAST when Carlton entered the dining room. Glancing neither left nor right, he walked straight to Father and presented a salver on which a news-paper rested.

I took a deep breath and waited for the hammer to fall. It didn't take long.

"Not again!" Father exclaimed.

"What's wrong?" Mother asked, alarm clear on her face.

He glared at me. "Is it too much to ask that one week go by without one of my daughters making front page news?"

"Oh, dear," Mother said. "Edward, try to calm down. You know what an upset does to your digestion."

He took in a breath, a second one, before he addressed me once more. "Would you care to explain this, this . . .?" He jabbed the paper without finishing his thought.

I desperately sought of a way out and settled upon the

most logical one. "As I haven't read the paper, Father, I can't possibly comment."

"Don't play silly buggers with me, young lady. You know very well what it is. You at Scotland Yard," he read from the paper, "conspiring with an inspector, interfering with an investigation." He fixed me with a hard stare. "Making a nuisance of yourself."

"It doesn't say all that, does it?" I asked, somewhat sheepishly, for I hadn't meant to anger him with my remark.

"It might as well. The insinuation is there. What were you doing at Scotland Yard?"

I hitched up my chin. "I was consulting an officer of the law."

"Who? As if I didn't know."

"Detective Inspector Robert Crawford."

"Not him again. That man is nothing but—"

"Helpful, Father. He's been very helpful." I could not allow Father to malign the man who'd been instrumental in advancing our knowledge of the facts.

His gaze bounced to Mother. "Did you know about this meeting, Mildred?"

"Yes," Mother answered, calmly buttering a piece of toast. "Kitty had my permission, and my approval, to consult Inspector Crawford."

His brows hiked up. "Why would you allow her to do such a thing?"

"Because we need his expertise to guide us with our inquiries. Surely, you can see that, Edward, since you're in a similar position. After all, people come to you to manage their funds. Your vast investment experience and knowledge are par to none."

"Well, harumph, you do have a point," he said, somewhat mollified.

"I'm glad you agree." She'd done a rather neat job of buttering him up as well as she had the toast.

In a much mellower tone, Father addressed me, "Did you interfere with the investigation into the duke's murder?"

"No. I did not. Inspector Bolton oversees that matter, and I did not talk with him."

"I'm sure dear Kitty did nothing inappropriate," Mother offered. "Newspapers write those lurid headlines to sell more copies. And as we all know, Edward, they blow things out of proportion. Only remember what they wrote about Ned."

He glanced at the paper once more. "I'm afraid this time some of it is the truth."

"What do you mean?" I asked. Had they found out about my journey to Winchester in the company of Inspector Crawford? Heaven help me if they had.

"It mentions Ned's trip to Scotland and the inappropriateness of Lily traveling with him."

Lily grew pale and bowed her head.

Now we were in the soup. It was one thing to discuss the Worthingtons. Having been raked over the coals before, we knew how to handle the notoriety. But Lily had no experience with that sort of thing. No wonder she was upset. "What else does it say?" I asked.

"It claims Sebastian is illegitimate—"

"What?" Margaret rushed over and grabbed the newspaper from him. She was not gentle about it, either.

While she read the article in question, her face heated up. "It says Kitty visited Scotland Yard to try and hush it up," Margaret said, "and hints at a bribe. How dare they?"

"I did no such thing!" Now it was my turn to snatch the paper from Margaret's hand. A quick read confirmed what Father and Margaret had said. "The nerve of those people. We should sue for slander."

"It's libel, Kitty, not slander," Margaret corrected me.

"Whatever it is, we need to take legal action against them," I exclaimed. "I'm tired of our family becoming fodder for every scurrilous rag in town."

"I'll consider it," Father said. "Right now, I need to determine the extent of the damage. I'll be at the office. If some other disaster unfolds, you may reach me there." After a quick peck to Mother's cheek, he marched out.

Goodness! He was in a mood.

Lily quietly approached me. "May I read it?"

"Of course," Handing the paper to her, I asked Mother, "What do you think we should do?"

"Go on as usual. We've survived slings and arrows before. We'll weather this storm as well."

"Well, I for one, am not taking it lying down," Margaret exclaimed, a militant light in her eye. I knew that look. It did not augur well.

"What are you going to do, dear?" Mother appeared rather unperturbed. Just as well. Someone in the family needed to keep her head.

"Write a strongly worded letter to the editor," Margaret answered.

"Wouldn't it be better to wait for the tempest to blow over? It will, you know. In time."

"Unfortunately, Mother, we don't have that luxury."

But Margaret's missive only made matters worse. If there had been a chance things would settle down, her message, printed on the newspaper's front page, scuttled it. It was the worst possible time for it to happen, too, since that very day we received word Sebastian's trial was to be held in ten days.

Things were downright dark and dreary in the Worthington Household. Even Sir Winston was feeling the strain. When I found him moping in the kitchen, turning up his nose at everything that was bad for him, I decided enough was enough. He needed a walk in the park, and I needed a respite from it all. At least for a little while.

A rare London day, sunny and cloudless, beckoned. I'd brought a book to read while Sir Winston gamboled with the squirrels. Even though he was a Bassett Hound, when properly motivated, Betsy could barely keep up with him. But my mind was in such disarray, the words made no sense. And soon, I gave up on the fruitless endeavor.

I'd just closed my eyes and leaned back my head to soak in the sun when I heard Betsy yell, "Bad boy, very bad boy."

Heavens! "What did Sir Winston do now?" I feared to find out.

"Why nothing at all, ma'am." A voice from my right replied.

Shading my eyes from the glare, I glanced toward the owner of the voice. A gentleman stood not far. In his late forties would be my guess, nattily dressed in a dark suit and wearing a bowler hat. He carried a fat cigar in his hand.

"I beg your pardon," I said.

"You seemed to blame me for something. What, I have no idea as I've done nothing wrong. At least not in the last five minutes."

His face looked familiar, but I was sure I'd never met him.

"I was referring to my—"

Sir Winston cut across our path, dragging my harried maid behind. As usual, he was chasing a squirrel.

"Sir Winston, stop," Betsy yelled, but the hound was on a mission and would not heed her command.

The man chuckled. "A hound, ma'am. You named a hound after me?"

"No, I—" The penny dropped. "Oh, heavens, you're Sir Winston Churchill, the Secretary of . . . something," I finished lamely.

"Secretary of State for the Colonies," he chuckled again.

"Not anymore, my dear." He pointed to the bench. "May I join you?"

"Yes, of course, sir. What do you mean not anymore?"

"I no longer hold that position. Nor am I a Member of Parliament at the moment. I'm writing my memoirs instead. Must keep busy and all that." His gaze bounced my way. "I've led a rather interesting life, if I say so myself."

"How splendid. I look forward to reading it."

"Thank you, my dear. Now what is a beautiful young lady like you doing all alone in a park?"

"Sir Winston" —I giggled— "the family's Bassett Hound, needed a walk and he loves the park so."

He took a puff from the cigar and blew the cloud away from me. "Somehow I sense that's not the whole story."

"Well, our family is in rather a pickle at the moment."

"How so?"

I explained about Sebastian, the duke's murder, the investigation, ending with the newspapers' muckraking.

He belted out a hearty laugh. "And here I thought my life was interesting."

"At the moment, I wish ours was less so."

"If I may give you one word of advice?"

"Please do."

"If you're going through hell, keep going."

I laughed so hard, tears rolled down my face. "How very apropos."

"It's stood me in good stead. Remember tough times don't last, tough people do." He took a moment to scrutinize me. "I think that's what you are. Tough."

"Thank you, sir. I shall remember that."

Nodding, he came to his feet. "Well, I better go. Clemmie must be wondering where I am."

"Clemmie?"

"Mrs. Churchill. Put her through the ropes. But she's

stuck by me. A good woman. A tough woman. Just like you. A pleasure to make your acquaintance." He duffed his hat and went on his way.

"Miss," Betsy arrived out of breath, a panting hound by her side, "do you think we may go back now? Sir Winston has gotten enough exercise."

And so had she. "Yes, Betsy, I do believe he has." In a much lighter frame of mind, I returned home. Good thing because what came next tested every ounce of my abilities.

CHAPTER TWENTY-NINE

ANOTHER VISIT TO WYNCHCOMBE HOUSE

*A*S SOON AS I RETURNED HOME FROM THE PARK, I retrieved my journal and reviewed all the information I'd written therein. Clearly, I would need to discover if the Duchess of Torrance had those letters in her possession. But I couldn't simply ask her. I'd need some evidence to back up my suspicion.

At the inquest, the butler Temple had hesitated when asked if there were any identifying marks on the envelope the duke had received. He'd testified he hadn't noticed any, but I suspected that was not the truth. He'd lied to protect someone, more than likely the Duchess of Torrance. I needed to talk with him again.

Since Lily had to be the one to request the meeting, I went in search of her. She was in her room quietly reading, although I suspected she was making no more headway into the book than I had with mine. When I explained what I wanted from her, she quickly agreed. But then she expressed a desire to accompany me. This I could not allow. Some of the discussion would be about her, and I did not wish her to become more upset than she already was. She gave in with grace and promptly sent a note to Mister Temple. Within an hour, he replied, and the meeting was set for the next day.

As before, he welcomed me graciously with yet another grand spread—scones, seed cake, and, of course the ubiquitous tea.

I could float a galleon with the volume of that beverage I'd drunk in the last fortnight. But one had to be polite, so I took a sip. "Thank you for agreeing to see me, Mister Temple."

"My pleasure, Miss Worthington. As I said before, I'm entirely at your service."

Hopefully, he was being honest because his offer was about to be tested. I retrieved the journal from my purse and reviewed the questions I wished to ask him. "Do you recall your testimony at the inquest?"

He seemed somewhat taken aback by my query but answered nevertheless, "I do."

"Wonderful." I followed my remark with a smile as I didn't wish him to turn hostile. "When the coroner asked you whether there were any identifying marks on the envelope," I said, reading from my journal, "you said you didn't notice any." I gazed straight at him. "I got the feeling that was not so."

"There was no name on the envelope other than the Duke of Wynchcombe's."

"Come, sir, I know prevarication when I hear it. You knew who sent that envelope, didn't you?"

His shoulders stiffened. "How could I when the name of the sender was missing?" he asked, all beetle-browed.

"Because you'd seen similar envelopes in the past. The party involved would have sent invitations and other messages to the duke, for they had known each other for a long time."

"I . . . don't know what to say."

"Mister Temple," I softened my voice, "I think you're trying to protect someone. But that will never do. Don't you see? The truth must come out, else the Duke of Wynch-combe, Sebastian Dalrymple, may very well hang from the wrong end of a rope. He's innocent. Of that, I can assure you."

I waited an eternity for him to speak. Finally, something seemed to ease in him, and he capitulated. "The envelope bore the Torrance crest."

"Ahh, I thought so. And I hazard to guess that it was not the only envelope the duke received that bore that mark?"

"No. As you have stated, there were numerous communi-cations, for his graces had been friends of long standing. Invitations to card parties were a regular occurrence."

Now that the flood had opened, I pressed my advantage. "Did the Duchess of Torrance ever visit the duke?"

"Yes. About two years ago when Lady Lily arrived. The Duchess of Torrance wished to sponsor her debut, you see."

"But his grace would not agree."

"Sadly, no. He had another, er, purpose for her."

"Yes, Lady Lily told us. He wanted to marry her off to someone with a fat purse and a title," I snapped out.

He cleared his throat. "That was apparently so. Her Grace protested such ill use of Lady Lily, but the duke would not budge from his chosen course of action."

"Of course not. He never allowed anyone else's opinion to interfere with his plans." Wrongheaded, misogynistic, arro-gant male that he'd been. "Did the Duchess of Torrance give up?"

He shook his head. "No. She kept trying to convince him, visited every other month. Earlier this year, he barred her entrance. Told us under no circumstances should she be allowed into the house." His whole frame stiffened. "That was an extremely difficult thing to do. One simply does not bar a duchess from entering a household."

"I'm so sorry you were forced into that situation," I commiserated with him. "Did the duchess accept the edict?"

"Yes. She left and never returned." He paused for a moment. "But something changed after that."

"What do you mean?"

"She started sending him letters. When he opened those envelopes, he'd laugh and toss them away. But one day, not too long ago, he received a message. And this time, he didn't laugh, he cursed. Begging your pardon, Miss."

"When did this happen?"

"About six weeks ago. All the envelopes bore the Torrance crest."

"Including the one that drove him out the night of his death?"

"Yes."

Irrefutable proof the Duchess of Torrance had sent that note. The problem was I didn't believe it. I could not see the duchess making an assignation at night with the duke in a garden off Westminster. She would have demanded he come to her house. And she certainly did not have the strength to plunge a dagger into the duke's black heart. No. Somebody else had managed to get his hands on her stationery and masquerade as her. And that required another visit to Torrance House. But first I had at least another person to interview.

"Thank you, Mister Temple, for your candor. You have been most helpful. Now I would like to talk to those staff members responsible for the upkeep of Mister Nevins' office and the surrounding area."

"That would be Martha. She's our downstairs maid, probably enjoying her tea about now, along with the rest of the staff. I'll need to explain what's required of her before she talks to you. If you'll excuse me, I'll go find her."

"Of course." I nodded.

While he was gone, I wrote down everything I'd learned. The duchess had been eager to sponsor Lily and tried to convince the duke to allow her to do just that. He'd turned down her offer but she'd pressed on, often visiting the duke. When she'd been denied entrance, she'd sent numerous notes. At first, the duke had laughed at them, but then the duke's reaction changed. More than likely after she received the letters from the Earl of Clarendon. Had she tried to blackmail him with those letters? Had she demanded Lily be allowed to make her debut or she would reveal the truth about Lord Percy's birth? I would need to find out.

I was so busy jotting down my thoughts, I failed to realize someone had entered the room. Someone who was not Temple.

"Miss Worthington," a silky-smooth voice declared.

My gaze bounced up. The so-called gentleman who faced me was no longer dressed as nattily as before. His tie was askew, his clothes were not clean and pressed. Furthermore, he seemed to be literally drunk as a lord.

"Lord Henry." I didn't bother rising and curtsying to him. He didn't deserve it.

"What the blazes are you doing here?" His lip curled with disdain. "Oh, let me guess. Prying?"

"I have some questions for the Wynchcombe House staff, yes."

"You and your family are a pain in my backside, putting your beak where it doesn't belong." He advanced into the room, his entire being hostile in the extreme.

I rose, for if there was something I'd learned from my

self-defense training, you could not fend off an assailant from a sitting position.

"Somebody has to help Sebastian. As opposed to you, milord."

"Why should I bother? He doesn't deserve the title. It should have come to my father, not him."

"The law says otherwise. He's been declared the Duke of Wynchcombe. And nothing you do or say can change that."

His lip curled once more. "Really? If he's found guilty and hanged, my father will become the duke."

I could tell him otherwise, but he was riled up enough as it was. "That's not going to happen. We have discovered enough evidence to raise the issue of reasonable doubt. A jury of his peers will find it difficult to find him guilty."

"What evidence?"

"Well, for one, there is the the issue that no one saw him near the duke that night."

He sneered. "A witness at the inquest testified a yellow-haired gentleman was seen around Westminster."

"He also reported that the gentleman was dressed like a toff. That description would describe you more than Sebastian as he doesn't possess any fashionable attire."

Fear flashed on his face. "Why you—" He bared his teeth and came after me.

But I was more than ready for him. I picked up the silver tea pot and beaned him on the side of his head. He stumbled, blinked, and crashed to the floor. Unconscious.

"Miss Worthington!" Temple stood by the open door, a wide-eyed maid next to him.

"Mister Temple," I remarked calmly. "Lord Henry seems to have, er, taken a faint. I suspect it's all the drinking he's been doing. He rather smells like a brewery."

"Is he breathing?" he asked, a note of alarm in his voice.

I observed Lord Henry's chest rise and fall. "Quite."

He appeared much relieved. "I'll ask our footmen to attend to him."

I held up the teapot. "Some more tea would not go amiss." Especially since a fair amount of it had spilled over the, more than likely, priceless carpet. Sebastian would forgive me as the damage had been done in the exercise of a good cause.

"Of course, Madam. Right away." Temple bowed before introducing the young woman next to him. This is Martha, the downstairs maid. I've explained what she needs to do."

"Splendid." I smiled at the servant for I didn't wish her to get the wrong idea about me.

Martha and I waited in silence while the footmen and Temple removed the refuse. A fresh pot of tea arrived shortly after.

"Please sit, Martha." I pointed to the seat across from me. "No need to stand."

"Yes, Miss." She rushed to do my bidding.

"I only have a few questions, so no need to be nervous."

She nodded, shoulders tight, her body stiff as a board.

I had my doubts I'd get anything out of her, but I soldiered on. "Now, your duties include cleaning Mister Nevins' office and the surrounding area. Is that correct?"

"Yes, Miss."

"Marvelous." She was wound up tighter than a wind-up toy. Maybe some sustenance would ease the way.

"I apologize, but did I interrupt your afternoon tea?"

"Umm, well." She shrugged.

"I did. How horrid of me. And here we have a perfectly lovely spread. Would you care for some?"

She looked at me with shock. "Oh, no, Miss. I shouldn't. That service is for quality, not staff."

"Who'll know? I won't tell, if you don't." I winked and shared a conspiratorial smile with her. "Go on. Help yourself."

She glanced over her shoulder, probably to assure herself Temple had not returned. And then poured tea into one of the porcelain cups.

"Try the scones. They're delicious." I pushed the platter toward her.

She placed one on a plate before gently taking a bite. It took her a few more seconds to finally relax.

"Now, Martha. I'm particularly interested in anything you may have seen or heard in the days before the duke's unfortunate demise." I bowed my head as in respect. She did the same. Once the proprieties had been observed, I asked, "Were there any conversations you may have overheard of a fractious nature? A row if you will?"

When she hesitated, I again urged the scones on her. "Take another."

Grinning, she helped herself. "Ta, Miss."

"You are most welcome."

Once she was done with the second scone, she sipped some of the tea. At this rate, it would take the rest of the afternoon to learn anything from her. "Mister Nevins?" I prompted.

"Yes, Miss. I did overhear a row. I wasn't trying to listen in, mind you. I would never do that."

"Of course not." She probably had her ear glued to the wall, as any self-respecting servant would.

"A couple of days before the duke's passing" —She bowed her head. I did as well— "I heard a right ole tiff between himself and Mister Nevins."

"What were they arguing about?"

"A bank draft, Miss. One had gone missing, and the duke wanted to know where it was."

"Really?" The duke would keep close tabs on bank drafts. He was a miser, after all.

"Yes, Miss. He was that upset. I never heard so much yelling."

I waited until she poured herself more tea and grabbed another scone. While she was munching, I asked, "What did Mister Nevins say?"

She swallowed hard. "He said he was sorry and would look into it. And then the duke stormed out. Almost knocked me on me pins, he did."

"Anything else?"

She sipped her tea. Gossiping was thirsty work, after all. "The next day, I was polishing the credenza outside Mister Nevins' office. The one right below the horse portrait."

They had portraits of horses. Amazing. But I guessed when they ran out of ancestors, something else was needed to hang on their walls. "Mr. Nevins and the duke again?"

"No, Miss. Mister Nevins and Lord Henry." The way she spit out his name told me what she thought of him. "They were arguing something fierce." She lowered her voice. "Mister Nevins was accusing Lord Henry of stealing a bank draft."

"Really?"

"Yes, Miss. And not only that. He said he'd had to lie for him and now his position was preca—preca—"

"Precarious."

She brightened up. "Yes. That's the one. What does that mean?"

"The duke was thinking about letting him go."

She turned misty-eyed. "Oh, that would have been downright awful. He has a wife and five little ones to feed."

"Awful indeed." Mister Nevins may not have been the pleasantest of individuals, but he didn't deserve to lose his position because Lord Henry had stolen a bank draft. But he'd also lied to cover it up. Something the duke would have never forgiven if he'd known. "Anything more?"

"No, Miss. I had to leave." Her face pinked up. "Nature called. By the time I returned, Lord Henry had gone."

Unfortunate she hadn't heard the end of that discussion, but I'd learned enough. "You did very well, Martha. Thank you for sharing your confidences with me."

"You're welcome, Miss. And if I may be so bold?"

"Of course."

A light came into her eyes. "I'm glad you knocked out Lord Henry. He's a devil, that one."

Just like his grandfather. I nodded toward the table. "Why don't you take the rest of the food? I won't be eating it."

"Ta, Miss." Coming to her feet, she wrapped up what remained of the scones and the entire seed cake in two of the huge napkins and tucked them away.

"If you could let Mister Temple know I need a last word with him," I requested once she was done.

Her gaze grew fearful. "You won't tell him what I said?"

"No, Martha." I pressed her hands. "I won't tell."

She curtsied and scampered off, her pockets bulging with food.

A few minutes later, Mister Temple returned, a placid look on his face.

"Miss Worthington." He bowed. "Is there anything else you desire?"

"No, thank you. Did Lord Henry recover from his faint?" I hadn't hit him hard enough to cause serious damage. Still, I wished to be assured of his wellbeing.

"He's departed, Miss. Hale and hearty. When he came awake from his, er, faint, all he wanted was to leave, as speedily as possible."

"That's good to hear." I stood. "I will mention your stellar cooperation to the duke."

He bowed again. "You are all graciousness, ma'am." Mister

Temple would make Sebastian and Lily a loyal and steadfast retainer.

I took my leave, for I was eager to get home so I could organize my thoughts. But, alas, that was not to be accomplished as quickly as I wished.

As soon as I arrived, I was accosted by Margaret. Lily was not far behind as she was just as anxious to hear what I'd discovered. By necessity, I gave them a somewhat edited version, for I couldn't reveal what I'd learned from Temple. But I did share my conversation with Martha and my interlude with Lord Henry which they particularly appreciated.

They both came to the same conclusions I had. Lord Henry had stolen a blank bank draft which he used to pay himself 10,000 pounds. And Mister Nevins had committed a wrong as well. Instead of owning up to the lost draft, he'd lied to the bank manager which put his position in jeopardy. Once the duke discovered the transgression, as he seemed likely to do, he would most certainly have fired Mister Nevins.

Would he have killed the duke to prevent that from happening? After all, he had a family who depended on him. And what about Lord Henry? He'd stolen money from his grandfather. Would the duke have allowed the theft without inflicting punishment? I doubted it, for the Duke of Wynchcombe had been a singularly unpleasant individual. He would have made Lord Henry's life miserable, at the very least.

The facts I'd learned today, and the conclusions which could be drawn from them, could be employed to convince a jury reasonable doubt existed. But we still had to account for the dagger. Without that bit of knowledge everything else could be ignored. And for that, I would need to talk with the Duchess of Torrance. She was in possession of the letters. Of that, I had no doubt. But had she also been sent the dagger? That was a question I would need to put to her.

"We have some news of our own to share," Margaret said glancing at Lily. When Lily hesitated, she urged her on. "Tell her."

"Viscount Tottingham has withdrawn his offer of marriage."

"Well, hallelujah. One less thing to worry about." She appeared worried, though.

"What's wrong? You didn't secretly wish to marry him?"

"No, of course not. I never could have. Thing is, the papers and the notoriety." She glanced down to fiddle with her fingers. "They've branded me a 'fallen woman.'"

"No! Which one?"

"*The Tell-All*," Margaret said, putting a piece of scone in her mouth. "I've explained to Lily nobody pays any attention to that scurrilous rag."

"Some people do, Margaret," Lily said. "You may not wish to marry, but I do. I want a family, children, a husband."

I sat on the other side of Lily and wrapped my arm around her shoulders. "Dearest, Margaret is right. People read those papers for the scandal. The rest take it with a grain of salt. They make up lies all the time. With your beauty and your pedigree, once you make your debut, well, you'll be beating them off with a stick. I mean, just look at Lord Marlowe. He seems quite taken with you."

"He's not serious about marriage, Kitty. He enjoys the thrill of the chase more than anything else." She gazed at me with a light in her eyes. "I'm not a horse."

Fighting back a grin, I pressed her hands. "No, you're not. But honestly, Lily, you have nothing to worry about. Trust me, I know."

But the doubt never left her face.

CHAPTER THIRTY

KITTY VISITS THE DUCHESS OF TORRANCE
AGAIN

"*T*HANK YOU FOR AGREEING TO THIS MEETING, YOUR GRACE." Once more I was to be found in the Duchess of Torrance's drawing room. I'd sent round a note the day before, and she'd graciously consented to meet with me today.

"I was glad to do so, my dear, as I was anxious to discover if you'd interpreted my note correctly."

"I did. Edith Clemson was quite forthcoming about the Duchess of Wynchcombe."

She sighed. "She was very close to Sophie. So it doesn't surprise me her maid would know her secrets."

"Not only did Miss Clemson know the duchess's secrets, but she was entrusted with some letters which spoke of those confidences."

"I know." She stood and wandered about the room. To me it seemed as if she was making up her mind as to what she would say. Having reached a conclusion, she turned back to me. "When she lay dying, Sophie handed them to Edith for safekeeping with instructions to send them to her brother, the Earl of Clarendon. He knew those letters had to be kept safe while the maid lived. They were Miss Clemson's protection against the Duke of Wynchcombe, you see."

"But things changed a few months ago when the Earl of Clarendon passed away."

"He'd been ill for a long time."

"Just so. When he knew his time was coming, he must have realized the letters needed to be forwarded to someone he trusted, someone who would keep them safe." I took a deep breath. "I can't help but think that person was you."

She returned to the cerulean settee. Softly smiling, she said, "You're a very bright young woman, Miss Worthington."

I knew prevarication when I heard it, and I was no longer willing to suffer it. Time was running out. "Do you have them in your possession?"

"I do."

I took a deep breath and let it out. Finally, I was getting the answers I sought. "Did the Duke of Wynchcombe know?"

"He did. I wrote him about them. Told him exactly what they contained."

"What did you hope to gain from doing such a thing?" I knew, but I had to hear it from her.

"That he'd end the engagement to Viscount Tottingham he'd forced on Lily. That alliance offended my every sense. No, it was more than that; it sickened me when I heard." She retrieved a handkerchief from the depths of her dress and, with a trembling hand, raised it to her lips. It took her a few moments to regain her calm. "I'd seen what he'd done to Sophie. I couldn't stand by and watch her granddaughter suffer the same fate."

"That's when you wrote him?"

"About this, yes. I'd sent other notes before and met with him as well. I'd offered to sponsor Lily for her debut, you see. But he wouldn't allow it. He said he had another purpose for her that didn't include her being introduced to society."

"I see. So, when did you mention the letters?"

"After our ball. That's when the engagement announcement was printed in the papers, as you know, Miss Worthington."

"Yes, I do."

"I tried to be politic about it. Informed him I had them in my possession, told them what they contained. At the start, I said nothing more. But when he ignored my pleas, I grew more forceful."

"What do you mean?"

The handkerchief was used again. "I told him, God help me, that I would make those letters public if he didn't call off the engagement."

"He refused?"

"Yes." Her fiery gaze found me again. "He didn't think I would publish them."

"Would you have?"

Her shoulders slumped. "No. They would have hurt Lord Percy. And Wynchcombe would have retaliated by marrying Lady Lily off anyway. But I wrote one last letter, or started to, anyway."

"What do you mean?"

"A couple of days before he was killed, I started to write a note right there on that desk." She pointed to the escritoire in the room. "I was interrupted by a caller, my granddaughter as it turned out. She had a masked ball to attend and wanted to rummage through a trunk in the attic. She wanted to dress as Marie Antoinette. She knew I'd once dressed up as her and had a costume. After we located it and she went happily on her way, I returned to find the note was gone."

"Do you have any idea what happened to it?"

"I searched all around, called in the footman who was on duty on the hallway. He said only the duke and the duke's man entered the drawing room."

"Did you ask your husband about it?"

"I couldn't. He knew nothing about the letters or my notes to Wynchcombe. If I'd asked, I would have had to reveal the entire distasteful business. And then Wynchcombe was murdered, and Lady Lily fled to you for sanctuary. The entire affair became moot at that point. And yet . . ."

"And yet?" I prompted.

"I can't help but feel I was partly responsible for his death. The papers said he was lured to that place of death by a note." Her gaze had a tortured look about it. "What if someone took my half-written letter, changed it somehow, and sent it to him?"

That supposition appeared likely since Temple admitted the note bore the Torrance crest. "How did you have the other notes delivered, your Grace?"

"My maid. She's totally loyal to me. She would never breathe a word about them."

"And the only persons who came into the room were your husband and his man? Meaning his valet?"

"That's what the footman said."

"Would you consider bringing him in? It's important that we find out exactly what he saw."

"No, of course not." She came to her feet and pulled the bell. When the butler arrived, she asked him to have John step into the room.

It took but a few minutes for a tall, strapping young man dressed in the Torrance livery to enter the room. "Your Grace. How may I be of service?"

"John, you remember when I asked you some weeks ago if anyone had come into the drawing room?"

"Yes, Your Grace. I remember vividly."

"Could you please explain it again?" She nodded toward me. "Miss Worthington may have a few questions.

"Of course, Your Grace. I was stationed in the hallway. As was my duty that afternoon." He faced me. "We take turns."

"Of course," I said.

"His Grace arrived from his club. He was handing me his outer garments when there was a knock on the door. I excused myself to attend to it. It was a gentleman, the duke's man."

Well, that was confusing. "I'm sorry. I do not understand."

"He came to call on His Grace. A previously arranged appointment, as I understood."

"Why would His Grace's valet need to make an appointment with him?"

John blinked rapidly for several seconds. "I beg your pardon. It wasn't the Duke of Torrance's valet, it was the Duke of Wynchcombe's man, at least that's what he said."

"The Duke of Wynchcombe's man?" the duchess asked. "Did he provide his name?"

"Yes. Mister Nevins."

Light was beginning to glimmer. "What happened then?"

"His Grace led him into the drawing room and closed the door. About fifteen minutes later, the duke's man—Mister Nevins—walked out and left. His Grace proceeded upstairs to his room."

"How did His Grace seem?" the duchess asked.

"Why his usual self."

"He didn't appear upset?" It was my turn to inquire.

"No, Miss."

"Thank you, John," the duchess said. "That will be all." Once he was gone, she asked, "What do you make of that?"

"I think Mister Nevins somehow found your half-written

note and took it for his own purposes. I can only imagine what he did with it."

"You think that was the note that lured Wynchcombe to that garden to be murdered?"

"I think it's a possibility. A strong possibility."

"But why would he want to kill Wynchcombe?"

I could tell her, but I felt it would be best to keep that information to myself for the moment. "That is a good question." Right now, I needed to discover the purpose of Mister Nevins' visit. "Do you have any idea why Mister Nevins would have had an appointment with your husband?"

Her brow furrowed. "Unfortunately, it wasn't the first time they'd met. You see, Torrance loved matching wits against his old friend in a game of cards. He probably lost, and Mister Nevins came to obtain the bank draft. He's done that more times than I care to count."

"Your husband wouldn't have paid the night he lost?"

She stiffened. "We don't deal in cash, Miss Worthington. Mister Nevins collects the draft, presents it to the duke's bank, and the amount is transferred."

She belonged to a generation who believed ready money never exchanged hands. It was always handled as a distant transaction. Unfortunately, that could lead to funds being stolen, as Lord Henry had done. But that was something to be discussed another day. Today, I needed to discover everything there was to learn about the Duchess of Wynchcombe's correspondence. "What will you do with the letters?"

"I suppose the best thing would be to burn them."

"I wouldn't if I were you. They might be needed as proof."

"As to what?"

"As to the impetus of what drew the duke to the garden in the first place."

"I could never make them public. Not now. They would hurt Lord Percy beyond belief."

"You might have no such option. The choice could come to hurting Lord Percy or condemning Sebastian to the gallows."

"If it comes to that, and only if it comes to that, I will hand them over to Scotland Yard."

"Unfortunately, the letters by themselves will not clear Sebastian. We need to find another dagger. Perchance, was one forwarded to you along with the letters?"

She shook her head. "No." Her gaze narrowed. "Are you telling me there was another one?"

"There should be at least two more." I explained the tradition of the dagger ceremony when one was awarded by every Duke of Wynchcombe to each of his sons. Since all the previous daggers would have been buried with their owners, the only ones in existence would be the ones belonging to Wynchcombe himself and to Trenton Dalrymple, his cousin, as well as the ones given to Lord Percy and Sebastian's father.

"That's extraordinary. I never heard of such a ceremony."

"Sophie never shared that information with you?"

"No."

So, I was down to the last piece of information I needed—the locations of the two missing daggers. Something I would need to figure out by myself, for I could no longer consult Inspector Crawford. My notoriety over my last visit to Scotland Yard precluded another visit.

At least now my choices had come down to Mister Nevins or Lord Henry. And I had enough evidence to damn them both.

"You have provided much for me to consider, Your Grace. Thank you for your candor."

She reached across the table and pressed my hands. "Miss Worthington, if you need anything, anything at all, please don't hesitate to contact me. I could not bear for Sophie's grandson to be condemned to death."

Unfortunately, it might very well be another grandson who would suffer that fate. But I couldn't share that with her, at least not now. "Thank you." I said goodbye and went on my way.

As the Rolls traversed the driveway of the stately home, I leaned back against the seat of the Rolls and rested my eyes. I was so close to identifying the murderer, and yet, I had a niggling doubt that I'd missed something, something important. When I arrived home, I would review my notes and hopefully discover what it was.

Unfortunately, it was not to be. During my absence, chaos had erupted at Worthington House.

CHAPTER THIRTY-ONE

LILY SUFFERS A CALAMITY

*T*HE GATE AT WORTHINGTON HOUSE WAS LOCKED. How very odd.

"What's happening?" I asked mostly myself as Neville, our chauffeur, wouldn't know any more than I would.

But he answered, nevertheless. "I don't know, Miss, but I'll get it open in a tick." He jumped out of the Rolls and, in no time at all, unlocked it. As our chauffeur, he carried the key with him.

While we rounded the fountain in the center of the driveway, I caught sight of two motorcars parked in front of the house. One was faintly familiar and the other—That was Doctor Crawley's vehicle! What was our physician doing here? Had someone grown ill or suffered an injury?

As soon as the vehicle rolled to a stop, I rushed up the stairs. Carlton was not at the entrance, but one of our footmen was. "What's going on?"

"Best go to the drawing room, Miss. The family is there."

I scurried in that direction to find Margaret and Mother sitting side by side on the sofa, both of whom appeared distraught. Strangely enough, Father and Ned were also present. Neither should be here this time of day. One person was missing, though, from this tableau.

"Where's Lily?"

"Oh, Kitty," Mother said. "She's been taken."

My thought immediately flew to Viscount Tottingham. But that couldn't be. He'd broken off their engagement. "I don't understand. Who's taken her?"

"We don't know," Margaret said. "She's been kidnapped."

Dear heaven! "How? Why?" I didn't even know what to ask.

"Sit, dear," Mother pointed to a chair. "Have some tea." Mother's solution for everything. But this time, it wouldn't do.

"I've spent an entire afternoon drinking Darjeeling. I don't think I could take one more sip. Now somebody, please, tell me what's happened."

Mother gazed at me out of stricken eyes. "Lily decided to take a walk in the park. She said she needed air."

No wonder. After being accosted by the reporters at Angelique's, the poor thing had been cooped in for days. Her only excursions had been to her brother in jail, and those in no way qualified as a fun outing. "That wouldn't be a problem. I've done it myself."

"That's what she said," Margaret offered. "Mother couldn't forbid her, of course, but she did advise Lily to take a footman for protection. But Lily didn't want anyone fussing over her, so she took only Hester, her maid."

"I should have insisted on the footman," Mother said, her voice trembling.

"Mildred." Father placed his hand on her shoulder. "You

cannot blame yourself. How were you to know somebody would steal her from a park in the middle of the day?"

"I insisted she disguise herself with a dark hat and veil," Mother said. "Unfortunately, that did not help. Whoever took her must have known who she was."

"Did they take her maid as well?"

"No. A bystander helped her home. That's how we found out Lily had been kidnapped. The poor girl was knocked down trying to save her mistress." Mother's tortured gaze found me once more. "She was bleeding from the head, Kitty."

The poor thing. "Was she able to tell you who took Lily?"

"No," Margaret answered. "She collapsed as soon as she stepped into the house. Doctor Crawley is with her now. Hopefully, we'll get some answers when she comes around."

"Did you notify the police? They must be alerted." The earlier they were informed, the sooner they could start searching.

Mother shook her head. "No. Not the police. Someone else."

"Who?"

Mother nodded toward the drawing room entrance. "Him."

I turned to face the man who'd just entered the room. "Inspector Crawford!" Of course. Who else would she depend upon to find Lily?

"Miss Worthington." Polite as ever, he bowed. "I'm sorry we have to meet again under these circumstances." And then he became all business as he faced Mother and Father. "The maid has regained consciousness. She's doing as well as can be expected given the injury to her head. Doctor Crawley believes she's suffered a concussion. He's attending to her now and will provide more details when he's through with his examination."

"Was she able to describe who took Lily?"

"Oh, she did more than that. She identified the kidnapper."

"Who was it?"

"Lord Henry Dalrymple."

My stomach sank. "This is all my fault."

His brow wrinkled. "How so?"

"I had more questions for the Wynchcombe House staff, so I visited yesterday. He arrived while I was alone in the drawing room. We exchanged words. When I . . . hinted he might be responsible for Thomas Hodgkins' death, he came after me. I hit him with the tea pot."

His lips trembled with laughter.

"It's not amusing."

"You're right. It's not. I apologize." And still, his eyes smiled. But then in the next breath, he turned serious once more. "Do you have any idea where Lord Henry would have taken her?"

"The Silver Slipper," I said. "They would ask few questions if he asked them to hide her there."

"What is that?" Father asked.

"It's a gambling establishment Lord Henry patronizes," Ned answered. "There are others, of course. But that's the one he prefers. And then there is—pardon me, Mother—his mistress. She lives in Covent Garden."

"How do you know all this?" Father asked, surprise apparent in his voice.

"Kitty, Lily, and I created a committee to investigate the duke's murder," Margaret explained. "Ned soon joined us, as well as Lords Marlowe and Newcastle and Lady Emma Carlyle. We discovered all sorts of information."

Father seemed taken aback by her words. "Committees require a place to meet. Where, pray tell, were you gathering?"

Margaret hitched up her chin. "Here, in the library."

"With my blessing, Edward," Mother added.

Father's only reaction was a raised brow. But he'd prob-ably have more to say after Inspector Crawford departed for Father was not one to discuss family disagreements in public. And it was clear from his expression, our revelations had upset him.

Inspector Crawford cleared his throat, recalling us to his presence. "Could you point me to the telephone? I need to contact Scotland Yard." He turned to Ned. "You'll have to come with me to provide details."

"Of course," Ned readily agreed.

"My study," Father suggested. "You'll have privacy there."

Ned led the way, and Inspector Crawford followed.

Once they stepped out of the room, I collapsed into the nearest chair. "I think I'll have that tea, after all."

"Margaret, ring for Carlton," Mother said. "We need a fresh pot and some sustenance. It's going to be a long evening."

Once she'd done so, Margaret took the seat across from Mother.

While we waited for Inspector Crawford and Ned to return, Father pelted Margaret and me with questions. We answered as many as we could.

Margaret concluded her share of the explanations by saying, "Not all of us are privy to the whole evidence, as Kitty has refused to share the information she learned from the Duchess of Wynchcombe's maid and her meetings with the Duchess of Torrance."

How long was she to harp about that? "You asked me to investigate, Margaret. Part of that responsibility is to know what I can and cannot divulge."

"How did you learn to do this, Kitty?" Father asked, seem-ingly more curious than anything else.

"Inspector Crawford provided a great deal of instruction and direction."

"I suppose that's what those visits to Scotland Yard were for?"

"Yes."

Amusement rippled across Margaret's lips. "That was not the *only* reason."

"Margaret. Now is not the time for such misplaced humor," Mother chided.

"I just want to know one thing." Father came around the sofa to sit beside Mother. "When did I stop being a member of this family?"

That remark drew a gentle "Edward" from Mother along with "Father" from Margaret and me.

"How can you ask such a thing?" Mother asked, kissing his cheek. "You are the head of our family. We love you dearly."

"Really, Mildred?" he questioned. "My entire family is involved in an investigation into the duke's murder. My wife provides her blessing for this endeavor. And I'm not made aware of what's going on?" His gaze found Margaret and me. "Why didn't you tell me?"

"I suppose," I hesitated, "we were afraid you would not approve. Or at least I was."

"And it was so very important we look into things since Scotland Yard was not," Margaret pressed on. "Inspector Bolton seemed perfectly fine with blaming Sebastian. And that was so very wrong. We simply could not allow him to be framed."

"Then you are to be commended for carrying out this investigation."

My shoulders released the tension I'd been holding.

A knock on the door preceded the arrival of two footmen, carrying more tea and sandwiches. By necessity, we waited until they departed before resuming our conversation.

"Have you discovered evidence of someone else's guilt?" Father asked.

"We're exploring several avenues of investigation," I said.

One brow winged up. "I know when a question is being dodged, young lady."

"The evidence points to more than one individual. Until I'm reasonably sure of someone's guilt, I don't feel comfortable divulging my suspicions. Heaven knows I've been wrong before."

After a long, piercing look, he nodded. "Very well, keep your secrets. I trust you to know what's best."

That's more than another member of the family was willing to do. "Thank you, Father."

"Have you come up with an explanation for the dagger, though? Without that, anything else you've discovered would provide only doubt of Sebastian's guilt, not certainty."

"I agree." I could have told him about the additional two blades, but I was not willing to share that information just yet.

He strode toward the mantle where he took a cigarette from his silver case and lit it. He was being courteous, as Mother abhorred smoke being blown on her face. "Somehow, I can't feel that a sleight of hand was performed, much as magic fools the eye."

Well, that was an interesting way of putting things. "What do you mean?" I asked.

"What if the dagger used to kill the duke was not the one inherited by Sebastian?" He was very close to figuring out the mystery of the weapon.

"How could that be?" Margaret asked. "There were only two."

I ducked my head lest my expression revealed the truth.

Unfortunately, my sister noticed. "Kitty. Were there more?"

"For the sake of argument, let's say there were," Father interjected, thankfully taking the focus from me. "How would that come about?"

For a few seconds, silence filled the space, and then a light came into Margaret's eyes. "What if that dagger ceremony was not a single occurrence, but a tradition that had been conducted for generations? I can't believe I didn't deduce that earlier."

"You had enough to worry about, Margaret." I sighed. "You've guessed most of it, so I guess I might as well share what I discovered. You're right. The daggers were part of a ritual from the time of the first duke. Daggers were created and awarded by each duke to his son or sons. When the owner of each dagger died, the weapon was buried with him."

"Which means there's another dagger." Margaret's face flooded with joy. "The one that belonged to the duke."

"The duke's funeral has been held, Margaret," I said. We'd received notice a week ago. Lord Percy had held a private ceremony, with only Lord Henry in attendance. Lily had neither been invited, nor would she have gone if she had been. "His blade must have been buried with him."

"But Lord Percy never mentioned it."

"Strange, isn't it? And no one has seen that blade, then or now. He had to have known not only about its existence but its location."

"But who's to say he buried the duke with it? Or that it wasn't the blade he showed Inspector Bolton?"

"We don't. But there is one way to find out. Scotland Yard will need to open the duke's coffin and determine if the dagger was interred with him."

Mother appeared horrified at that suggestion. "Would Scotland Yard do such a thing?"

"They'll have to when we bring them the evidence." The fierce look in Margaret's eye was back.

"What evidence?" I asked. "All we have is conjecture."

"Then we're back to square one," Margaret said in a despondent tone.

"Not quite." I could share this much without revealing the question of Lord Percy's legitimacy. "Another dagger exists, one which belonged to the duke's cousin. You see, the duke's father had a younger brother. When the brother passed away, he took in his son. From all accounts, he dearly loved his nephew. So, when it came time for the dagger ceremony, he awarded one to him as well."

"Where is that dagger? Do you know?"

"No." I shook my head. "That is a question which must be answered."

A rattle at the door alerted us to the return of Inspector Crawford and Ned.

"I've arranged for a search to be carried out," the inspector said. "The places Mister Worthington mentioned will be explored, along with Lord Henry's residence, and his father's, as well. I doubt he would take Lily there, but one can never tell."

Awareness flooded in. "Lord Percy. *Oh, heavens.* Why didn't I realize?"

"What?" the inspector asked.

"He has a conservatory in which he grows flowers and plants with quite unique properties. Some quite poisonous. Lord Henry must know about them. What if he used a distillation from one of those plants to hurt Lily? What if he used one to drug Sebastian's wine?"

He fixed me with an avid stare. "Why didn't you tell me this before?"

"We had so many other things to discuss, and the investigation into Thomas Hodgkins' death had been assigned to Inspector Bolton." Neither excuse would do. He was right. I should have told him. "I'm sorry."

"When we find Lady Lily, and we will find her, you and I need to review all the information you've uncovered."

"You may use our library, since Scotland Yard is off limits for the moment," Father said. A quite surprising offer since he'd been so vehemently opposed to Inspector Crawford.

The inspector cast a questioning glance at Father. "It's not off limits. Miss Worthington has not been barred."

"Trust me. It is." It'd be a long time, if ever, before Father would allow me to visit Scotland Yard again.

He was quick on the take. "The library it is then."

"Thank you."

"I'll make Lord Percy's house my first stop," he said.

"I'd like to come with you," Ned declared.

Inspector Crawford shook his head. "Mister Worthington, you are not a member of the London Metropolitan Police. Your participation would be frowned upon."

"You make use of consultants, don't you? I could be one for the extent of this search." Trust Ned to come up with a valid argument.

Inspector Crawford appeared doubtful.

"She's much more to me than a friend. I . . . care about her."

Margaret and I shared a glance. We'd sensed his growing attachment to Lily which now had been decidedly confirmed.

"Very well, but you are not to interfere. You'll be there in a consulting capacity only."

"I understand. Thank you."

Inspector Crawford glanced at his wristwatch, and, for the first time, I realized what it was. A Rolex Oyster. Its gold encasing, which made it waterproof, gave it away. Another piece of evidence that hinted he was well off.

"We best go. I'll keep your family informed as best I can. Morning would be my guess."

Mother approached him. "Inspector. I know this investigation is in the best of hands. Please don't fail us."

"I'll do my best, ma'am." And then he was off with Ned by his side.

Supper was an almost silent affair as tortured thoughts about Lily filled our minds. Rather than take coffee afterward in the drawing room, Mother suggested we retire to our rooms. It'd been a long day, and we needed our rest. Not only that, but we would need to preserve our strength in case the news was not what we wished. I thought I'd review my notes, but exhaustion soon claimed me.

What seemed like minutes later, I was awakened by Betsy, white curling papers blossoming around her head.

I blinked at my bedside clock. It was barely past three. Dismay stirred in my gut. No one was ever awakened at this time to night to good news. "Is something wrong?"

"Inspector Crawford is downstairs, Miss. He's asking for you."

CHAPTER THIRTY-TWO

INSPECTOR CRAWFORD REPORTS

*J*UMPED OUT OF BED and dashed toward the door. But Betsy intercepted me before I could reach it.

"No, Miss. Here." She held up my robe, nodded toward my slippers.

I slipped into both, but when I tried to leave again, she stopped me once more. "Your hair, Miss, and your face."

"Of course." It wouldn't do to be seen less than groomed, never mind it could be calamitous news. I rushed to my en suite bathroom and hurriedly drew a comb through my flyaway mane, tossed some water on my face, brushed my teeth. Done, I turned to her. "There. Will I do?"

She nodded. With that final approval, I raced out. Carlton, dressed in his butler attire, stood at the bottom of the stairs. Had he slept in those clothes? "The drawing room, Miss Worthington."

Inspector Crawford sat in the sofa Mother had occupied

yesterday, sipping from a porcelain cup. Unbelievably, someone had already managed to provide him with something to drink. Coffee by the smell of it. He stood as I flew into the room.

Breathless as I was, "Lily?" was the only word I could manage.

"We found her. She's safe."

"Thank heaven." I collapsed on the sofa, next to him. "Where? How?" I asked, once I'd managed to regain my breath.

"We found her at Daisy Todd's place. She's Lord Henry's mistress, if you will recall. He'd abandoned Lily there."

My heart was still beating wildly. After my mad dash, it would take a moment for it to find its normal rhythm. "But where is Lily? Why didn't you bring her home?"

His gaze turned somber. "She'd been drugged, Catherine."

I gasped. "That dastard. How could he do that to his own cousin?" I was beyond outraged. If he'd been present, I'd hit him again with the coffee pot. "Hanging is too good for that worm."

He grinned. "Bloodthirsty little thing, aren't you?"

I scoffed. "How can you find this situation humorous?"

"It helps to get through the rough patches of life."

And heaven knew he'd seen enough of them. Not only had he almost died defending Lord Rutledge from a gang of ruffians, but he'd been injured during the Great War. And here he was trying to lighten a moment, only for me to find fault with him. "I'm sorry. I shouldn't have yelled."

"To finish answering your question, I took her to Doctor Crawley so he could examine her. It'll be up to him to determine whether she can come home or needs to recuperate at hospital. Your brother remained with her."

"She would welcome his company."

"She not only welcomed it but asked him to stay. If it's

any comfort, she was coherent and lucid when I left her. She, much like you, desires a pound of Lord Henry's flesh."

Well, that was indeed good news if she was demanding retribution. "That's good to hear. What will happen to him once you apprehend him?" I refused to so much as consider he'd evade capture, not with Scotland Yard on his trail.

"He'll be charged with kidnapping. Since the evidence is quite clear, he'll be imprisoned for a long time. At least ten years would be my guess."

I turned to face him. "What did he hope to gain from kidnapping Lily? Does she know?"

"Money. Apparently, he planned to ransom her."

"That's insane."

"He's desperate. According to Daisy Todd, he doesn't have a ha'penny to his name."

"Well, no wonder. His sole source of funds dried up with the duke's death."

"Not only that, but, as we discovered tonight, his debtors are on the hunt for him. The piper must be paid, after all." Much as he'd done at Lord Rutledge's supper, he placed his arm on the sofa's back rest, allowing his hand to hover close to me.

And, of course, I grew breathless once more. "What will they do if they find him?" I asked, once I was able to speak.

"Nothing good, I'm sure."

I shuddered. The man was beyond despicable, but I did not desire such rough justice for him.

"Daisy Todd is furious with him."

"Because he left her holding the bag, or in this case, Lily?"

His lips quirked. "Exactly so. I pressed her on Lord Henry's whereabouts the night of the duke's murder. She denied he was with her."

"Well, there goes his alibi for that night." I took a deep breath. "I believe he killed Thomas Hodgkins."

My statement did not seem to surprise him as he did not even blink. "But not the duke?"

"I was wrong about that." I grinned. "You were right. I allowed my ill opinion of Lord Henry to influence my thinking. But I've come to realize he wouldn't have killed his grandfather. It would have cut off his only source of funds. No, his scheme required the murder of Thomas Hodgkins so the blame could be placed on Sebastian's shoulders. Once Sebastian was found guilty and hanged, Lord Percy would have become the duke's heir."

"Except he can't ever inherit the title."

"But Lord Henry doesn't know that."

He gazed off into the distance before turning it back to me. "What do you think happened? Exactly? I have a reason for asking."

I was flattered he wanted to know my opinion for it meant he was taking me seriously. Still, I was curious as to what precipitated the question. "What reason?"

"Inspector Bolton is no longer heading the Thomas Hodgkins' inquiry. After tonight's events, the Detective Chief Superintendent decided that he'd taken on too much and will be reassigning that case."

"To you?"

"Maybe." And that's all he would say on the subject.

But I knew. More than likely, it had already been decided he would be charged with that responsibility. Good. He would get to the truth of the matter.

"Well, the way I see it, Lord Henry probably asked Thomas Hodgkins to invite Sebastian to that supper at Cherubs. My guess is he'd provided the bottle of wine to the club earlier that day. And then, more than likely, he arranged to meet Thomas Hodgkins later that night to make sure Sebastian had drunk the wine and had lost his sense of recall. When Hodgkins showed up, Lord Henry killed him and tossed his body into the Thames. He now only needed to point the blame toward his cousin. Since Sebastian was not able to remember what happened that night, he appeared to be lying. With all that evidence against him, it wouldn't take long for Scotland Yard to arrest him and charge him with the crime."

"The question now becomes whether all that can be proven."

"A yellow-haired man provided the bottle, according to the Cherubs waiter."

"That's not nearly enough. But there might be a money trail as I doubt Thomas Hodgkins would do such a thing without compensation. I looked into his background. He was not exactly flush. I'll look into the money side of things."

He had just confirmed he'd been handed the case. "I'm sure you will."

A rattle at the door preceded the arrival of Carlton, carrying a tray laden with ham, a loaf of bread, cheese, and sundry pastries. A footman followed with a pot of tea, porcelain cups, plates, and silverware. "Per your request, Inspector Crawford, the master, and mistress, as well as Miss Margaret, have been alerted to your presence. They will be down presently." After they placed the food and drink on a side table, they retreated, leaving Inspector Crawford and me alone once more.

"Before they arrive—" Inspector Crawford rushed to say.

I pointed to the food. "Don't you want something to eat?"

"The coffee is more than enough."

"Inspector." I pierced him with a glance. "When was the last time you ate?" I was willing to entertain the notion that it had been hours. Long enough for him to be experiencing hunger.

He pondered my question a second too long.

I came to my feet and chose some choice fare from the

offerings before placing the plate in front of him. "You need to keep up your strength if you're to catch Lord Henry."

One corner of his mouth lifted. "Thank you."

I nodded in acknowledgment. Since it would have been rude to pelt him with questions while he enjoyed his food, I remained silent while he ate.

"Satisfied?" he asked once he had finished every morsel.

"Yes. But more importantly, are you?" I retorted for I was not willing to let him have the last word.

He grinned. "Shall I resume my report?"

"Of course."

"When I visited Lord Percy, I asked him to show me the dagger." A light came into his eyes. "It differs from the one that killed the duke."

I came upright. That was a momentous discovery. "But Inspector Bolton said it was identical."

"The inscription on the dagger was in Latin, a language he doesn't know. You see, he never obtained a classical education." Another reason why Inspector Bolton should have never been assigned the duke's murder investigation.

"But you did, since you attended Oxford."

"Don't forget, my father was a scholar." A touch of pride tinged his voice. "I learned my Latin from him."

I smiled softly, glad he'd been treasured as a child. "So how did the daggers differ?"

"The one used to kill the duke bore the motto—*Fortuna audaces iuvat*—Fortune favors the bold. The one in Lord Percy's possession retains the same meaning but has a different inscription—*audentis Fortuna iuvat*."

"You'd think Inspector Bolton would have noticed."

"Yes, one would." He could say no more because just then my family arrived.

I stepped away while he reported tonight's events. They were all horrified Lily had been drugged.

Once all their questions were answered, he excused himself as he needed to return to Scotland Yard to continue the search for Lord Henry. But he promised to come back when he had further news.

I retired to my room to properly wash and dress for the day. While I did, I mentally reviewed the evidence. With Lord Henry no longer a likely suspect, I was left with Mister Nevins. The duke would have fired him once he realized he'd vouched for the lost draft. Mister Nevins couldn't afford to lose his position, not with a wife and five children to support. But did he possess the physical strength to stab the duke? He seemed rather a weakling. To my eye, he didn't appear powerful enough. But desperate men have been known to do desperate deeds. Who knew what he'd be capable of doing?

But he wasn't the only suspect. There was one more—Lord Percy. Problem was he had a solid alibi—supper at Lord Mountford's and an evening of playing chess. Even though Inspector Bolton had verified Lord Percy's whereabouts, I would need to talk to the aristocrat myself. As I'd come to realize, Inspector Bolton tended to accept people's testimonies without digging deeper.

But why would Lord Percy want to kill his father? He didn't appear eager to inherit the dukedom but seemed perfectly happy in his role as the duke's son. Maybe that was the answer. What if he'd learned about the letters and the Duchess of Torrance's threat to reveal them? Much like his father, he took pride in the family's title. If the letters were made public revealing he was nothing but a bastard, all of that would be lost to him. What if he had asked his father to end the engagement and the duke refused? But I didn't have to wonder about that last question. He had done that in plain sight at the ball, and the duke hadn't listened to him. Was it then and there he formed his scheme? Did he confront his father one last time in that garden? And when his father refused him again, would he have realized he had no other choice and driven the dagger home?

Many questions with few answers. And none of my suspicions would bear fruit unless I was able to destroy his alibi. And for that, I would have to visit Lord Mountford. He wouldn't see me, of course, if I requested a meeting, for we were not acquaintances. But he wouldn't so easily turn down the request of the Duchess of Torrance. She'd offered to help in any way she could. Well, she was eminently suited for this task for Lord Mountford would not want to offend Her Grace.

I sat at my desk and once more penned a note explaining what I needed from the duchess. Having written it in my best copperplate hand, I rang for Betsy and asked her to have a footman deliver the note. Now all I had to do was wait for her response.

CHAPTER THIRTY-THREE

HAPPENINGS

*E*ARLY IN THE AFTERNOON, my bedroom door burst open to a much-welcomed sight.

"Lily!"

She rushed forward to embrace me. "Oh, Kitty. I'm so glad to be home."

I was so overcome with emotion, it took me a moment to speak. "And I'm so very glad you're home." I took her hand and led her to the bed. Might as well make ourselves comfortable since it would take some time for her to provide her account. But most importantly, I needed to ascertain her state of being. "How are you feeling?"

She brushed a hand across her brow. "I have a small headache, but Doctor Crawley said it would fade with time." Her expression turned stormy. "That dastard chloroformed me."

"He didn't! That worm! Tell me everything!"

"Well, I went to the park for a stroll. Took Hester with me. It was such a lovely day, Kitty."

"Yes, it was." Too bad it was ruined for her.

"After a couple turns around the paths, I set about returning home. I was about to cross the street when he accosted me, He put a rag over my mouth. It smelled horrid."

I pressed her hand. "How awful for you, dearest."

"Before I knew it, the world faded away. I woke up in a dark, dingy room that was filthy beyond belief."

"Inspector Crawford told us he took you to Daisy Todd's home."

"That was not a home. A pig sty is better kept. When I came to, Henry and that woman were arguing. He wanted to leave me there with that, that slattern. If that is his notion of a mistress, he has the poorest taste."

"Probably all he could afford seeing how he doesn't have a ha'penny to his name."

"Oh, Kitty." She laughed. "I love your sense of humor. It's so welcome after—"

She didn't get to finish as Margaret rushed in just then. "You're home." Tears of joy flowed once more, and, of course, Lily needed to repeat her story. But once my sister was caught up, she resumed.

"Since Henry and that woman were occupied, I made a dash for the door. There were only two rooms, you see."

"Excellent!"

"But Henry caught me before I could get away. I screamed and screamed, but nobody heard."

"Oh, they probably did, but people who live in that area are not the kind to interfere." As I'd discovered not so long ago.

"What happened next?" Margaret prompted.

"He tried to put that nasty rag over my mouth again. But before he could do so, I bit him."

"How marvelous!" How very brave she'd been in the face of such adversity.

"I kicked him on the shins, too. And then I told him if he tried to knock me unconscious again, he would live to rue the day. He settled for tying me up and wrapping a cloth over my mouth. Not the nasty one, thank heaven."

"That ape."

"But I didn't give in to despair. I knew sooner or later someone would find me." She took a deep breath and let it out. "Although I must admit, I was a little scared."

"As anyone with a working intellect would have been," I exclaimed.

Margaret hugged her. "We're so proud of you, dearest."

"Anyhow," Lily said, offering her brightest smile, "That's how Inspector Crawford and Ned found me, trussed up like a Christmas goose."

If she was able to make fun of her ordeal, she was fine indeed.

"After they made sure I wasn't seriously hurt, Inspector Crawford asked one of the police officers to drive me to Doctor Crawley's surgery. He remained behind to question Daisy Todd." She shyly ducked her head. "I asked Ned to accompany me."

"Of course, you did." Not that she would have needed to do so. He would have volunteered on his own.

"And Doctor Crawley provided a clean bill of health?" She'd explained that before, but I wanted to make sure she wasn't leaving anything out.

"Except for the headaches I would suffer from the chloroform. But, other than that, I'm as right as rain." Her bright smile faded. "I'm worried about poor Hester, though. He said she'd suffered a concussion?"

"I visited her this morning," Margaret offered. "Her head aches, as would be expected, and she's seeing double. And she's not too sure on her pins, either. Hopefully, with time, all of it will right itself."

"I hope so. Doctor Crawley is with her now. Maybe he'll provide good news when he's through with his examination."

For a while, we cosseted her, propping her up with a pillow, offering her chocolates, a gift from one of my admirers. But eventually she laughed us off, claiming she wasn't made of china and wouldn't break.

Just as she declared herself fit, Betsy knocked on my door. The family was gathering in the drawing room to hear Doctor Crawley's report. The three of us linked arms and descended the stairs.

His report was mostly a positive one. Hester was coming along. He didn't think she would suffer lasting damage. But he recommended she continue to rest since she was suffering from dizzy spells and double vision. And then, after promising to return the next day, he took his leave.

The rest of the afternoon proceeded at a more sedate pace. Lily, of course, had to visit her maid to reassure herself of her wellbeing. But once she had done so, Mother suggested a warm bath, a meal, and a bit of a rest in that order. While Lily took Mother's advice to heart, Margaret withdrew to the library to do more legal research. Since I'd received word from the Duchess of Torrance that the meeting with Lord Mountford had been arranged for the following day, I remained in my room going over my notes and planning the questions I would ask him.

Just as we headed to supper, Inspector Crawford returned with the news Lord Henry had been apprehended.

"Thank heaven!" I said, "Where did you find him?"

"At the docks trying to stow aboard a ship bound for Argentina."

"But he doesn't know Spanish!" Lily exclaimed.

"I don't think that mattered to him as much as it was the earliest departing ship. It's set to sail tonight."

"What will happen to him now?" Lily asked. Of course, she was not aware of my earlier discussion with the inspector.

"He'll be held in custody until he's charged. As he's liable to flee if released, the judge is not likely to grant him bail. You'll need to visit Scotland Yard at some point to provide an official report."

"Of course. Anything I can do to put him permanently behind bars."

Although her kidnapping hadn't been a pleasant experience, it seemed to have lit a fire under her.

"We're just about to enjoy our supper, Inspector," Mother said. "Would you care to join us?"

"I thank you, but I have reports to write."

There were shadows under his eyes. I wondered how long he'd gone without sleep. "If that's all that's pending, your responsibilities can wait," I said. "Unless I miss my guess, you've been on duty more than twenty-four hours. You can certainly take an hour or so to enjoy supper."

That charming grin of his made an appearance. "Well, when you put it that way."

"I do."

We proceeded into the dining room with Mother on Father's arm and Lily and Margaret on Ned's, who'd returned earlier in the evening. Inspector Crawford and I brought up the rear.

Since we were *en famille* as it were, I didn't waste such a golden opportunity to discover more about the good inspector. We soon learned his father taught school at a boy's prep school which Inspector Crawford was allowed to attend for free. His mother had treasured books and imbued in him a love of reading. At some point, he became interested in law and justice and eventually joined the police force. His career had been cut short, however, when he'd defended Lord Rutledge against a gang who'd seen an easy mark in the aristocrat. Although Lord Rutledge's injuries had been minor, his hadn't been. It'd taken him six long months to recuperate. Once he'd done so, Lord Rutledge had insisted on paying for his education at Oxford, claiming his was too bright a mind to waste.

"What did you study at Oxford?" Ned asked.

"Jurisprudence at Magdalen College."

That was a surprise. "You wanted to become a barrister?"

"Not that so much as I wished to learn the more intricate aspects of the law."

A police officer would only be required to know the rudimentary bits. So even then he must have had his eye on Scotland Yard. "Ahhh."

"After graduation, I was considering my options. But then . . ." A shadow crossed over his face.

"The Great War," I said.

"Yes, I felt it my duty to volunteer."

"Ned and Richard helped with the effort as well," I said.

But Ned stopped me from saying more. "No, Kitty."

Lily's questioning gaze bounced from him to me and back again.

Unfortunately, an explanation would not be forthcoming. Ned had been asked to join the War Department. We'd never found out what he'd done as he'd been forbidden under penalty of law from discussing it. Adventurous Richard, who had a facility for languages, had been sent overseas on several trips, the nature of which we never discovered. Other than those bare facts, the family knew nothing more.

Inspector Crawford, who would have known there was more than one way to serve, simply nodded.

Mother broke into the uncomfortable silence. "Shall we

adjourn to the drawing room, ladies, and leave the men to their port and cigars?"

"Of course," Margaret said, following Mother's lead.

"I must beg to be excused from further activities," Inspector Crawford said. "I still have those reports to write." He brushed a hand across his brow. Tired did not begin to describe him.

"Inspector," Mother said. "I understand your sense of duty. But you're exhausted. Wouldn't it be better to go home and get some sleep?" As always, she was a strong proponent of rest. In this instance, I strongly agreed with her.

"I can do that in my office."

"Where would you sleep?" I exclaimed. "There isn't enough room to swing a cat in there, much less a cot."

He offered a tired grin. "I wouldn't say that."

"You caught the villain of the piece," I said. "What's the rush of writing the reports? Doubt there's someone there to read them at this hour of night."

"Very well," he raised his hands in surrender. "I wave the white flag."

Father laid down his serviette. "Good. Glad that's settled. I'll ask Neville to drive you to your place."

"You don't need to do that. I can hail a cab."

"Nonsense," Mother said. "It's the least we can do after you brought our own dear Lily back to us, safe and sound."

"I find it best to agree with Mother," I whispered to the inspector. "She's relentless, especially when she's right."

"Then I shall accept."

Once the Rolls had been brought around, I accompanied him to the front door to bid him goodbye. "Thank you, again."

"It's my duty, Miss Worthington," he said, adjusting the dark fedora Carlton had just handed him along with his outer garments. The dent crown, with its grosgrain ribbon band, single bow, and feather, suited him no end.

"Ahhh, but would anyone else have done it with such style?" I pointed to the hat.

He captured my hand and kissed it. "Goodnight, Miss Worthington." And then he was gone, leaving me . . . breathless, trembling, wanting more of whatever existed between us.

Intending to join my family, I headed toward the drawing room. But something stopped me. There was bound to be a conversation about Inspector Crawford, or, worse, gentle probing about my feelings toward him, none of which I wanted to discuss. So, rather than face them, I sought the refuge of my bedroom where I could be alone with my thoughts.

CHAPTER THIRTY-FOUR

AN INTERVIEW WITH LORD MOUNTFORD

*M*Y DISCUSSION WITH LORD MOUNTFORD WAS NOT GOING WELL. "What I want to know is what the devil you have to do with any of this?" The earl, a short, pugnacious fellow with not an ounce of grace to him, asked.

Regardless of his attitude, I needed to maintain my calm if I wanted to get the information I needed from him. "As I informed you, milord, I'm looking into the death of the Duke of Wynchcombe."

"But why you? You're not Scotland Yard. You're not the police. You're nothing. Less than nothing. You're a woman." His upper lip curled with disdain.

Now with that, I took offense. "Are you saying women are not supposed to investigate murders?"

"Exactly," he huffed. "Females are supposed to stay home, take care of their children, cook, clean, and so forth." He nailed me with a gimlet eye. "You're not even married, are you?"

He was an obnoxious, repugnant reptile, an aristocrat of the worst sort. "No, I'm not. And, for the moment, I have no wish to be."

"Ha! As if any decent man would have you."

"I'll have you know, sir, I've received numerous marriage proposals."

"From who? The neighborhood rag collector. No, let me think." He snapped his fingers. "I know, the night soil man."

"Night soil man? You are aware we're living in the twentieth century where there is indoor plumbing."

"Of course, I'm aware. I just don't know if, dressed as you are, your family can afford such a luxury. Your garment is missing some cloth."

I'd worn one of my most stylish dresses for I'd wanted to impress him, and he was complaining about the length of my dress. Unbelievable. "Milord, if you would but answer a few questions, I'll take my offending presence from your sight and be on my way."

He'd welcomed me, if that was the right word, in his drawing room, a space that opened into a very small garden through a pair of French doors.

"What do you want to know?" he asked.

"Was Lord Percy with you the night of May 31st?"

"Yes, he was. We ate supper and then enjoyed a game of chess. Anything else?"

"And he never left?"

"Why the devil would he?" He bit out. The boor probably thought his rudeness would deter me.

But I was not so easily thwarted. "You didn't answer the question, sir."

He stared at the rug beneath his feet before answering. "Of course, he didn't."

He was lying. I was sure of it. "What did you have to eat for supper?"

His head jerked up. "A good English beefsteak and boiled potatoes. The beef was overdone, and the potatoes were mush. We threw it all back with some claret."

His round belly and red-veined nose told me he ate too much and drank in excess.

"Anything else?"

"Who won the chess match?"

"He did. Blast his eyes. He's just as adept at chess as his father was at cards."

That was a revelation. "You played cards with the duke?"

"Once upon a time. Can't afford it anymore. Not too plump in the pocket at the moment. I'll need to marry some rich heiress if I want to come around. Know any?" His version of a smile was closer to a grimace, as he was missing some teeth, and those he still possessed appeared ill-kempt.

"No. I don't." I wouldn't wish him on my worst enemy, if I had any. "What time did Lord Percy leave?"

"I didn't keep track of the time, gel."

"But you told Inspector Bolton Lord Percy had been with you until close to midnight."

"Did I? Can't remember. Must have been if I did."

He was hopeless. Beyond hopeless. But clearly, I would not get any more from him. I thanked him and walked out of the room.

The butler, a tall, dark-haired fellow, escorted me to the front door. He offered my outer garments and my purse with all the manners and grace Lord Mountford lacked. Maybe he'd be more forthcoming than his employer. "Were you here on May 31st?" I asked, slipping into my gloves.

He nodded. "Yes, Miss. I was."

"Do you recall the events of that night?"

"Lord Mountford requested supper be set for two, as he'd invited Lord Percy."

"What time did Lord Percy arrive?"

"Around eight or so."

"When did he leave?"

"Well as to that, Miss, I don't know. Lord Mountford excused me right after supper. Told me my services would not be required for the rest of the evening."

"Was that usual?"

"No. I normally remained on duty until Lord Mountford's guests left. You see I lock the front door and keep the key. No one could leave without me knowing about it."

"And that didn't happen that night?"

A slight shake of his head. "I was up half the night waiting for the bell to summon me. But it never rang."

"So how did Lord Percy leave? Do you know?"

"My guess would be the French doors in the drawing room. They open into the garden, you see. From there, it would be a relatively easy exit to the street."

If Lord Percy had departed that way, the butler would not know the time he left. How very unfortunate.

"But the thing of it is, Miss, next morning there was mud on the drawing room carpet."

Well, that was interesting. "Was there?"

"Yes. The maid had to scrub for hours to get it out."

"But how did the dirt get there?"

"I've thought about it. It'd been raining that night, so I doubt they would wander into the garden, and if Lord Percy left that way, well, there wouldn't be any footprints."

Daylight was beginning to glimmer. Lord Mountford's Georgian-style townhouse, located as it was in St. James Square, was not far from Westminster. A motorcar could have been driven there and back in no time. "But if he left and returned?"

"That's the way I figure it. One of them must have gone somewhere and come back."

"Why only one?"

"There was only one set of footprints."

"How very clever of you to notice, Mister—I'm sorry, I did not get your name."

"Brougham, Miss."

"I'll remember that. Why would either of them leave and return?"

"I don't know, Miss. But I did wonder."

I was doing more than wondering. I was formulating a theory. "You've been very helpful, Mister Brougham. Lord Mountford mentioned he wasn't too plump in the pocket. Would you happen to know anything about the state of his finances?"

"Very poor, Miss. He hasn't paid the staff in three months. Most have moved on to other positions. Only ones left are Cook, the maid, and me. And I'll be gone by the end of the week."

Well, that explained why Mister Brougham was willing to talk. He wouldn't suffer any repercussions from his discussion with me.

"He'll lose the house next if he's not careful. It's not entailed you see."

"How did he come to be in such dire straits?"

"Gambling, Miss. Horses, cards, whether it will rain next Tuesday. He'll bet on anything. That's how he gained possession of this townhouse. He won it at a card game."

I retrieved the journal from my purse, wrote down my name and address, and handed the page to him. "You've been very helpful, Mister Brougham. If you would forward me the address of your new domicile, I would greatly appreciate it." I slipped him a ten-pound note. "Thank you for your assistance."

"Will do. Thank you, Miss." He bowed.

As I made my way to the Rolls where Neville was waiting for me, I reflected on my recent exchange with the butler. What a happy surprise he'd turned out to be. He'd be a good man to have in your corner. Observant, smart. Willing to share his employer's dirty linen. Of course, it would depend on his situation. I doubted he would be as accommodating if his employer treated him right. For his sake, I hoped he would land at a more pleasant household than he now had.

CHAPTER THIRTY-FIVE

THE CURSE IS COME UPON ME

*T*HINGS ADVANCED RATHER QUICKLY AFTER THAT DAY.

After dear Lily provided her report to Scotland Yard, Lord Henry was formally charged and the matter set to trial.

Inspector Crawford was formally assigned to the Thomas Hodgkins' matter. Since, of course, he couldn't discuss it with me, I kept abreast of the investigation through the newspapers. Sadly, it was not enough, but it was what it was.

And as for me, I analyzed all the information the investigative committee, Inspector Crawford, and I had unearthed and reached a conclusion as to the Duke of Wynchcombe's murderer. I requested an audience with Inspector Bolton to present my findings, for it'd be up to him to arrest the villain. To my surprise, he agreed.

On the day of our meeting, I presented the evidence. He asked many questions. I had to give him that. And then he politely thanked me for the information and bid me goodbye.

For days afterward, I waited to hear something, anything, but the only thing that arrived at our house was an invitation from the Duchess of Torrance. She was holding an exclusive supper and wished me to attend. Oddly, the invitation was addressed to only me.

I thought to decline, but Mother, being Mother, said I could not possibly turn down such an honor. An exclusive supper at such an august personage's home was something devoutly to be wished. When word got around, and she'd be sure it would, I'd be the envy of every debutante. And then she reminded me how very accommodating the Duchess of Torrance had been with our endeavors. I could not possibly wish to offend her. In the end, I had no choice but to accept.

On the night in question, I dressed in my finest evening gown, a black silk gown with a small train. Lord Rutledge's pearls were displayed to advantage around my neck while a feathered band adorned my head. The entire family, every one of them smiling, stood by the front door to bid me adieu. I should have known right then and there something was up. But I was so preoccupied with my thoughts, I failed to take in its significance.

The supper party was exclusive indeed, as the only guests were Lord Percy and me. Odd, but it was our hosts' prerogative to invite whomever they chose. The Duke and Duchess of Torrance kept the conversation light during the splendid meal, avoiding such uncomfortable subjects like his father's death and his son's arrest. When it was time to retire to the drawing room, his Grace suggested that, rather than remain behind to enjoy their port and cigars, he and Lord Percy join the ladies instead.

Quite a surprise greeted us when we walked into the drawing room.

Every member of the investigative committee was there along with Inspectors Bolton and Crawford.

292

"What's this?" Lord Percy asked when he stepped into the room.

"You will find out soon enough," the Duke of Torrance said, firmly closing the door behind them.

"Sit." Inspector Bolton slapped down a chair in the middle of the room. Strategically placed, it wasn't one that would lend comfort, but a common kitchen one, seemingly made from good English oak.

Adopting a casual air, Lord Percy eased into it, as if he was perfectly comfortable with what had been asked of him, but his gaze did not share that same belief. It darted madly about the room, more than likely trying to find a way out. I doubted there'd be one. Unless I missed my guess, two police officers would by now be stationed outside the door.

Inspector Crawford held out his hand for me. After I rested mine in his palm, he led me to a comfortable chair positioned a few feet across from Lord Percy, facing him. Once I sat down, he handed me my journal, the one which detailed every nugget of information we'd discovered, as well as the methodology I'd employed to reach a conclusion.

But how had he obtained it? I'd locked it inside my desk. "How—"

"I gave it to him, Kitty," Margaret said. She was seated next to Lily on a blue settee on the far side of the room. "I knew where you kept the key."

I would need to find a better place to hide it then.

"Miss Worthington, if you would," Inspector Bolton said.

"But—"

He nodded his encouragement. "Explain it the way you explained it to me."

Before I spoke, I took my time skimming over my notes for I did not wish to miss an important point. When I was ready to begin, I took a deep breath and dove in. "When our family learned the Duke of Wynchcombe had been murdered, we were horrified. That horror turned into despondence when Sebastian was arrested. We didn't know what to do, how we could help. But my sister, Margaret, and Lady Lily did. They asked me to investigate for they knew Sebastian could not have done it." I glanced up from the journal, toward Lord Percy. "When I visited your home, you seemed to concur with that sentiment."

He nodded. "I did. Not for one second did I believe he was responsible."

Of course, he didn't. "And then the situation went from bad to worse when Thomas Hodgkins' body was discovered, and that investigation was assigned to Inspector Bolton." I didn't mention Inspector Crawford's temporary involvement. It'd been so brief I wouldn't have known about it, except for the message he'd sent me. "The implication was clear. Scotland Yard believed the deaths of the duke and Thomas Hodgkins were somehow connected."

Lord Percy raised a brow.

"The added complication meant I could no longer conduct the investigation on my own. I needed help. So we formed a committee to investigate the duke's murder. Those you see here were involved. Margaret and Lady Lily, as well as my brother Ned. Lords and Newcastle and Lady Emma all agreed to assist as well." I nodded to each as I mentioned them.

Lord Percy sniffed. "How very enterprising of all of you."

Ignoring him, I continued. "Initially, our investigation focused on your son, Lord Henry."

He rushed to his feet. "How dare you? Of all the unmitigated gall!"

"Sit down, Percy." The Duke of Torrance's tone demanded obedience.

This time Lord Percy didn't ease into the chair but flopped down in a snit.

"There was much evidence against him, you see. Did you know he'd stolen a bank draft from his grandfather's bank account?"

"He'd never," he huffed out.

I nodded toward the duke's man of business. "Would you care to explain, Mister Nevins?" He'd been trying to make himself invisible in a corner of the room. But I had noticed him.

"Miss Worthington, I would . . ." And then he stopped.

Inspector Bolton fixed him with a gimlet stare. "I'm aware of the facts of the matter—all the facts. Need I say that revealing the entire truth will be a point in you favor?"

"Well, sir, when you put it that way."

"I do."

"The first I learned about it was when I received a phone call from the bank manager. Apparently, Lord Henry had presented a draft drawn on the duke's account in the amount of ten thousand pounds. He was demanding it be paid in cash. As I understood it, the bank did not have such a large amount readily available, so they contacted me to verify the duke had indeed authorized the large withdrawal. I" —he cleared his throat— "I mistakenly thought the duke had approved the transaction."

"But that was not true," I said.

"No, it wasn't." He ran a finger under his rapidly wilting collar. "His Grace became very agitated when he discovered the missing draft."

"What happened after your discussion with the duke?"

"Well, nothing. The duke's demise precluded any further discussion."

Yes, death would do that. "And you did not provide that bank draft to Lord Henry?"

He stiffened. "No, Madam, I did not."

"Ned, would you care to shed some light on the subject?"

Along with Lords Marlowe and Newcastle, he'd been standing behind Margaret and Lily's settee, in a way guarding them in case matters went awry.

Rather than come forward, he spoke from where he was. "After I obtained Sebastian's permission, I discussed the matter with the bank manager. Even after the conversation with Mister Nevins, he remained doubtful of the authenticity of the instrument. So, I arranged for the signature to be verified. The expert leaned toward the signature being a forgery. But he opined that it could simply be the result of old age catching up with the duke."

"There, you see. Not conclusive evidence," Lord Percy said, crossing his arms across his chest.

"Then how would you account for the duke's anger when he discovered the missing draft?" Inspector Bolton asked. "No, sir. That dog won't hunt."

"He could have forgotten," Lord Percy offered somewhat subdued.

"Forgotten?" The Duke of Torrance blurted out. "Wynchcombe had the memory of an elephant. He never forgot a thing. Just witness his expertise at cards."

"Thank you for bringing up that subject, Your Grace," I said. "By all accounts, the Duke of Wynchcombe was an avid gambler. And a very good one at that. Apparently, several gentlemen owed him a great deal of money. We looked into them as well." I briefly glanced at my notes. "Lord Marlowe, I believe you oversaw that aspect of the investigation. Could you please share what you discovered?"

"Well," he strolled to the front of the room to take center stage. After giving Lord Percy a dismissive sniff, he said, "Wynchcombe had formed a committee, comprised of those gentlemen who owed him money, for the express purpose of subverting votes at the House of Lords."

"I say," the Duke of Torrance exclaimed, seemingly affronted.

"Afraid so, sir." Lord Marlowe said a note of apology in his voice. "He employed the threat of calling in their vowels if they didn't follow his lead. It was easier for them to go along with the duke's scheme than to pay."

"He never demanded such a thing of me," the duke blurted out.

"You paid him, dear," the Duchess of Torrance reasoned. "There was nothing he could hold over you."

"So, Lord Marlowe, did you discover anyone likely to murder the duke?"

"No, I did not. The reason was made clear by one of the gentlemen. Apparently, they held a mutual belief that, since they were all younger than the duke, he would shuffle off his mortal coil before they did."

"And why was that important?"

"Because once he passed away, their debts would die with him. No one would owe money to his successor."

Lord Percy scoffed. "Wouldn't that provide a motive?"

"No. Not really," Lord Marlowe responded. "He never demanded money from them. Apparently, they paid what they could when they could. They were perfectly satisfied with that arrangement."

"Thank you, Lord Marlowe," I said.

"How long are you going to keep this up?" Lord Percy asked.

"Only a little while longer. And now we come to the matter of Thomas Hodgkins."

Lord Percy stiffened up.

"Lord Newcastle was in charge of that enquiry." I nodded toward him. "If you would, milord."

Newcastle and Marlowe changed places. "I visited Cherubs, the gentleman's club where Thomas Hodgkins and

Sebastian Dalrymple enjoyed supper the night of the duke's murder. The waiter who served them informed me a gentleman visited that afternoon. He'd asked him to serve Hodgkins and his guest the wine he brought with him. The waiter didn't think it odd. Seeing how the stuff the establishment serves is pure swill, patrons often bring their own spirits. For a small remuneration, the staff is happy to pour such for them."

"Did he describe this gentleman?"

"Tall, blond-haired. Oh, and he'd worn fancy dress. Formal wear, in the parlance."

"Thank you, Lord Newcastle," I said. "So now we come to the crux of the matter. Two murders that happened more than likely the same night."

"You don't know that," Lord Percy exclaimed.

"The medical examiner revealed Thomas Hodgkins' body had been in the water between" —I consulted my notes— "ten days to two weeks before he performed the postmortem. And then there was the evidence of the witness who saw a yellow-haired man tossing something into the Thames the night of the duke's murder."

"He was drunk!" Lord Percy protested.

"You don't know that, sir," Inspector Crawford tossed Lord Percy's words back to him. "Some men have a great capacity for drink."

"Why would Henry kill his grandfather? Give me that."

"Ned, would you care to explain?"

"Well, Lord Percy," he said, taking over from Lord Newcastle, "after he used the ten thousand pounds to pay off his gambling debts, he incurred more of them, to the tune of five thousand."

"Ever the fool," Lord Percy mumbled under his breath.

"You had to have known about them," I said.

"Not the amount. I counseled him against gambling heavily, but he never listened to me."

"Your father didn't listen to you either, did he?"

"How would you know?"

"The night of the Torrance Ball. You tried to convince him to listen to Sebastian. He refused."

"Father was ever one to follow his own counsel."

"Yes, he was. In more than one matter, as it turns out."

"What do you mean?"

"Your Grace," I said, gazing at the Duchess of Torrance, "would you care to explain?"

The duchess, who'd been sitting in her favorite cerulean settee, took a deep breath and let it out. "I was friends with your mother."

"I know that."

"She wrote to me often. She was deeply unhappy about her marriage, Percy. About the way your . . . father treated her. She was so very lonely in that big castle, with only your brother, Thomas, and the servants to keep her company. Wynchcombe never allowed her to travel without him, and his only interests lay in London—gambling and Parliament."

"One day, one summer, I should say, your father's cousin arrived, Lord Trenton Dalrymple. He'd been raised by the old duke, Wynchcombe's father, after his own father died. By all accounts, the old duke loved him like a son."

"Yes, I know. Where are you going with this?"

"Percy, you will keep a civil tongue in your head when you address the Duchess," Torrance said.

Lord Percy seemed to shrivel. "I didn't mean to offend. My apologies."

"Trenton and Sophie, for that was your mother's name, spent a magical summer together. And then the duke arrived. He'd heard from a neighbor that his cousin was visiting. When they returned from a ride in the estate, he dragged Lord Trenton from the horse and whipped him until he bled. He then ordered him to leave and never return. Well, he got his wish. He never did. Trenton Dalrymple had joined Her Majesty's army. He was dispatched to the Boer War where he was killed in a skirmish." The duchess paused for a second, and then, with great deliberation, she said, "You were born eight months after he left." The implication was clear. Lord Trenton had fathered Lord Percy.

Someone in the room gasped.

"My father was there, wasn't he?" Lord Percy exclaimed. "They must have been intimate."

"Yes, the duke made sure of that," the duchess bit out in a bitter tone. "She lived for seven more years after that, mostly for you, as Thomas was old enough to fend for himself. And then, as she lay dying, she gave a set of letters to her maid and asked her to forward them to her brother, the Earl of Clarendon. This was done for the maid's protection, for the duke was sure to come after her. You see, she knew everything. She was aware of every secret, every confidence of your mother."

The man whose entire life was being revealed as a sham remained silent.

"But then the Earl of Clarendon became ill. When he knew his time was coming, he sent those letters to me. He knew I would keep them safe."

"He should have burned them."

"He couldn't do that. The maid still lived, Percy, and so did your father." The duchess raised a trembling hand to her brow. Clearly, this was becoming too much for her. But from somewhere she drew on some strength because she raised her head and carried on. "I read those letters. They confirmed what I suspected from all those years ago. You are not the Duke of Wynchcombe's son."

He rushed to his feet. "I am his son, damn it. He gave me a dagger as proof."

"Sit down, Lord Percy," Inspector Bolton demanded.

Lord Percy grunted but, nevertheless, obeyed the command.

"Two years ago, you brought Lily to town," the duchess carried on, "presumably so she could enjoy her debut. But Wynchcombe had other plans for her. He sought to marry her off to someone with a title and a fortune. And all that time the poor girl was kept a prisoner in that mausoleum of a place."

"Father didn't see the need for a debut."

"I wrote him," the duchess continued. "I met with him. I tried my best to convince him Lily should have her season. But he refused. And then he affianced her to Tottingham. I was desperate to stop that marriage. I didn't want Lily to suffer her grandmother's fate. So, God help me, I found a way to use those letters to force his hand. I told him I would make them public if he didn't end the engagement."

Lord Percy's eyes blazed with fury. "You shouldn't have done that."

"And he still refused," she continued as if he hadn't spoken, determined to spill the whole sorry tale for everyone to hear. The truth would set her free. "I started to write one last letter to him, claiming this was my final demand. But I was interrupted when my granddaughter arrived seeking a costume I'd worn long ago. When I returned to my escritoire, the note was gone. I subsequently discovered Mister Nevins had visited. I suspected he'd taken it."

"He didn't, my dear. I did." The Duke of Torrance approached and placed a hand on her shoulder. "I intended to discuss it with you. But then Wynchcombe died, and the point seemed moot."

She glanced teary-eyed at him. "Oh, Torrance. I wished you had told me."

"This is all very touching," Lord Percy said, with a curl to his lip. "But what does all this have to do with my father's death?"

The Duke of Torrance turned to him. "You must have been aware of the letters Wynchcombe had been receiving, as well as my duchess' visits. You visited Wynchcombe House often enough. Even if Wynchcombe had not told you who was sending them, you would have recognized the stationery, for you've received many invitations from us."

"Of course, I knew how eager the Duchess was to present Lily to society. I assumed that's what the visits and the notes were about."

I picked up the narration, for the next bit was pure speculation. "Maybe so. At the beginning anyway. But then you discovered the duchess' threat—that she would make your mother's letters public. And you panicked, for you knew what they contained."

"How could I?"

"Once upon a time you were a little boy, an inquisitive one. And one day you went hunting in your mother's chambers for treasures, as all little boys do. That's when you found them."

Fear rolled over his face. "You have no proof. No proof."

"Oh, I wouldn't say so, Lord Percy. You see, your mother's maid still lives, and she would have been quite aware, don't you think?"

"She didn't know I read . . ." He must have realized he'd given himself away because he stopped talking.

"You'd dealt with the Duke of Wynchcombe your whole life. You knew how stubborn he could be. When the duchess threatened to expose your illegitimacy, he weighed the odds and gambled that she would not make the letters public. But you couldn't take that chance. Your way of life, your status, your entire existence was in peril. And there was only one way out—to murder your father."

Lord Percy looked about the room. "Does anyone believe this fantastical tale?" When no one answered, his gaze wandered back to me. "You're insane."

I continued as if he hadn't spoken. "But the thing of it was, you couldn't figure out how to keep the blame away from you. Until Sebastian played right into your hands. A visible disagreement at the Torrance Ball with most of British high society in attendance. A public argument captured by the press in front of Westminster. And then you knew exactly who to frame."

"How could you, Uncle Percy?" Lily cried out.

"Hush, dearest, let Kitty finish," Margaret said, in a calm tone.

"How do you account for the note Father received? It bore the Torrance crest."

"How would you know that, sir?" Inspector Bolton asked. "Neither the envelope nor the note was ever found."

"But Nevins said . . . and the duchess . . ." Lord Percy's shoulders drooped. He'd fallen into the trap.

"It would have been easy enough for you to obtain both on one of your many visits, Percy," the Duke of Torrance said. "And to think we welcomed you into our home when all the time you were planning . . ." The duke brushed a trembling hand across his brow.

Lord Percy attempted one final salvo. "How could I have killed him? I was at Mountford's playing chess. He vouched for me."

Inspector Bolton stepped forward. "Not anymore."

"What?"

"He now claims you left a few minutes after ten and returned before midnight. The front door had been locked.

So, you were forced to leave by way of the French doors that open into his garden. You left mud prints on the carpet when you returned."

"Who told you such a thing?"

"Mountford's butler," I said. "He was quite clear about it. Apparently, it took ages to remove the stain."

"I could have simply stepped into the garden for a smoke."

"It was pouring that night."

His eyes took on a wild look. "The dagger. How do you explain the dagger? It belonged to Sebastian."

"No, sir, it did not," Inspector Bolton said. "The duke was killed with a different dagger, probably his own."

"I buried that dagger with him," Lord Percy bit out. He was perspiring now. His eyes had the look of a cornered rat.

"Maybe. Or maybe you buried him with the one that belonged to Lord Trenton Dalrymple, the duke's cousin."

Lord Percy hissed. He was well and truly caught, and he knew it. "How the devil do you know that?"

Inspector Crawford stepped forward. "The military are very good about keeping records. When Lord Trenton died, they sent his possessions to your mother which included all the letters she'd sent him. And a dagger which bore the inscription *Fortuna audaces iuvat*, a match to your father's. You see, the old duke had awarded one to him as well. Sebastian's dagger, as you yourself testified, was identical to yours. And yours bears the inscription, *audentis Fortuna iuvat*. So, no, sir. He was not murdered with Sebastian Dalrymple's dagger."

Lord Percy hanged his head in defeat. "I never wanted the dukedom."

"But you wanted everything that went along with being a duke's son," I said.

He raised his gaze toward me. "I had no choice. Don't you see? She would have made those letters public."

"No, Percy," the duchess said. "Wynchcombe was right. I never would have published them. I would have found another way."

"I murdered my father for nothing."

Nothing much could be said after that. Except for one thing.

"Why did you return to Lord Mountford's?" If he'd stayed away, his alibi would have held up.

His left brow rose in arrogance. "Why, I had to finish the game, of course."

CHAPTER THIRTY-SIX

ALL'S WELL THAT ENDS WELL

*I*T TOOK BUT A DAY to release Sebastian from jail. The entire Worthington clan was waiting outside for him. Lily, of course, was the first to welcome him to freedom, their warm reunion bringing tears to our eyes. And then Sebastian's gaze found Margaret, and she fairly flew to him. Lily rejoined us so they could enjoy their privacy. Not that there was much to be had, as they were out in the open. I doubted they noted their surroundings, however, for they only had eyes for each other. When they turned toward us, the rest of the Worthingtons swarmed them with many cries of congratulations, pats on the back, smiles and, of course, more tears.

That night we enjoyed a private supper, *en famille*, with only our family and, of course, dear Sebastian and Lily. The next day, they reluctantly moved into Wynchcombe House. Something that had to be done. After all, he was now the

Duke of Wynchcombe, and that was where Lily and he belonged.

Upon their arrival at Wynchcombe House, they were properly greeted by the staff which lined up across the front of the house to welcome them, a stark contrast to their past treatment of him. But then, they'd had no choice since they'd been under strict orders from the duke.

Most of the staff chose to remain, even before Sebastian announced an increase to their salaries commensurate with the Worthington household's. Mr. Farthington, the valet, however, decided to accept the offer of a fashion-conscious peer as dressing him would be much more in keeping with his expertise. That, of course, left Sebastian without the services of a valet. He didn't seem to think he would need one, but Mother reminded him he was now a duke and, whether he liked it or not, his worth would be measured in great part according to the way he dressed. So, of course, one was found who came highly recommended and looked forward to dressing a duke.

Mister Nevins had proven a particular conundrum for Sebastian to solve. For years, he'd done stellar work keeping track of the duke's personal finances, including all the gambling matters, which was no small feat. When it came right down to it, he'd done nothing wrong, except for the lie he told his employer which made it difficult for Sebastian to trust him. In the end, he settled a sum on Mister Nevins which would provide sufficient funds until he found another position. But as it turned out, he wished to retire to the county where he'd grown up. The sum provided him with the means to buy a house in which he and his family could live comfortably.

Along with the title, Sebastian had inherited a great many properties as well as a sizable fortune. Initially, he wanted to turn over the management of everything to Father and Ned for he didn't have the foggiest notion as to how to go on. But Ned recommended he keep his man of business, as he was a solid, prudent man who would do right by the extensive Wynchcombe estate. Worthington & Son, however, would handle the investments, since the man who'd been managing them was not up to the task.

Mother spent the next few weeks providing instruction to Lily as to matters pertaining to the Wynchcombe household, something that Lily dearly appreciated as she'd never been taught.

In short, our family remained entwined with Sebastian and Lily even after they moved into their own home.

The resolution to the Hodgkins' murder was handled quietly and efficiently by Inspector Crawford who, according to the newspapers, obtained a confession from Lord Percy. When I subsequently thought about it, I realized it made sense. Lord Percy needed Sebastian out of commission for the night in question so he could frame him for the duke's murder. More than likely, he'd warned Hodgkins not to drink the wine he'd provided to the Cherubs waiter, laced with some drug he'd distilled from one of his plants. He'd probably arranged to meet the hapless Hodgkins by Westminster Bridge later that night so he could pay him. At that point, Hodgkins' life was forfeit, for Lord Percy could not afford to have him live. Not when he could provide evidence against him. He'd killed his father and Hodgkins on the same night, all for the sake of preserving his legitimacy.

The newspaper reporters were indefatigable in covering the courtroom proceedings for the murders. As we wanted nothing to do with the notoriety, we stayed away.

But, unfortunately, the press was not quite done with us. Someone leaked information about the investigative committee. My guess? One of the servants. Not ours, of course. Probably someone from one of the households I visited. Since we were busy with other endeavors, we managed to ignore most of it. But I guessed it would not be forgotten and would rear its ugly head at some inopportune time.

In the meantime, we carried on for we had better things to do. Margaret picked up where she'd left off with her projects, volunteering her time at the newly-built women's health clinic. Mother continued her work with the Ladies Benevolent Society, and, of course, Lily had an entire household to manage. She hoped to entertain within a month after they moved into Wynchcombe House. Nothing outlandish since they were in mourning. After a brief consultation with Lady Kingsley, the arbiter of etiquette, Lily decided a small supper party with a few select friends would not flout any rules. Anything more elaborate would need to wait until the following year.

There was nothing to stop us from holding our own celebration, though. Two weeks after his release, the Worthingtons held a supper party made up of family and close friends which, of course, included all those who'd involved themselves in the investigation. Besides the Worthingtons, Lords Newcastle and Marlowe, as well as Lady Emma, were invited. And we couldn't leave out Lord Rutledge, Father's friend and Inspector Crawford's mentor. I, of course, insisted on issuing an invitation to Inspector Crawford, not that there was any resistance on Mother's part, since he'd been instrumental to our cause.

The Duke and Duchess of Torrance declined our invitation, however, as Her Grace felt her actions had led to the duke's death. She might have acted with good intentions, but the effect had been catastrophic. But she did leave the door open for future gatherings once some time had passed and the memories were not as fresh.

The night of our party the mood was festive for we had

much to celebrate. After supper, as tradition dictated, the ladies retired to the drawing room, leaving the men to enjoy their port and cigars.

"How is Wynchcombe House coming along?" I asked Lily once we'd settled into the drawing room. With Sebastian's blessing, she'd decided to redecorate the family rooms. Guided by Mother, she'd spent a fair amount of time visiting furniture warehouses and such.

"There's so much to do. It can be overwhelming, but thankfully, I've had Mrs. Worthington to rely upon."

"She loves redecorating," Margaret said. "Last year I returned from Oxford for the winter holiday to discover my entire bedroom had been refurbished. New paint, new bed, new everything. I hardly recognized the room."

"She did it without first gaining your permission?"

"Oh, no. She asked. She told me it needed a small retouch, nothing major."

Lily's laughter rang out.

It was so good to hear it. She'd missed enough of that growing up.

"I don't even want to think about Wynchcombe Castle. I don't think it's been renovated since the Middle Ages. Well, except for installing indoor plumbing, that is."

"Maybe you could leave that for the future Duchess of Wynchcombe? Sooner or later, there's bound to be one." I winked at Margaret who pinked up.

To our surprise, no movement had been made on that front, although Mother remained ever hopeful. Maybe Sebastian's ardor had cooled while he'd been in prison. Margaret's certainly hadn't. She still lit up every time he walked into the room. Or maybe he hadn't quite acclimated to the fact he now had the means to take on a wife. While he still made the occasional appearance at Worthington House, it wasn't the breakfast-to-supper presence we'd been used to seeing. It made sense, but we sorely missed him.

Before too long, the gentlemen arrived in the drawing room, some with strange looks on their faces. Something was up. And it took no time at all to find out.

Sebastian walked up to Margaret and got down on one knee.

The oohs and aahs filled the room.

"Margaret, since the moment I spied you at Oxford's Bodleian Library with your nose firmly stuck in a book over your diminutive spectacles, I knew you were the one for me. I can't imagine my life without you by my side. You are not only beautiful, but intelligent, a fierce warrior, and I do believe somewhere in there you've reserved a piece of your heart for me. If you can imagine living your life with a duke, who's also a farmer at heart, I promise to make your life as wondrous as I possibly can. Dear, dear Megs, I offer my heart and everything that is mine. Will you do me the honor of becoming my wife?"

I waited with bated breath to see what she would say, because, for the first time in my life, Margaret was speechless.

A few seconds later, she finally found her voice. "I must finish my degree at Oxford."

"I never doubted it for a second."

"And I have my causes, women's rights and health. I won't give those up."

"I'll stand firmly behind you and support you all the way."

"Children?"

"As many or as few as you wish, although there must be a male to carry on the line."

"In that case, I accept."

"Well, thank heaven, that's over," I exclaimed.

"Kitty!" Mother whispered.

Sebastian drew Margaret to her feet and wrapped his arms around her like he'd never let her go. And then he kissed her. Fully. On the mouth. Something about that kiss told me they'd done that before.

We'd barely caught our collective breaths when Carlton walked into the room followed by two footmen carrying champagne and flutes. Soon, the bottles were being popped while everyone milled round Sebastian and Margaret to congratulate the happy couple.

I walked up to Mother whose shining eyes were most decidedly anticipating the wedding. "You got your wish. A daughter married to a duke. A definite triumph, Mother."

She harumphed. "It's not a done deal yet, Kitty."

"I can't imagine either crying off. Look at them. They're perfectly suited for each other."

"Yes, but as you know, anything can happen." Her gaze settled on a blushing Margaret and her handsome duke. "We'll need to hold that wedding as soon as possible."

"But you wouldn't be able to have a grand affair since Sebastian will be in mourning for another few months."

"Yes, there is that."

And then the entire question was settled by the two parties most closely involved.

"The wedding can't take place for another year, maybe two. I must first finish my degree," Margaret said.

But Sebastian showed his mettle. "A year, that's all I'm willing to wait for you. It will give me time to learn everything there is to know about Wynchcombe."

"But you said—"

"I'll move to Oxford. We'll make it work, Megs." He brought her hand to his mouth and kissed it.

It took me a few minutes to notice Ned and Lily were missing.

CHAPTER THIRTY-SEVEN

THE SHAPE OF THINGS TO COME

"*A*NYTHING WRONG, MISS WORTHINGTON?" Inspector Crawford asked. He'd followed me to the balcony where I'd escaped after seeing a blushing Lily and a confident Ned return to the drawing room. The implication was clear. They'd been doing something untoward away from prying eyes.

I plastered on one of my false smiles. "Why, nothing at all, Inspector. I just came out for a breath of fresh air."

A frown, clearly visible from the light of a full moon, expressed doubt. "I beg to disagree. Something seems to be troubling you." He was too observant by half.

"It's nothing, really."

He stood there, in all his height, staring down at me, not saying a word, waiting for something.

He wasn't the only one. The evening's soft breeze, fragrant with the scent of blooms, was perfect for what I wished to be doing, which wasn't getting a breath of fresh air. "I better return to the drawing room. If I don't, someone will come looking for me. It will not do to be caught here in the dark with you."

A small smile curved his well-shaped mouth. "Ahh, I see."

"What does the all-knowing Inspector Crawford see?" I peevishly remarked.

"You're upset about the growing closeness between your brother and Lady Lily."

"No, I'm not. I wish them all the best."

"But something about them is bothering you."

"Not them. Exactly. It's what they've been doing. Her rosy cheeks and his smug look gave them away. Clearly, they were kissing in the garden."

A small shake of his head. "You don't know that's what happened."

"I know my brother and Lily. She's been smitten with him from the start."

"Maybe all he did was ask to court her, after obtaining her brother's blessing first, of course. Your brother would not do anything that isn't right and proper. He's a stickler for the rules."

I huffed a complaint. "Why are you always so reasonable?"

"I'm trained to think that way."

"While I jump to conclusions, and sometimes act impulsively. Yes, I know. It's gotten me into trouble more than once."

"Really?" He quirked a brow. "I hadn't noticed."

I laughed for he knew better than anyone the trouble I'd gotten into. "Oh, please, don't make me laugh."

"You'd rather sulk instead?"

"I was not sulking." All evidence to the contrary.

Once more, he allowed silence to fill the space.

"Very well, I was. But I'm over it now. Mostly."

"I can't help thinking there is more to this story."

"You'll think me petty."

"I'll think you human."

I strolled away from him, placed my hands on the parapet, and stared at the full moon. "A year ago, I was sent to finishing school when I was caught in the garden with a gentleman. I'd been hoping to be kissed."

"Ahhh, I understand now. You want to be kissed?"

My face heated up. How could I have confessed such a thing to him? "No. I mean. Not really. Maybe. Oh, I'm going back inside now."

But before I could flee, he caught me and spoke but a single word, "Catherine."

I stood trembling waiting, wanting, so much wanting, while he peeled off my glove one finger at a time. Turning my hand over, he slowly kissed the palm. His warm, firm lips spoke of things I'd never experienced before.

Lifting his gaze, he asked, "Will that do, Miss Worthington?"

"It's a start," I whispered breathlessly, while happiness pulsed out of me.

Cradling my face, he brushed a thumb across my cheek. "And so, it is."

* * *

Follow the adventures of Kitty Worthington, Inspector Crawford, and Kitty's friends and family in the next book, Murder at the Masked Ball, Book 3 in The Kitty Worthington Mysteries, available from Amazon Murder at the Masked Ball

Amateur sleuth Kitty Worthington once more investigates when a dear friend is suspected of murder. Can she find the villain before her friend swings from the wrong end of a rope?

London. 1923. When an invitation arrives to the premier event of the season, the Midsummer Masked Ball, Kitty Worthington does not even think of declining. Not with a mother on the hunt for a noble husband for her. But no sooner does she curtsy to her hostess at the masquerade than tragedy strikes. A very dead earl is found at the bottom of a staircase, and it's clearly the work of foul play.

Scotland Yard Detective Inspector Robert Crawford is soon assigned the case. In no time at all he hones on Lord Newcastle, who'd earlier in the season pummeled the dead earl for sorely abusing his wife. But does he have the right man? The evidence seems to suggest so, but not everything is as it seems.

Afraid her friend may wrongfully pay with his life, Kitty once more organizes her ace team, including her maid, Betsy, her siblings, sundry members of the nobility, and, as ever, Sir Winston, her mischievous Bassett Hound. From the seediest parts of London to the glittering mansions of Mayfair, they fearlessly pursue the truth. For if they fail to find the killer, their dear friend may very well dance one last jig at the end of a rope.

Murder at the Masked Ball, the third book in The Kitty Worthington Mysteries, is another frolicking, historical cozy mystery filled with quirky suspects, a wicked villain, and an intrepid heroine sure to win your heart. Available from Amazon.

Also available from Amazon, **Murder on the Golden Arrow**, the first book in The Kitty Worthington Mysteries. A lighthearted cozy mystery set among the glittering world of British high society. For lovers of Downton Abbey and Agatha Christie alike.

ISBN-13: 978-1-943321-12-4 (EBook)

ISBN 13: 978-1-943321-15-5 (Print)

Hearts Afire Publishing

First Edition: January 2022

CAST OF CHARACTERS

Kitty Worthington - Our amateur sleuth

The Family
    Mildred Worthington - Kitty's mother
    Edward Worthington - Kitty's father
    Ned Worthington - Kitty's oldest brother
    Richard Worthington - Kitty's next older brother, in Egypt
    Margaret Worthington - Kitty's older sister

The Worthington Household
    Betsy - Kitty's maid
    Mr. Carlton - the family butler
    Mrs. Simpson - the family housekeeper
    Neville - the family chauffeur and Betsy's beau
    Cook - Betsy's aunt
    Cummings - Mrs. Worthington's lady's maid
    James - Footman
    Sir Winston - The family's Bassett Hound

The Wynchcombe Family
    Hugh Dalrymple, the Duke of Wynchcombe
    Sebastian Dalrymple, Marquis Thropplethorpe, grandson and heir to the Duke of Wynchcombe
    Lady Lily Dalrymple, Sebastian's sister
    Lord Percy Dalrymple, Duke of Wynchcombe's second son
    Lord Henry Dalrymple, Lord Percy Dalrymple's son
    Thomas Dalrymple, Sebastian's father
    Trenton Dalrymple, the old duke's nephew, and the current Duke of Wynchcombe's cousin

The Duke of Wynchcombe Household
    Mr. Temple - the duke's butler
    Mr. Farthington - The duke's valet
    Martha - a maid
    Mr. Nevins—the duke's private secretary

Other Notable Characters
    Detective Inspector Robert Crawford
    Chief Detective Inspector Bolton
    Lord Marlowe - An Earl
    Lord Newcastle - Another Earl and Ned's friend
    Lady Emma Carlyle- Debutante and Kitty's friend
    Thomas Hodgkins - Sebastian's friend
    The Duke and the Duchess of Torrance
    Edith Clemson - Maid to the Duchess of Wynchcombe

Made in United States
Troutdale, OR
06/02/2023

10397311R00194